THE SET UP

First Edition 2025
ISBN 978-1-953368-94-2

Belt Publishing

6101 Penn Avenue, Suite 201
Pittsburgh, PA 15206
www.beltpublishing.com

Book design by Jordan Koluch
Cover art by David Wilson

THE SET UP

JON WYNN

Belt Publishing

THE SET UP

PROLOGUE

1995

CAL

He watches a man with deep, welled eyes plead to the tailored pant cuffs of a passerby from behind his wrinkled cardboard sign: "I bet I can guess the day you were born." His voice barely disturbs the desert morning air.

The Guessing Man casts his pitch, over and over. Ten feet away, Cal makes his own pitch. As the suit passes to his lonely bubble of sidewalk space, Cal mumbles, "I'll sell you this necklace. Cheap?" But the man walks on without a glance.

Over time, Cal and the Guessing Man work into syncopation, in a kind of bartering music: ". . . day you were born . . ."; ". . . necklace . . ."; ". . . day you were born . . ."; ". . . necklace . . ."

Cal watched the Guessing Man emerge from the tunnels, an entrance a few blocks away. The six-hundred-mile storm drain system serves as a de facto shelter for hundreds of homeless men and women in Las Vegas. The tunnels scare Cal, mostly because he knows they'll be his next stop if he doesn't get out of town.

Someone pauses. The Guessing Man's got a live one.

"I'll guess the day you were born for a dollar," he repeats, before hastily adding, "within three days." Cal can't hear the woman's response, but he hears the reply. Given with more pizzazz than he previously exhibited, the Guessing Man says, "Wednesday," while waving dirty fingers. It's a flicker of showmanship, of some long-lost career, perhaps.

Unimpressed, the woman shakes her head and turns to go. "Get it? 'Within three days!' No, wait, how about this? I can guess which state you were born in." The woman turns back to him and gives a little shrug of an invitation, eyebrows raised. The street man proffers, "A state of innocence."

At that, she hands over a bill from her purse. It disappears behind the cardboard sign as if to erase the awkwardness for everyone involved. "Have a magical day, ma'am," he says.

After thirty fruitless minutes, Cal realizes he cannot compete with the simple trickery of his sidewalk competitor. Might as well head to the pawnshop.

He doesn't get very far. Distracted by the sunlight, his vision partially obscured by the neon yellow cap he bought at the gift shop, he doesn't notice the family until he sees four sets of feet blocking the sidewalk. Khakis, black belt, a modest gut to his left. Two pairs of shorter legs with bright white sneakers to the right. A woman's legs between them. Cal looks up.

"Excuse me," the mother says. "Binion's?" Her voice is soft and hesitant. Cal reads the father's stiff body language at asking a stranger for help, and it makes him relax a bit.

"Sure. Sure," Cal says, smiling at the children. "Two blocks. On the right." He adds, "Check out the million-dollar display."

With a thank-you, they pass, and he hears the mother say, "Hear that? A million dollars! $1.99 breakfast buffet, here we come!"

The thought of family draws his hand down to his pocket, to his mother's gold necklace. It made her feel pretty, and he'd wanted to steal that bit of happiness from her. Now, it's his only means of escape.

Cal's been running for a long time—from the Blue Ridge all the way to Las Vegas—but this is the first time he's felt truly in danger. Which is confusing, because until recently, living with a group that called themselves the Third Family, he'd felt the safest he'd felt since fleeing his papa's belt.

They had taken him in from the street and given him a place to live, a clean bunk in a room with six other men. Warm meals. Clothing. A daily rhythm. They'd told him they saw a light in him, a light he'd hidden even from himself. It had all felt easier than being alone. And with the temptations and dangers of Las Vegas just beyond the doors of the compound, the world cleaved easily into the sacred and profane by the knife of their conviction. Month after month, they bound him with an invisible rope.

But after a year, something has felt different. There have been whispers of a move, perhaps south, out of town. Gossip about an upcoming wedding. The leader, the Reverend, was a slight, middle-aged man with a mask of a face, who spoke in the kind of calm voice Cal remembered hearing on the Midwestern radio, fading in and out as he drove down the highway. When he delivered the news, it was as if he were giving another work detail: Cal would marry someone from the compound. A nice enough girl he had paid little attention to before. The Reverend's hands were still, but Cal felt that invisible rope pulling taut.

Cal knows what can happen when families move, and when people marry in haste—in his experience, almost never anything good. So, he started to plan and to gather his few belongings.

On the way out—impulsively, and perhaps driven by the same malice with which he'd stolen his mother's necklace—he'd taken a ledger from the Reverend's desk. He doesn't really know what he was thinking.

He headed to the bus station first but got spooked by two men in matching khakis hovering near the ticket counter. Do religious men dress like off-duty cops, or is it the other way around? The waiting room felt tight, and there was nowhere to hide. Cal considered a flophouse—Bridger Inn or Little Hotel—before slipping into the closest hotel, the Four Queens. He's been holed up there for two days in a room with a view over the brand-new Fremont Street Experience. At night, the twelve million-bulb light show runs a few times an hour, fighter jets with American flag contrails and cheerleaders with winks and pom-poms set against a jet-black sky. He's watched the light show two or three dozen times from his tenth-story perch.

But his cash is running out. If he's going to try to get out of town, he needs to go now.

This morning, he took stock of his meager belongings: a couple T-shirts, the necklace, his driver's license, the ledger. He flipped through it a few times: lists of addresses, names, and appraisals. It looked to him like an inventory of properties near the southern tip of the state. He thought about sending it to the newspaper—it's pretty clear there's something not entirely aboveboard about the Third Family—but maybe he'll just toss it when he gets to wherever he's going. He slipped the ledger into a plastic souvenir bag from the hotel, put his license and the necklace in his pocket, and headed down to the street.

He's memorized the route: two rights and a left. First to Pete's EZ Pawn to hock the necklace, then back to the bus station, three blocks to the west.

Halfway down the block, he sneaks a glance at the pawnshop. "Jewelry! Watches! Diamonds! Cash! Layaway Today!" He tucks his chin to his chest.

From under the brim of his cap, he sees another pair of khakis pass, and then he feels a shoulder jam into his left side, throwing him off balance. Cal stumbles off the curb and into the street before turning to catch a look at the man. He looks familiar.

Then, from behind, Cal hears the roar of a car's engine. He spins to see a '79 Buick Regal bearing down on him. He throws his hands up, like two delicate fans. In one, the necklace is woven between his fingers, and the thin plastic bag with T-shirts and the notebook hangs from the other.

PRESENT DAY

MONDAY

1

MARSHALL

"Like Norwegian Death Metal," Marshall Grant says, his regular joke to the barista. Coffee black and clothes gray, like a less committed Johnny Cash, he takes his Café Chroma travel mug and crosses the street to the university.

He hopes he'll keep the coffee in his system today. The first two weeks of his Intro to the Metro Desk course have been bumpy, and twice last week his nerves led him to vomit up his breakfast in the first-floor bathroom at Greenspun Hall. Sometimes, the vibes are just off, but this feels different. If he's honest, this summer session has made the growing distance between his and his students' lived experiences apparent to everyone involved, and Marshall finds he's not so interested in building bridges. His jokes about not being able to open a pdf were one thing, but last week, he allowed himself an ill-advised rant about social media as an unreliable news source. To put it mildly, his students didn't appreciate him mocking their favorite platforms. And he should have let their good-natured ribbing of his old-school ways wash over him. Calling him "Professor Grantenberg"—a mash-up of his last name and the name of the fifteenth-century German inventor of the printing press—was actually fairly clever. But it was his regrettable quip—calling TikTok "ADHD-CNN" in a weak moment—that transformed that day's class into a production of intergenerational cultural awareness theater. Now, he just wants to get through the remaining two weeks with enough self-esteem to be able to get back to being a freelance journalist.

Marshall pauses at the wooden doors of the lecture hall to adjust his belt buckle in a way that allows him to surreptitiously determine that his fly is up before entering. Time to put on his best college professor impersonation. "Showbiz," he grumbles to himself, and swings open the doors.

He starts in, projecting his voice to fill the cavern-dark, casino-chilled hall: "If you're early, you're on time. If you're on time, you're late. And if you—" He stops as he sets his travel mug down. A printout of an old news article from the *Las Vegas Record* rests on the lectern. His byline. The date: October 15, 1995. A Sunday issue, almost thirty years old. One of his first pieces to hit the front page. Maybe the first.

He looks up as if he could tell which of the 250 students placed the article there. He finishes his customary welcome.

"And . . . and if you're late?" he asks.

"You're in trouble," a third of the class responds.

But Marshall doesn't notice them. He takes the first sip from his mug and keeps his eyes on the article. As the hot coffee hits his empty stomach, he puts his satchel at his feet and surveys the printout.

The full headline reads: "Sidewalk Calamity: Suicide Darkens Fremont Street Experience Opening." A midsized piece. The operatic headline contrasted a tragic John Doe death with the glitzy opening of downtown's latest attempt at attracting a meager slice of the city's overstuffed tourism pie. He's written hundreds of articles since, and he always believed more than his fair share made it to the front page. But why is this one here today?

His teaching often draws on his experiences working his old beat at the *Record*, but this is taking that a bit farther than he'd planned. Scanning the near-capacity lecture hall, he catches some yawns and no knowing smiles. Folks are still unpacking their bags, opening laptops and notebooks. A few are still settling into their seats. The overhead lights make it difficult to see the top rows.

"Who?" escapes his lips.

Tom, perhaps the least bored of his TAs, looks up from the first row. "Professor?"

"I'm not a professor, Tom. But . . . nothing." He looks at his other three TAs—Jennifer, Aaron, and Shuyin—as they earnestly position their pens above their matching yellow legal notepads.

His eyes flick to the clock to confirm the time. 8:30 a.m. Better get this show started.

"Okay," he says, opening with an invitation. "What do you think makes a 'good' story?" And then he waits. Starting a discussion is like starting a fire. You need a little kindling but also a little air.

Finally, one student near the front of the room offers, "Something counterintuitive. A puzzle."

"Alright, yes," Marshall says, exhaling slowly. "Something that draws the reader in. What else?"

Answering with a question, from the center, "A beginning, middle, and end?"

"Structure is important. Arcs are the backbone of narrative, but ends are often scarce in journalism, and sometimes you start in the middle. Still. Good, workmanlike answer. Let's keep going." He wants a little more wood.

"There's a lesson?" another adds, quietly.

"Alright . . . If there's a puzzle, there should be a solution, perhaps? A takeaway?" He's sensing a slight dip in collective interest. He's often torn between teaching the fundamentals of the craft and keeping the students entertained with salacious and scandalous stories. He looks at the photocopied article again. Paper, he thinks, works as an accelerant.

"Here's a story to consider," he restarts, moving back to the lectern and lifting the article momentarily over his head.

"So, this is a story about a young man—about the same age as some of you. He came to town and got lost." Marshall scans the article and continues, "I couldn't find his home address, or an employer. Maybe worked illegally. Seems he blew his money at a casino the last week of his life, before, one morning, stepping out into traffic. The recent closing of Fremont Street disoriented an out-of-town driver."

Marshall spools outward from the lectern again, like the article does for its middle third. Tall and awkward, he prefers to lean on a stool, folded in on himself, but moving around the room gives students something to watch. "With little to go on, I used the story as a metaphor for the changes in the city: a sad demise. Suicide by sedan." He's momentarily pleased with his younger self's balance of tragedy and the wider story of a changing city. He surprises himself with a rare spark of pride. The framing, if a little too strained, was possibly what landed the piece on the front page.

"The final third rests on suicide rates before returning to an eyewitness account," he says. Reflecting on it, looking at the text and driven by that growing flame of vanity, he adds, "This was the article that launched my career."

"So, you have your career thanks to this person's death?" a student asks from the middle left. Oof.

"Well," Marshall struggles to respond, "like most journalists, I don't relish tragedy, but—"

"The question isn't if you enjoyed it," a student says from the other side of the room. "She was asking how you felt owing your career to someone's actual death."

He wants to say that his is hardly the first career—journalistic or otherwise—launched by tragedy, but he isn't sure of the right tone for it. "I'm still not happy about it. But all you can do, in this job, is to try to be as decent and respectfu—"

Another student, from a middle row, cuts him off. "What was his name?"

The class has Marshall back on his heels yet again. Only this time, it's not about social media creating echo chambers of questionable content. It's about . . . him. He looks at the clock and sees plenty of time remaining to the class, and he's far outside the margins of his rough sketch of a lesson plan.

"At the time, I didn't know his name. I . . . I can't recall," he says. He retreats toward the shelter of the lectern.

The same student: "Why did he commit suicide?"

"I . . ." Marshall says, "I never found out." He backs up more, toward the lectern, grimacing. Wrong response. His spark of pride extinguished, he thinks of the ambitious rookie reporter who wrote the article, and then looks to the door.

From the second row, another student asks, "Isn't curiosity, especially about someone's misfortune, a sign of respect?"

At that, he holds up his hands. "Well, look. Look. There were fifteen people near the scene, and one was a key informant." He pauses. He hasn't thought about any of this in a long time. "She provided the needed details, having seen the man leap in front of the car." Marshall is momentarily distracted by the memory of the witness in that moment. Her tearful eyes and his desire to comfort her.

From the front left, a student asks, "Fifteen people, and only one eyewitness?"

From the middle right, another student asks, "Was the witness credible? How long did you interview her?"

He wonders if the student would say that if he had said the witness was a man? He sees the pathways out of the conversation get consumed in the flame of raised arms.

In his peripheral vision, he sees a few phones rise above knee level. It's possible they're checking the weather or launching a dating app. Maybe they're texting each other in some group chat. But maybe—every college instructor's worst fear—they're recording his blooming public frustration in real time. He desperately wants to avoid a comeuppance on #professorsofTikTok.

While he loots through his memories, even more students raise their hands at the collective sense of some deeper story. A rare and genuine moment of enthusiasm for the class, he marvels. Too bad it's at his expense. He looks down, scrambling for another topic.

From the back, someone shouts, "Did you care more about the kid or your career?"

Most of the hands fall, and a few heads turn. Being a journalist requires a certain comfort with blood but not outright bloodlust. And with the unwelcome trip down a tragic memory lane, the pressure from students pushes him too much.

"We all act based on self-interest," he says. "Like, if I told you all to stop asking me questions about this or everyone's going to get a full letter grade reduction on class participation, would you keep throttling me with questions?"

The remaining hands quickly drop. He feels a twist in his empty stomach, and his cheeks heat nuclear. Sometimes you're an arsonist, sometimes you're a firefighter. Either way, you risk getting scorched.

He looks at the clock. Twenty-five minutes left. A bead of sweat falls on his glasses, leaving a wavy streak in his line of vision. Who left this article here? Why?

He wipes his brow with his sleeve, then stands to his full height. "I did the best I could, considering. For what it's worth, I . . ." He hears his voice trail off.

In his six years as an instructor, Marshall has always taught until the very last minute of class, so students "get their full money's worth." But he quickly lifts his satchel, stuffs the photocopy into it, grabs his coffee mug, and walks through the side door without another word.

2

ALLY

Out of the corner of her eye, Ally Parks catches a dark hand reaching over the fitting room door to pull her clothes off the peg. This shopping expedition is a test, she realizes too late. No use in yelling now. Ally looks around and settles on her reflection in the mirror. She's wearing nothing but ill-fitting Target underwear, a splatter of freckles, and a familiar expression of slack-faced annoyance.

The only other thing in the room is a lavalliere-neck draped dress in checked silk in a tiny pile on a chair. "Lavalliere-neck" isn't in Ally's everyday vocabulary, but that's what the tag says, right above the price that isn't in Ally's everyday bank account: $3,990. Ally knows her budget couldn't cover so much as an earlobe in this store.

Figures, she thinks. Now, how to get home without giving a show—and a sad one, at that—to the city's tourists and their smartphones? This is not the kind of acting job she was looking for.

Two hours earlier—and fully clothed—Ally had pulled up to an address sent via text. The Taj M'all Plaza, on Desert Inn, one of many Las Vegas streets named after a long-gone casino. The towering sign at the street listed the tenants, though not the one she was there for.

World's Largest Beauty Supply World's Smallest Prices
Caps Lock Computer Repair Shop
Laundry Coin Op

ComixXchange

Tattoos

Jack's Pot

Jimmy's Wok 'n' Roll

The sun was baking cars like macarons on the sheet pan parking lot. From her dingy white Nissan Altima, Ally watched yellow pollen swirl over and in between them all, looking for purchase. She asked herself again what she was doing here.

It's just another audition, she told herself. But she rated her anxiety as a "5" on her personal comfort score. Just a tick above an average first date score of 4.5. She wasn't sure why, though. She probably wouldn't get this job, just like every other job she's auditioned for. Even in Vegas, she's just another dirty blonde in an oversaturated market.

She'd hoped she would be a plucky fish in a smaller pond here. She knows how to play up certain natural qualities and play down others. Back in LA, she'd enrolled in classes where she'd learned some good tricks: improvisation, physicality, interacting with audiences. She took to the basics. Audition after audition, however, sapped the reserves of confidence she stashed away in those classes. Each little colorful Lego of self-assurance stolen and replaced by a gray brick of doubt.

Until yesterday.

It was an audition for a local appliance store commercial, and the production company paired her with a guy a little older than her. Midtwenties. They exchanged their lines—he was selling a dishwasher; she was a coy but enthusiastic customer. He had about five inches on her, and when she looked into his eyes, she could see he was handsome, even if he wasn't her type. He had a dark complexion, an artful fade, and a habit of touching the divot above his lips with his second knuckle when he was struggling with a line. She thought he was a good actor. There was a chemistry there, actually. He'd followed her out after the audition. Said his name was Webster but that he went by "Web."

Prior experience prepared Ally for being hit on, but then he surprised her.

"I might have a gig for you," he said.

"Y'okay," Ally said, only half believing him. "Go on."

He told her he worked for a company called the Set Up. It was "almost like a reality show." He said they did performances "in actual situations."

"How do I get an audition with this Set Up?"

"You just did, kinda. I'll recommend you."

"Are you an actor or a talent scout?"

"Maybe both? Tap your name and number into my phone."

"Aha. Okay, okay," she said, backing up. "I get it. And here I thought I heard unconvincing lines in that audition. Look, if you—"

Web offered a warm, laid-back laugh, and despite herself, she relaxed just a little. Shaking his head gently, he said, "No, no. It's real. Not a scam."

She looked at him for five seconds before taking his phone out of his hands. After once having a man immediately call the random number she gave him only to receive an auto dealership's automated response—that was awkward—she was ready to give her girlfriend, Phoebe's, number to quickly extract herself from the situation. Web got a real number, just not an immediately refutable one.

"You have WhatsApp? That's the only way the Set Up communicates." He winked at her. "Don't worry about that. Hope to see you soon," he said, and walked to a white GMC cargo van. Not really riding in style, Ally thought. Must be a work van.

Ally definitely needed the cash, so here she was at the address from the text that Phoebe forwarded her a couple hours after the audition. "Tomorrow 1 pm 2305 E Desert Inn Road Suite 37."

Actually, she was early. She wanted to see what she could find out.

Obviously, she had searched for the Set Up online. No one lowballs their own intelligence, and Ally prided herself on her incredulity. But there was nothing.

Ally thought this strip mall wasn't doing much to convince her the Set Up was a real business and not some kind of sketchy front. Sad signs hung in the windows, either faded or yellowed images of cartoon characters or General Tso's chicken. Only the marijuana dispensary seemed to have a new sign.

She pulled around back, matching the back door with suite #37 in the front. She parked behind a dumpster and watched the door in her rearview mirror.

Just as she had almost convinced herself that this was nothing more than an elaborate gag, the door swung open. A middle-aged woman, maybe in her midforties, walked out. She had long, straight brown hair, an oversized bag, and sunglasses. As the woman approached a green Subaru, she retrieved a pair of white oven mitts from her purse and opened the driver's-side door. Ally watched as she cranked the AC, put the mitts on, and, after a minute, drove off. *Well, that's one way to avoid burning your delicate digits on a hot steering wheel,* Ally thought.

Nothing else happened for the next half hour, so Ally returned to the front of the plaza and parked in the row closest to the street.

At 12:50, Web pulled up in the white cargo van, parked, and walked in. Eight minutes later, Ally flipped her stick to "D" and drove through the lot, crossing yellow lines to avoid speed bumps. She parked at the glass door, reflecting the lot, empty save for the cargo van. On either side of #37 were vacant storefronts.

She stepped out of the car and into the hot air with a headshot in hand and a handbag over her shoulder. As she approached the door, Ally saw a surveillance camera tucked under the overhang and imagined what it recorded. As she reached for the door handle, she heard a buzzing sound and a metallic click. Someone was watching her.

Rubbing her arms against the blast of air-conditioning, she took a quick inventory of the vestibule. Maybe ten by ten feet. Blue-gray floor tiles. Another door straight ahead and, directly above it, an envelope-sized vent. More business park than strip mall. As she started to offer a "Hello?" to the void, the interior door opened, and there was Web.

"Good to see you, Ally! Come in. Leave your headshot on the table," he said, leading her through the second door. Ally heard the door click shut behind her. She felt her pulse race and took a breath. *It's just another audition*, she told herself. *You've got this.*

The second room was three times the size of the first and almost as unadorned. Web motioned toward two chairs, a black coffee table between them. On the table were two glasses and a pitcher of ice water that hadn't had time to collect condensation.

With an open palm, Web invited her to sit, and Ally chose the chair closer to the door. She balanced herself on the edge of her seat, just in case she had to get up in a hurry. Web sat back with a "what-do-ya-think?" smile.

There was another door opposite from the one she came through, and a long mirror along the wall to her left. She noticed the air, smelling of cut lumber and that slightly sugary tinge of fresh paint. Like a film set... or at least what she imagined a film set would smell like, if she'd ever catch a whiff of one.

After scanning the room, she settled on Web's face. Squared up, Ally took him in again. Neither muscular nor scrawny, on the tall side but not imposing. Not unattractive. Ally made herself uncomfortable taking a few seconds trying to guess his ancestry before settling on the fact that he was what her grandmother would have called "ethnic." She guessed he could play characters from a handful of different backgrounds, depending on the lighting.

On the whole, she decided, he would be hard to pick out of a crowd. Like herself.

Might as well see where this goes, she thought.

If asked, Ally would say her low-wattage improv superpower was her ability to fill awkward silences with more awkward jokes. "You spared no expense to charm up your office park interrogation room," she said. "Was Lowe's out of plastic plants?"

She looked at the mirror, and Web met her gaze, making her blink twice before turning back to him. "It's a city of mirrors, Ally," he said, smiling. "There's a mirrored pyramid. Mirrored walls turn small casino rooms into infinite caverns."

"No, I know," she said while settling back into the seat. "It's great. Someone has a real future in black site interior design."

"So," Web continued unfazed, "this isn't a normal audition." She watched him shift in his seat and glance at the mirror. "Tell me. When did you realize you wanted to act?"

Ally pushed her feet in front of her and let herself slouch a bit. She considered telling the truth, but why start now?

"Really?" she asked.

"Really," he responded. "Tell me the story."

"Both of my parents were analysts," Ally said. This story came easily for her. She'd rehearsed it on Greyhound buses and over first-date drinks. "Elite. Upper West Side. Their offices were on the first floor of our brownstone. During dinner, my parents would prattle on about the psychoses and neuroses walking through their doors. Oppressively depressive disorders. Ego deaths. Fears of phobias. Traumas. Motivations. I'd memorized most of the disorders in the DSM by middle school."

"Okay," Web said, leaning forward, interested. She felt loose and in control.

"When . . . when you're ten, eleven years old, burning for independence, and the magical world of the city is right outside your door, well, you want to get out. If it's possible to get cabin fever living in a city of eight million people with a gross domestic product of Canada, I had it. And because my parents both worked from home offices, all it took was a couple mid-session meltdowns to convince them to let me to escape the house on occasion."

"Sure," Web said, in a way that made her feel he was buying it.

"And so," Ally continued, "my parents had a dilemma that all New York parents must face: keep me confined or build a protective barrier. They let me explore, piece by piece. First on my block, and after a few weeks, they added another block. Then another. After that, they allowed me to walk alone to school, with them pacing a block behind me. For a few months, they paid a sidewalk vendor to keep tabs on me. They hung a map on the door and drew boundaries for each stage, adding odd concentric squares over time."

She took a sip of water, and Web used the pause to interject. "Okay, keep going, but less decoration."

"I—" Ally started, looking at him for a moment and puzzling over how he wanted her to perform before continuing. The details were her favorite part, but she could pull back if that would get her the job. "I saw them when I explored Chelsea. First, it was at a pocket playground on Tenth Ave. I had a *Goosebumps* book. On a bench ten feet away was a woman with a long, dark-haired wig, bug-eye sunglasses, and a bulky trench coat. An emu in a red felt fedora would be less obvious. She was more of a spy movie caricature. I finished my book and walked home. Twelve minutes later, my mother got home. I didn't talk about it and neither did she."

"It was your mom?"

"Obvs. It went on that way for a few months. Mustaches and makeup. Slowly, their costumes got more subtle. When I couldn't easily see them, I would stare at strangers to the point of discomfort. That kept people away from me. I'd guess that was more of an unintended consequence. One person called the police on me."

"You never talked about it?"

"Of course not. I wasn't going to be the one to give up the game," Ally said. "The final exam was some next-level coercion."

She gave the impression that she was considering it all and realized she was enjoying the banter. This was why she loved acting. When she was able to be someone else, her anxiety almost completely disappeared. She felt in control.

"They gave me ten dollars to go to Gristedes and get a loaf of bread for dinner. In line, a man stood behind me and started chatting me up, commenting on the weather or whatever. But then he invited me to see a movie with him."

"What movie?"

"Some comic book movie," Ally said, quickly. "My father's appearance impressed me. His hair looked a little grayer, the lines on his face were a little deeper. I didn't recognize the suit he was wearing. After a few minutes, I lost him in the performance."

"He was successful, then?"

"Skipping dinner and seeing a movie was appealing. I remember wanting to in the worst kinda way. He asked questions and listened to the answers. He was more attentive than my actual father." Ally gave a bittersweet little laugh.

"What did you do?"

"Well, I didn't go, of course. I couldn't let them win." Ally looked down at her hands. "And then, at dinner, my father barely even acknowledged my presence at the table."

Ally tucked her feet under her chair, crossing her ankles as if she were back at her family's table. She looked up at Web, making eye contact. "I realized how coercive acting could be. I figured I wanted to be the one doing the coercing. After high school, I moved to LA."

And scene. Ally held her gaze steady.

"How much of that was true?"

"Some," she said firmly. Then, "Most."

There was a knock on the mirror that made her knees reflexively bump together. Web said, "Sorry. I'll be right back," and, looking around the room, added, "Have some more water, I figure." He left through the interior door.

Scanning the room, she looked at the empty chair. Did the middle-aged woman sit there? Was she auditioning for the same gig? Hearing the knob click broke her concentration, and Web returned to his seat.

"How would you rate your technological aptitude?"

She shrugged. "I'm a Mac person."

"So, not much. Social media use?"

"Age appropriate."

"How attached are you to your phone?"

"On a scale from 'Disinterested' to 'It's an Inseverable Appendage'?"

"Sure."

"A step shy of 'Appendage.'"

"Can you drive a moped? Like a Vespa?"

"I consider myself a quick learner."

"Drug use?"

"On the regular."

"Yeah?"

"Can't get out of bed without 'em." Ally grinned.

"Coffee."

"Right."

"SAG? AFTRA? AEA? AGVA?"

"No, and also no, no, and no."

"LinkedIn?"

"No."

"You say you moved here six months ago?"

"A little longer, but I'm new to town."

"From New York?"

She gave an "um hm" and hoped he didn't notice.

"Twenty-one."

"Yes." She smiled but had a flicker of a thought: How did he know that?

Web took a breath and continued. "You have a job. Can you juggle more?"

"Like a carny with a habit," Ally said. Web wasn't just asking questions. He was telling her the things he, and whoever was behind the mirror, already knew.

"Okay, look, so here's the deal," he said, leaning forward. "I work for an elite group of CIA operatives who live as double agents, working against the SD-6 to maintain world peace."

Ally felt a wad of spit get stuck in her throat. "No way."

"Yes, no way. I think that was *The A-Team*? *Alias*? Look, the Set Up pays actors to act IRL. In Real Life. Here's the rub: it'll never go on your resume. It's not a union gig. Las Vegas is a city of excess, and it has an oversupply of at least three things: out-of-work actors, uncomfortable situations, and desperation. The Set Up hires the first to help with the second."

And Ally wondered just how much she had of the third.

Web's tone relaxed. "Look. Do you want acting work? You want experience?"

"Yes."

"Well, this is it. No stage. Real audience work. Improv." He smiled again.

"What kind of gigs?"

"Performances."

"What kind of performances, then?"

"Well, as I said. Sometimes we're just selling a product, being a brand ambassador. Sometimes clients have awkward situations and will pay well to have things be, well, less awkward. Delicate social problems. Retirement parties, weddings, funerals.

"We call the work 'the ruse.' It's deception, of course. But, like, for pay."

She asked, "How regular is this ruse work?"

"Irregular in every way. Mostly an evening gig, some afternoons. We have a big week coming up."

Ally winced. "I work most afternoons."

"Call in sick. You'll get paid quadruple what you make slinging quad espressos over ice."

"And what, leave showbiz?" she chirped before pointing to the mirror with her chin. "Who runs this?"

"If you mean 'Who's behind the mirror?' that's just Erv," he said. "Erv likes punctuality, buffets, long walks at sunset, and buffets. You'll meet him later. If you mean 'Who runs the entire operation?' I honestly couldn't say."

"Doesn't that seem a little . . . fishy?"

"Everything's acting, Ally," Web shrugged. "We operate on 'the Etcetera Principle.'"

"The what?"

"The Etcetera Principle. We get limited information and kinda 'etcetera' the rest."

"A lot of etceteras," Ally said.

"There are two kinds of people in this world. Those who can handle incomplete information."

After waiting too long, she said, "Okay, cute." Web chuckled at his own joke.

"It's no different than the rest of your life, and we get paid to manage the etceteras. We work in those indeterminate spaces, and that's where we get to be creative."

"Are you saying you really don't know who runs the Set Up?"

"Yes, I don't know. Somebody. And somebody hired them, and on and on. I don't know. See? Etcetera."

Ally slumped back in her chair. This was all a lot more than she had expected. But it also didn't sound completely uninteresting. In fact, it sounded like a blast.

"What do you say?"

She looked at the ceiling tiles, pretending to consider it all before responding. She forced herself to wait an appropriate time, not to seem too enthusiastic.

"I'm in."

"Good. Let's go shopping."

"Shops at the Crystals," on the Strip, was a world away from the Taj M'all, with jagged po-mo architecture and designer brands well beyond the reach of Ally's barista income. As she and Web walked past the stores—Fendi, Ford, Choo, Vuitton, Zegna—and a light installation by some famous artist, Ally felt her anxiety rising again. Possibly triggered by class angst, she thought. She was wearing a gray utility tie-belt shirt from Old Navy, and the only thing she could afford at the mall was a small coffee at the Starbucks.

Web, however, floated through with ease in tapered joggers, a light blue linen shirt, and a pair of gray slip-ons. He casually steered her into Saint Laurent. Her only point of reference was that it looked like an uncrowded Apple store, with thin piles of clothes instead of iPads.

After a little consideration, Web collected a short dress, held it up to her body for a half a second, and escorted her to the dressing rooms. Ally didn't think twice when he said, "I want to see you try this on. Put your clothes here," pointing to the hook on the door. "I'll hold your bag." She handed it to him, like a dummy.

Now, sans bag as well as a good portion of her pride, she marvels at how quickly she succumbed to Web's breezy directives. She admits to herself again that he's a capable actor. His hand reaching over the top of the door, lifting her clothes, was a fitting next step to her day, better than any pin-straight Saint Laurent skirt would ever suit Ally's slightly curvy tomboy physique. She's more deflated than distressed.

Well, she can't stand here in her underwear all day.

"Hellooo?" she sings.

A polite, servile voice responds at the door: "Yes?"

"Yes," Ally says. "Hi. Do you work here?"

"Yes?" the voice says, again, less assured.

Ally considers describing Web, asking if he's there, but she knows he's gone.

"You wouldn't happen to have, like, some clothes someone left behind, would you?"

A nervous laugh. "Excuse me?"

"Any chance you have loaners?"

"Loaners? Miss, are you okay?"

Ally sighs. "I don't have any clothes in here."

"Did something happen to our dress, ma'am?"

"The dress is here. It's fine. What isn't here are my clothes." After a moment of silence, she adds, "Someone . . . took them."

Ally senses the confusion morph into concern through the fibers of the wooden door. "I'll get my manager."

"No, no. Please." Ally realizes the attendant needs help helping her. "Listen. You have garment bags, right?" Ally asks, saying a silent prayer that they're opaque. "You've gotta help a girl out."

Ten minutes later, Ally emerges from the store, wrapped in four black cotton garment bags: one twisted into a narrow band over her left shoulder and fanned out over her breasts, anchored with two bags wrapped around her torso and one more cinched around her waist as a skirt. White "SAINT LAURENT PARIS" letters run up her thigh.

Web is waiting for her on a bench, twenty feet away. He's covering his mouth with a hand. As she approaches, he wipes away a tear.

"Do I send my therapy bill to you or directly to the Set Up?" she asks, walking past him without pausing. He jumps to meet her pace. "The cashier wanted to call the cops."

"Why didn't you let them?"

For that, she doesn't have a good answer. She only has a bad one: She's desperate to see what will happen next.

Web moves on. "Well, anyway, you did it!"

"Did what?"

"Improvised," he says, still chuckling. "You walked out with a Saint Laurent dress."

She wonders just how much of her body is blushing, but she musters a laugh.

Web sobers up and tells her, "Look, that looks great. Way better than what I came up with."

She stops. "You had to do it too? What did you do?"

"Me? I had my bank card memorized and walked out shirtless in $500 jeans, like an Abercrombie model."

She rips her bag out of his hands.

At the garage, Web pays for a taxi to take her back to the Taj M'all. Before she steps in, she says, "Well, thanks."

"You'll hear from them," he says. "If they like my report." She can tell he's trying to be reassuring.

Ally shakes his hand, surprised by her formality before realizing that the gesture is how she would end an audition.

"Thank you for this opportunity," she says.

As the cab pulls away, Ally sees her first honest smile all day reflected in the cabbie's rearview mirror. For the first time in a long time, she feels like she's nailed something.

3

WEB

"She's basic," Erv says matter-of-factly, finally looking up from his plate.

Web wishes Erv would just stay in the van, but when Erv wants to eat, it usually eclipses his dispositional preference for letting Web do most of the fieldwork. Erv enjoyed watching the entire Saint Laurent scene through the window at the Prada store, and he wasn't going to pass up the Bellagio buffet if they were only a block away. Erv rarely misses an opportunity to visit a buffet.

Web sighs. He likes Ally, he thinks. She's intuitive. Or at least a good sport. "Don't be thick," he says.

"Why fight against my nature? She's a background extra with all the self-confidence of a newborn fawn," Erv grumbles, adjusting his boxy frame in the booth.

"She's exactly the demo you told me to look for, and she's the best of the bunch. Plus: that story about her parents? C'mon."

"They sound like psychos," Web's bear of a partner mumbles into his salmon. "I can't tell what would concern me more, Dub: if that story is real or if she made it up."

He hates it when Erv tries to be cool with nicknames. "Dub" is fine, just not coming from a dude so white he's almost translucent. Web continues, "Look, truth or not, we don't need the next Emma Stone. You said we just need to hire a young blonde woman, new to town. A blank slate. We'll train her. She's good."

"She won't play along," Erv continues.

"She will, and she's got the tools. Following rules isn't exactly what we do here, either." He knows, however, that Erv has a few edges Ally almost certainly doesn't.

"Okay, fine," Erv sighs. "What kind of tool *does* she have in her kit?"

"The thing with the garment bags was great," Web counters, looking out over the casino floor on the other side of the booth. Most locals do their best to avoid the Strip, offended by its gaudy everything and the millions of visitors, or by the sanitized pop culture jazz those millions of visitors are attracted to. But Web loves it: the pull of the Plastic Mirrorland, the Caverns of Perpetual Daylight. He lets the explosions and performances that spill onto the sidewalks sway him. He fools himself into walking through Paris, New York, Venice, or Rome. He happily suspends disbelief watching the tricks, enjoying the artistry of the sleight of hand. He's studied the partnerships: Penn and Teller's smug, smirky know-it-all-ism, Siegfried and Roy's ill-fated spectacle.

When he can find the switch to turn off the conscious part of his mind, his more animal self easily accepts the magical dreamscape. Talking with tourists, he can be what he wants to be, which is usually someone he's not. The mostly white crowds on a busy summer day have their faces turned up, mouths gaping, and they don't pay any mind to a Black man flanked by his uncertain past and more uncertain future.

Other days, Web can't switch it off. He knows he can't be just anyone. He knows he doesn't have the unearned social ease and unacknowledged luxuries most tourists have secreted away.

But maybe everyone knows they're being manipulated. To know the ruse is to love the ruse. Perhaps.

Web and Erv head to the buffet for round two.

Seemingly self-regenerating bubbles of food rise from carefully arranged ivory platters. Piles of ribs and noodles and rice that even a plague of khaki-trousered locusts could never deplete. Erv queues up at the head of the line with all the tourists, but Web walks to the end. Gotta make the $40.99 worth it.

The buffet is the pinnacle of a casino's delicate social engineering. Weighted plates make you believe you're holding more food than you are. Pricier items like crab legs are at the end of the line so that you've already filled your plate with rice, potatoes, and other cheaper fare by the time you get there. Rice is for suckers, if you ask Web. Identify the fresher food and leave plenty of real estate for the luxury items. He assembles a respectable but not embarrassing mound and beats Erv and his accumulation back to the booth.

When Erv returns, he brings Web up to speed with the conversation he's been having with himself. "There is a Venn diagram of the people who don't have what it takes for this job," he says, "and the high school drama club Bernadette Peterses of the world, and it makes a circle, Web. Or more like a zero. What about Number Four?"

"Four couldn't improvise her way out of a cubicle."

"We need boring. Someone who tops out as 'Protagonist's Best Friend.' We don't need main character energy."

Web takes a beat to not dial up Erv anymore. They both ponder Erv's plate and its cantilevered potato—another poor move strategically.

"Erv, we've gotta pick someone fast, and you know it."

Erv carefully excavates a shrimp. “If the zero fucks up, we lose money.”

Web gives up. “Let’s talk about it in the parking lot.”

“Fine. She’s a temp anyway. Pick your new girlfriend,” Erv says, getting up to go to the bathroom and leaving Web to his thoughts.

A low blow. And Erv knows it.

These interviews—auditions—cannot help but trigger Web’s memories of how he got started with this whole gig in the first place. Until Ally’s adventures in Saint Laurent, he hadn’t thought about it in a while.

He’d been working in the service industry. He was a pretty good waiter; playing the interaction game was in his blood. Both his father and grandfather worked up and down the hospitality biz after military stints. Unlike Ally, or Erv—from whom he’s detected the slightest Canadian accent—Web’s local. His parents raised him in the history, in crossing the lines. Web’s pop, Mike Cayton, never rose higher than shift supervisor. On smoke breaks, though, he got to know a pretty Korean coworker who finally agreed to a date and, after a few months, marriage. She and Pop often worked double shifts, sometimes together, but they always had a meal for Web on the table, even if it was usually leftovers in Styrofoam from a casino buffet.

The military didn’t interest Web. He wanted to be an actor, but it was much easier to back into waiting tables. And it was interesting. As customers studied their menus, he studied them. He could read a face like a chyron. At the Flamingo’s cheapest restaurant, he learned how to size up a table, sensing the need for flattery or a story, or whether they wanted to be left alone. He was all easy jokes when sensing lightness, and "Yes, Sirs" and "Right away, Ma'ams" when a raised eyebrow meant the mood was off. His mom used to tell him that it says a lot about a person if they see service work as anything less than highly skilled labor.

He ascended the ladder of the casino's restaurants, from the more informal buffet to formal fusion. Then came an offer from an upper-scale casino group, and he shifted to the Cosmopolitan. With each stage, he moved into whiter and whiter spaces.

At the Cosmo, he couldn't shake the sense that he was auditioning for roles only his customers understood. Most of it he chalked up to people treating servers as a race of semi-advanced robots, testing their glitchy AI. Some customers were rude. Others saw him as another hired entertainer. There were blowups over the Tan Tan noodles being too spicy, and there were fat tips that floated him for a week. In hindsight, he couldn't guess which of these everyday misadventures in table service was a charade organized to test his aptitude to join the Set Up, but he remembers the Tuesday afternoon he found a note on one of his tables requesting a meeting and promising a better gig.

Like Ally, Web had been hesitant. He'd met with a middle-aged white woman named Ruth. After a preliminary audition, she'd ditched him in a Prada dressing room. She could not have known that he harbored some attachment issues.

But after he passed that test, Ruth quickly swelled into charm-mode and offered him a job. She introduced him to Erv, who said he had been working for the Set Up for about a year. Web, apparently, was the replacement for another Black man named Gibbs. Two weeks later, he had his first official gig, advertising Fitbit knockoffs at the Consumer Electronics Show. And then Ruth built up his swagger over the course of the year as he modeled clothes on the sidewalk, worked as a secret shopper in casinos across town, and on and on. The free company phone, new clothes, and handsome pay were only part of the appeal. It all made for a fairly swank life that pasted over any lingering childhood insecurities. He's surely no less confident than the next con man on the street.

Once, in a rare moment of intellectual curiosity paired with talky inebriation, Erv had posited that the company prefers trios: a burly type (flattering himself), a woman, and an African American. It seemed to be true.

Then, shortly after the mass shooting at the Route 91 music festival, Ruth disappeared. They were informed that they had to find and train a twentysomething blonde to be their third. He guessed they wanted a younger model. Different demographic. He and Erv had settled on Alice, and they worked together for two years.

And then, a string of jobs—pretending to be in love to sell products, pretending to fall out of love to make a distracting scene—required him to act like Alice's boyfriend. They performed their relationship in a series of short plays set in the bars and convention halls of the city. Although each gig had its own discrete audience, they came to believe the overarching, albeit disjointed storyline was theirs alone. A secret thread. And then, after Erv caught them being a little too fond of each other, they had to replace Alice too. Web assumes Erv reported it, somehow, although he never asked. Even in a trio, no one wants to be the third wheel.

With all communication conducted through the company phone, he had never contacted Alice directly. He gravitated toward the restaurants, habits, and neighborhoods she had mentioned while they were together, without success. Could be that the stories she told him weren't true. Still guarded after his parents' abrupt departure, Web wasn't in a confessional phase of his life, either, so no judgment there. Sometimes he'd flatter himself and fantasize that Alice had looked for him. If she did, however, he hadn't noticed. With every interactional gig, he found that the Set Up didn't exactly nurture a healthy view of relationships.

He stopped thinking about where people go. There wasn't much point in it. For all he knew, Ruth, Gibbs, and Alice were working as a team in Albuquerque now. Now they must replace Alice, and that's the outer limit of his known social universe. Etcetera, etcetera, etcetera. Someday they'll replace him too.

But for now, the money is great. No taxes. He has a high-rise condo behind the Aria casino and a nice car in the lot. He doesn't need to be a superspy Tom Cruise or an unhinged con artist Tom Ripley. He just has to be himself. Mostly.

Erv returns, and Web looks at his plate. "You know the Bellagio sends two thousand tons of food waste to pig farms every year?"

"Where are these pig farms?" Erv responds.

Web watches him polish off two-thirds of his plate in silence before Erv grabs the bill. "What's 2 percent of sixty-eight bucks?"

It's his worst joke. "Who's the Basic Bernadette now? Let's go," Web says pulling out a $100 bill and putting it on the table. Erv collects his phone and the GMC van's key fob. They leave their half-eaten plates for the busboys.

Before the parking lot, they head to the reception desk. Even if he hadn't memorized his way, Web knows how to move through a casino: keep your eyes above the machines. That's where the guideposts are. Casinos are designed to obliterate both time and space, but the invisible hand of the layout administers movement. He knows the architectural pinch points, the mirrors, and the hidden walkways. In a casino, as in life in general, he knows there are many ways in and many ways out.

When he's with Erv, Web feels more conspicuous. He dodges through the slots to keep Erv's lumbering presence a few paces back. They pass lines of dealers standing at attention at empty tables. Staring into the distance, the dealers rely on wide peripheral vision, like owls dressed in white shirts and red vests, ready to snap to raptor-focus when someone approaches. And then, as Web and Erv pass by without stopping, the dealers settle back into position with an almost imperceptible ruffle of feathers and a slight adjustment of their stance.

Web shakes his head and continues past the cage, the baccarat tables, the elevators, the pool, the fine art gallery, the high-end shops, and the slot machines chiming in the key of C major. Finally, they reach the front desk, under an inverted bouquet of two thousand hand-blown glass flowers. The receptionist's face blossoms into a warm smile as if she and Web are old friends at a high school reunion.

"How can I help you?" Web also registers a second emotion in her face: a dash of relief, as if she knows Web recently experienced a death in the family and has returned from having to settle affairs. It's a nice service industry touch, and he makes a note of it.

Web tells her there is a package waiting for him. "For Conor Shaughnessy," he says.

At that, she steals a look into his eyes, as if to read whether he's having a laugh at her expense before giving a quick nod and slipping behind a wall, like a dancer heading offstage.

Web has visited a lot of hotel receptions for Set Up jobs. They're ideal for drop-offs and pickups. Packages flow from place to place. Web has come to realize there is an entire shadow UPS system that flows behind the hundred-plus reception areas in the city. Three or four times a week he gets paid—well—to pick up a package at one hotel reception desk, only to drop it off at another one across town.

The Set Up arranges everything. Contacts, plans, exchanges. Every assignment is transmitted through simple directions via WhatsApp. At first, Web enjoyed guessing what or who was behind it all, but over time, and with so little data to go on, he lost interest. It's shadowy, but he's gotten used to the idea that there is a great deal happening behind the scenes in Las Vegas. And it isn't mysterious enough to outweigh the income.

The receptionist emerges with a padded manila envelope and a charming smile.

"Can I have a plastic bag?" Web asks.

She keeps her smile rolling and produces a serviceable bag from below the counter, and he slides her a twenty-dollar bill, which she slips behind the counter—all in a well-practiced move. The tips flow, exchanges made. One, two, three.

Once they return to the van in the parking garage, Erv puts the key fob and his phone in the cupholder while Web opens the padded envelope. He finds a smaller manila envelope inside, with a name and address on it.

"Well, looks like the Set Up agrees with me," Web says as he flashes Ally's information to his partner.

Erv sighs and backs out of the spot fast as Web reaches for the dashboard to brace himself.

4

ALLY

The building where Ally shares an apartment with Phoebe is like hundreds of others in the valley—a hundred-unit complex with a central pool, thin walls, popcorn ceilings, a disinterested manager, and a resident who claims to be the brother of Engelbert Humperdinck.

After a nap and a three-block stroll to pick up her paycheck from Café Chroma—south of $300 for three shifts slinging coffee—Ally pushes through the iron gate. She stops to pick up a short stack of mail, all bills and a coupon book.

The triple-digit heat makes the double-diamond-shaped pool almost tempting. It would be more enticing if not for the three retired men permanently installed there, baking themselves in the pool by day or in the hot tub after dinner. They radiate low-key heckler vibes.

With her high school theater experience on her mind after this morning's weird audition, Ally imagines the radiantly tan trio as the hags from *Macbeth*. The Neon Witches. She deploys her sunglasses as involvement shields and gives an autopilot wave as she passes on her way to the stairs.

Inside the second-floor apartment, Ally tosses the mail on the counter and calls out, "Beep, your coupon book is here!" The nickname comes from Phoebe's outgoing voicemail message, "Leave a message after the Phoebeep."

Ally and Phoebe met working at Café Chroma. Phoebe was a bit of an enigma to Ally, and isn't that always a turn on? There were folks who needed shifts to pay the bills, and she was the other kind of employee. Phoebe has a disposition—taking no more than two shifts a week, not wanting to spend money on a car, and yet still making rent easily—that Ally guesses only a trust fund can support, although she hasn't found the appropriate time to ask about this. Injecting class warfare into the relationship would be a touch premature. They've just recently flipped the script: moving in together after equally exhaustive searches for a roommate, and then quickly realizing they could sell Ally's barely used bed for an easy hundred bucks.

Ally prepares a simple dinner of cold soba noodles and sesame seeds with steamed vegetables while Beep provides commentary about the coupons from the mail—an ongoing narrative joke about the lives they don't lead. ("Honey, do we need our gutters cleaned?") Then they unpack Phoebe's day, highlighted by the kind of magical exchange that can only happen in the vast underground-favor economy of the city's service industry: two tickets to Cirque du Soleil's new show for eight iced lattes.

And when Beep asks about her day, Ally paints with the broadest of brushes. That audition she got the text about for the unconventional acting group. Mostly marketing. She decides the less said about Saint Laurent the better but mentions—casually, she hopes—that Phoebe just might get another mystery text on her phone.

To Ally's relief, the conversation moves on as they land on opposite ends of their secondhand couch with their used books. Ally is working through *Slouching Towards Bethlehem* and, although Ally knows she is burning to binge on *Naked and Afraid,* Phoebe's reading a worn copy of *The Magus.* As Ally looks up to watch the sun disappear over the tops of the palm trees, they both hear Phoebe's phone vibrate.

"Holy bagels," Beep says, grabbing it. "You were right." She reads the text aloud: "You're hired Be @ 2305 Desert Inn @ 7pm tomorrow Check your door Confirm."

Ally tries to act casual as she leaps to the door to peek out the peephole. No one is there.

"Al?"

Ally opens the door. There, on the doormat, is a manila envelope. She closes the door, locks it, and returns to the couch.

She unfolds the flap and looks in the pouch. There is a smartphone and nothing else.

Ally studies the blank device and her reflection in the glass as she flips it around in her hand. There is more than one way to make a buck in this town, and Ally's suddenly unsure if this is the best way to do it. Servers squeeze into all kinds of outfits to act a part. There are plenty of dancers paying for college in pasties. This, she tells herself, isn't any different.

Ally realizes she hadn't told them her address. She goes back to Phoebe's phone and texts, "how do you know my address??" but deletes it before clicking send. Instead, she responds, "confirm."

Beep grabs the new phone from Ally's hands. "This is not 'unconventional.' It's shady," she says, before handing it back. "I wouldn't turn it on if I were you."

It's hella shady, Ally agrees, but maybe not call-the-police shady. She looks at her reflection in the smartphone again and says, "I didn't think I'd get the job."

"You said you didn't want to be an actor anymore. We have rent to pay."

Ally thinks of the three-digit balance in her bank account. "Everything's acting," she says, noting that she's already repeating Web's lines.

"First you'll have to buy all the supplements," Phoebe says, looking around the living room as if to question where the packages will go.

"Okay, okay."

". . . then you'll have to recruit 'independent distributors,' who'll then recruit their own 'distributors' to maximize your earning potential," Phoebe says, being sure to act out the scare quotes.

"*Okay*. Dial down the scam sarcasm. It's weird, I get it," Ally sighs. She thinks about Phoebe's cavalier attitude toward the expenses they now share. It's also money.

"Having a normal conversation with a man at a bar is weird. This is more 'multi-level marketing scheme' weird." Phoebe shakes her head and adds, "Herbalife weird."

Ally's too busy contemplating a passcode to respond.

"Yeah, I'm gonna say a big 'no' to this, Al."

"Paying the bills isn't as effortless for me as it is for you," Ally says, doing a poor job of modulating her tone. "Three months doesn't give you veto power, Beep." She regrets it at once.

Damage done, Phoebe tosses her book and heads to the bedroom without another word. Ally hears the door close and, after a few moments, the chime of Netflix queuing up.

Her eyes flick to her tuition bill before turning back to the new phone. Ally needs a few tries before tapping a password from the only data she has: the address and suite number for the office at East Desert Inn. 230537.

It's a very new iPhone—actually, the same model Phoebe has—only there are no familiar factory-installed apps. Instead, there are icons for four apps: a calendar (the date in red), WhatsApp (a green phone image), CashStache (a blue dollar sign behind a green handlebar mustache), and PicSnapR (a rainbow vortex). She looks in the envelope for a charger and doesn't see one.

The phone only adds to the shadiness of the whole situation, but that makes her want the job even more. More than that, she wants the story. She wants to see where the weird leads.

First, though, she must repair. Ally walks to the back bedroom and hears anxiety-stoking reality television music through the door. She rests her head on the thin plywood. "Hey, Beep? Pheebs? I'm sorry." And then she says, "I think I know how we can compromise."

TUESDAY

5

MARSHALL

At 5:15, Marshall gives up on sleeping. He's spent the night tracing a loop.

First, the last few moments of yesterday's class. Even though he's sure the students walked up the aisles and into the bright sun to flirt in the food court or to study deep in the stacks before heading off to their part-time jobs or back home to their families, he regrets how he behaved. Just the latest in a series of regrets—some minor, requiring minor corrections. Some bigger, requiring apologies. And then the really big one, requiring a resignation.

But why is this story showing up now? What was the kid's name? What was he doing holed up in a hotel? If lost souls made news, the local paper would be three times as thick.

Might as well start the day. Marshall rolls out of bed and heads to the second bedroom. For the last ten years, this room has mostly been a storehouse for an unused guest futon, unfolded laundry, and boxes of paper. His "archives"—the boxes that store two dozen years of research and notes from his time at the Metro desk—are deep, high, and well labeled. Now, all of it could be stored on a pinkie-sized flash drive, searchable in a millisecond but ripped entirely out of a legible context of time.

"Analog is slow, and megabytes collect no dust," he says to the room. Scanning the scene, Marshall allows himself to feel some pride in his organizational aptitude.

For years now, he has been working on a biography of the casino magnate Milton Prell. (Working title, either *Bingo Palaces* or *American Aladdin*, after Prell's *Arabian Nights*-themed Sahara hotel.) He's amassed six boxes of transcribed interviews and notes on Prell and the city's old and behind-the-scenes power elite. To his disappointment, the boxes have produced not a single measly line of text on their own accord. No literary agent has expressed interest in this book, and, to be fair, it hasn't generated much interest in Marshall recently, either.

With a little effort, he finds the box of notes from his earliest assignments in the back bottom left of the stack. There are dozens of mini-cassette tapes and notebooks inside—comforting artifacts from the prescreen age. The thought of destroying them is as horrifying as the thought of digitizing them. No one will mistake Marshall for an early adopter. He sifts through the pile before locating a pocket notebook and a cassette tape, both with the date of the incident in black Sharpie on the label.

After rummaging for a set of AA batteries, he presses play on the recorder and rests it on the arm of the futon, letting it play while he thumbs through his notes, still on the floor. A ring of folders and notepads surrounds him. "What did you see this morning?" he hears his recorded voice say. He sounds so young, his voice halting. He presses stop and turns to the files.

He finds an article from 1979 noting six pedestrian deaths along Fremont. A court office supervisor told the paper she couldn't remember ever issuing a jaywalking citation, and Judge Seymour Brown added that cracking down on jaywalking would only harm the tourism industry. People "think they can walk anywhere," said one Metro detective. There are other clippings. In 1987, there were nineteen fatal pedestrian-automobile accidents, none filed as suicides.

As the sun seeps through the blinds, he finds the page in his notebook dated October 15, 1995. He reads his descriptions of the scene, initial thoughts, and a list of interviewees. After four pages of notes written with a black pen, there are two names written in red ink, apparently added days later. "Randall Carter" and "Cal Rothman." Driver and victim.

He puts his notebook next to his copy of the "Sidewalk Calamity" article in his satchel. His TAs can scan them both before class.

And then he can't put it off any longer. He excavates the cassette player from under the stacks of paper and presses play again, leaning on the dumpy futon. Auditory details fill in what was in the notebook. The idle of the ambulance's diesel engine. The chatter from nearby gawkers, starting with distinct voices before elevating to a loud murmur. The whoop of a second police cruiser arriving to break up the crowd. His own breathing. He remembers shepherding interviewees to a sidewalk in front of a dirt lot to avoid the gawkers, there as if it were just another Las Vegas show. Then he hears Brenda Dentner's voice, and suddenly, he can remember how she looked: hands on hips covered in black shorts, red cheeks veiled in fresh tears. Exposed.

He remembers her hand reaching for his forearm, as if to stabilize herself.

Marshall stops the tape as she starts to cry. He remembers her long hair falling forward. Her shoulders shuddering slightly. He rewinds the tape recorder, queues it up, and plays it again.

Details get students talking. "Good kindling," he says aloud. "At your own peril, Marshall."

8:30. "If you're early, you're on time. If you're on time, you're late. If you're late . . . ?"

About 30 percent of the class responds: "You're in trouble." He hasn't lost them entirely. That's good.

"First, your interview question exercises are due on Sunday night. Remember that you should also be working on your final projects, your draft of an investigative journalism story with a local angle. Work with your TAs if you have any concerns, okay?"

He pauses, counting to seven. No hands are up. "Okay, good. Here's the story from yesterday's class." He clicks on his computer, and the front page of the *Las Vegas Record* from October 16, 1995, projects on the screen behind him. "It doesn't sound like it had legs, but the article went above the fold."

His TAs move up the two aisles of the lecture hall, distributing photocopies of the article. "I'll give you a beat to read it." While they read, he scans the students.

When most seem to have finished reading the article, he starts the conversation. "So, there was nothing inherently special about the story. A nineteen-year-old pedestrian stepping into traffic. Tragic, yes. Over five thousand pedestrians died from car crashes that year in the US. One every six minutes. Today, that number has increased, due in no small part to distracted pedestrians with their eyeballs glued to Instagram."

A nervous chuckling bubbles through the class. Gallows humor. He remembers seeing the blood bloom on the street. Not bright red, but thick and dark. A neon yellow hat, with a venous stain edging up its brim.

"Since you asked, his name was Cal. Cal Rothman." The class quiets. "I looked through my notes, and it appears I discovered his name later."

"There were a few people on the scene but only one witness," he continues. "The driver didn't flee. As officers interviewed the driver, I worked the crowd. A young woman approached me."

At this, Marshall holds his mini-cassette recorder up to the microphone and presses play.

"I . . . I was jogging on the sidewalk, you know? The driver must have been distracted before hitting that man when he stumbled into the intersection . . ."

Listening to her voice for the second time this morning brings a swell of feelings, surprising him. He remembers taking her out to an early lunch at Vickie's Diner, trying to comfort her instead of following up with the nearby hotels, the gas station across the street, the pawnshop, cycling through the crowds. An instinct skirting an ethical line.

Brenda's voice shakes to a crescendo on the recording: "It's . . . It's the worst thing I've ever seen in my life." He stops the recorder.

"And so, I write in my notes that the EMTs could not save the pedestrian from significant head trauma."

He clicks on the PowerPoint to project a scan of two pages from his pocket notebook, filled with details in the scrawl that comes from writing while standing. "Here's contemporaneous notes from the scene," Marshall says, turning to read some sections aloud.

> Oct 15. 9:52am. Low of 52 overnight. Clear. Two EMTs CNT. DOA. Carson and 6th. the time of the ACCT roughly @ 9:08am. 15 people came out after.
>
> Interview after being debriefed by officers. Car headed west on Carson. No stop sign/light.
>
> Pavement is hot already Blood stain on the street the size of a bathmat. Suicide by car.
>
> Driver=~40yo white. CA plates.driver-gold late 80s Buick Regal. Officer says the driver was "lost" turned around due to changes in traffic patterns. From San Pedro,CA.
>
> Vic= Name unknown AP. Sgt says vic had an envelope of cash, gold necklace, no wallet, no ID. Blond. Baseball cap. Only distinguishing mark: self harm on right arm.
>
> Interview1=white woman. late 20yo. jogging by. Saw the vic in traffic. "couldn't be his fault" driver was crying. black running shorts. FQ bag. Contact #: ███████
>
> Interview2= hispanic male. Early ~50yo . Going to work @ Binions. heard hit, came running to the victim. Jogger arrived after. Didn't see the impact, only the. Witness-tight jeans. Bolo tie and rangers bball cap. Contat #: ███████
>
> Vic was midblock. No cars packed on the north side of street.
>
> TODO: talk mgmt @ Px, FQ, LL, BH, Pnr, GN. Check bizs: gas station, pawnshop, carson flophouse.

"Shuyin helped me block out the numbers," he says, nodding to his TA. "You see a lot of shorthand, a few spelling errors. You'll develop your own shorthand. Spelling errors too," he adds, rewarded by a few giggles from students. "For me, ACCT means 'accident,' S is 'south.' YO is 'years old.' AP is 'at present.' The letters at the end are casinos I left my number with. Plaza, Four Queens, Lady Luck, Binion's Horseshoe, Pioneer, and the Golden Nugget.

"Today, our phones geotag almost everything, and we can access details in a snap. It was all pen and paper back then. You had to get the whos, whats, hows, whys, wheres, and whens in real time. Some of these were unknown, and some I never discovered."

From there, Marshall walks through the case. "The first officer to arrive on the scene, McCall. She told me the victim had no ID, only an envelope with a little cash. It took five tries before I learned that the John Doe was staying at the Four Queens under a false name. Housekeeping offered no clues. He left nothing behind. 'Only a nice tip,' they told me.

"What," he asks, "do you do next?" He pauses, counting to seven.

No one answers, so he keeps going. That's bad teaching, he knows—he should wait for someone to proffer an idea, get a discussion going—but he forges ahead.

"With little to go on and a hard deadline, I wrapped the everyday tragedy in the wider cultural and historical landscape. Remember what I said last week? Pieces from the Metro desk should always be a conversation with the past. It's a challenge anywhere but especially in this city that celebrates imploding casinos.

"Let's go back to the article. Front page. Notice the headline story: The opening of the Fremont Street Experience, the otherwise seedy pit of a cherub city. Why's that matter?" At this, he points to the screen and pauses.

A student from the front left speaks. "It was a major undertaking by the downtown casinos? To clean up the area, attract tourists?"

"That's right," Marshall says, relieved.

The student continues, "So you built a contrast."

"Even the jogger. The jogger signified neighborhood changes too. Back then, one-third of its population made less than $15K a year, and three-fourths of the population was nonwhite."

Another student, middle center, says, "So, a gentrifier?"

"Yeah, although that wasn't as common a term back then." He feels a conversation warming up, relaxes ever so slightly.

Marshall offers other details. The tourist driving the Buick was from LA, on his fourth trip to the city. Closing Fremont Street messed with his understanding of the traffic patterns, and while he was looking at the street signs . . . boom.

"Bad luck," one student says.

"Believing in luck doesn't get you very far," Marshall says as he walks up the left side aisle. "All these various forces, known and unknown, set the stage for this moment, and I wanted to contextualize it. Give it relevance." At that, he pauses and waits again.

From the front, behind him, a student asks: "What was with the false name?"

Marshall stops, "I'm sorry?"

"You said the victim used a fake name at his hotel. Why?" Marshall returns to the front to face the student, a brunette.

"Good question. I found it odd, but it's not illegal to use a pseudonym at a hotel. Suspicious, though, sure."

He was missing something, indeed. *Is* missing something. Who dropped this damn article on his lectern in the first place? Why?

After class, Marshall walks back to his office. Students used to comment that his office had all the ambiance of an unused storage closet, so he now keeps a few talismanic objects there to make it look occupied. A fountain pen and a jar of ink. A yellow notepad. A local classic, *The Green Felt Jungle*, on his desk to hold his favorite quote handy: "Las Vegas is a city in statistics only. In every other aspect, it is a jungle—a jungle of green-felt craps tables, roulette layouts, and slot machines . . ."

He opens his old notebook again and flips to his scribbled notes from 1995. He considers calling Brenda, but he deleted her number long ago. He pulls out his flip phone to dial the investigator for the DA's office, Tracy McCall.

Tracy was the officer on the scene, and she tipped him off to the accident on her way there. Over the years, they've exchanged favors, developing the kind of friendship common enough for people in complementary professions. Something's camping out in a corner of his mind, perhaps something he's tried to forget, and she's as good a place as any to start.

"McCall," she says.

"Trace?" She hates the nickname, which opens her to "Leave No Trace" McCall. Low-hanging fruit.

"What's up, Mar?" Multiple forms of mutually assured irritation: another necessary hallmark of a friendship with someone in law enforcement.

A student peeks into the office. Marshall cradles the phone in the crook of his neck, giving the "one minute" gesture with an index finger.

"Got time?" he asks. But the student thinks he's talking to her and walks in, taking her backpack off her shoulder. Marshall waves his arm, and mouths "sorry" a few times.

"This can't be good," says Tracy. "I see your byline when I think to look for it."

"A few old friends keep me in print. Happy I don't see your name in print."

"You and me both," she chuckles.

He watches the student silently get back up and walk to the hallway. "Listen," he says, a little quieter, "I want to start up an old conversation. One of our first, actually."

"Ugh, it sounds like you doing work is wanting me to do work."

"It's not like that." Then, he says, "Fine. Kinda. Someone in my class is . . . To be honest, I'm not sure what they're up to. But someone dredged up my first article, about a kid who got clipped near Fremont. It's got me thinking."

"Kinda refresh my memory, Mar."

"It was a black eye at the opening of the Fremont Street Experience. Back in '95."

"Okay?"

"I need more details. I had him initially as a John Doe, but later I changed my notes. I'm guessing you gave me the name. Cal Rothman."

He hears Tracy move her phone in her hands. "Old cases are bad mojo for the city po-po."

For him too, Marshall suspects. But he waits. Of all his contacts in law enforcement, Tracy has the clearest moral compass. As a cop, she had to walk a narrow path between exceling in every way to prove to her colleagues that a woman belonged in the force, and tactically relaxing to avoid being perceived as an ice queen. But toward the end of her rookie year, she got a call to a bar fight that included some off-duty officers—half in the bag, and fully in the wrong—taunting two African American tourists. Tracy talked when no one else would. That, paired with mounting representation fatigue, supercharged her desire to complete a night school law degree, and the DA's office threw her a life preserver in the shape of an inspector's badge. The DA needed someone with some street background, and Tracy was happy to get her ass off the beat. Ever since, she's enjoyed the LVMPD more from a distance.

"Well, I definitely couldn't say here and now," Tracy relents. "Give me a day or two. I'll go back to the home office."

"Yeah?"

"Yeah, I'll look. Reports were nothing like what they are today, Mar. But I recall thinking the kid was on the run. You're not going to like revisiting what came of that case."

"You mean Brenda."

"I mean any number of things, but yeah."

"Who's laying it on thick now?"

Tracy's not the rookie cop who showed up on that street in '95. She's well practiced. Even with him, even after all this time, she can keep her guard up.

Well, so can Marshall.

"Thanks, Tracy. Call me back when you've got something."

He snaps the phone shut and gets up to look for his student, but she's long gone.

6

ALLY

Ally's nerves bring her to the Taj M'all lot a half hour early. She grabs a box of gluey General Tso's tofu with rice from Jimmy's Wok 'n' Roll and eats it in her car, parked well way from suite 37. There's no sign of Oven Mitts or her green Subaru, Web or his van.

At 12:57, she drives slowly across the lot and parks. She puts the white waxed-paper box and plastic fork on the floor mat. She grabs her bag and a lightweight sweater from the back seat.

She's buzzed through the first door, then the second. But instead of the small coffee table and two chairs from yesterday, there's a long conference table with people seated around it, and a screen with a projector.

She pauses with one foot in the door. A man at the end of the table offers a stiff smile. "Ally, good. Please," he waves her in. Ten people—five on each side of the table—turn to stare. She feels she missed a memo.

"S-Sorry I'm late," she says, although she doesn't know why she's apologizing. She drapes her sweater and bag over the single empty chair at the end of the table. She sees a "Hello, My Name is . . ." tag at the seat, already filled out. Everyone has one. There's a sheet of paper and a pen in front of each seat, and a glass of water. Some are empty—they've been here a while. Ally quickly puts on her name tag.

"Okay," the man at the front of the room says. "Now we can start. I'm Don. I'll ask questions about various products for upcoming ad campaigns. In return for your ruthless honesty, we'll pay you via CashStache. Good?" Everyone nods.

"Great, let's have those waivers," Don says. Ally watches everyone pass their sheet of paper forward, and she scans the one in front of her. There's an unfamiliar company logo at the top, followed by paragraphs of dense font. There's a line to sign and date the form. The quiet in the room makes her look up to see everyone staring at her.

"Sorry, I—" Rather than completing the sentence, she grabs her pen and scribbles her signature.

Ally wonders how these people came in. Did they arrive before 12:30? When she was at Jimmy's getting lunch? Did they enter through the back door?

Everyone is turned away from her, and she cannot read their name tags nor their expressions. There appear to be five men and five women. Two Black men, two Latinas, and six white people. Mostly young people, two over fifty. To Ally, the group approximates a cross-section of Las Vegas. Don has all the personality of an appliance. A cardboard-box robot with thinning hair and a terrible tie.

"First, I'll ask three baseline questions. Okay?" He touches his tablet and grimaces when he looks up. Ally senses Don is a little put out to have to talk to people. Like a teacher with a lower back issue.

"Raise your hand if you can name five or more of these ten corporate logos."

On the screen is a group of ten corporate logos. Just symbols, no words. Ally recognizes two of them: one for a sports drink, and the rainbow PicSnapR vortex icon. The others are all unfamiliar. A green square with a black diagonal line through it. A sun with a winking face that looks like Don's wince. A lilting speckled robin's egg with a green arrow escaping from the top. Most look half-baked. Two look hand drawn.

Ally watches as all ten of the other participants raise their hands. Her eyes dart around the screen, hoping to recognize other logos.

Ally asks, "Don, you make two of these with your nondominant hand?" That gets a few chuckles, but Don's face only hardens.

Her stalling tactic doesn't spark any recognition. She sees Don's gaze and then senses everyone else's, one by one. She raises her hand.

"Eleven out of eleven. Perfect."

Don swipes the iPad, and a new slide appears. Four lines: one by itself on the left; three to the right, labeled A, B, and C.

"Which line—A, B, or C—is the same length as the one on the left?"

B is very clearly the same length as the line on the left; A is obviously shorter, and C is obviously longer. Ally realizes she's seen this test before somewhere.

"A," one of the women says immediately.

Everyone agrees with her; there's a chorus of As as Don goes around the table. When he gets to her, Ally repeats it. "A."

Don makes eye contact. "Ally, you've done enough. Or not enough. You can go now."

Everyone turns to her again. Her shoulders reflexively fold at the attention.

"Oh," she fumbles out as she stands. She takes two steps before remembering her bag. "Oh, okay." She turns to walk to her car.

"This way, please," Don says, pointing to the door to the left of the screen. Feeling the weight of everyone's gaze pressing on her as she walks the length of the table, Ally offers a forced parting smile before making her escape.

And there's Web, grinning and gesturing for her to close the door behind her.

"Aces! Come watch," he says. They're in a room that shares a wall with the conference room. There's another door at the far end. Same smell of fresh paint and cut wood. Silver vents pumping cool air above. She sees the two chairs and coffee table from yesterday, pushed against a stack of moving boxes. Web's sitting at one of four seats around a smaller, square table, facing the mirrored window.

"What's going on?"

"Just watch." Web turns a knob on a box the size of a pocket dictionary, resting on the table, and she hears Don say, "Now that she's gone, we can finish." She winces at the collective laugh.

Ally sucks air through her teeth. "Uncalled for, Don."

"Totally, but don't sweat it." Web says calmly. "It's part of the act. That's Erv."

She remembers he said she would meet Erv if she got the job. "The grumpy freezer chest with arms?"

"Yup," he says. "Erv has an aptitude for construction and precision. People skills ain't in his lane. Every performance needs a crew, and Erv's our techie. Transportation. Costuming. Operations. I think they plucked him from the production side of one of the big Strip shows."

"And you're front of house, then?"

"Yup." Web continues, "You and I will do the 'face work.' Acting in place. People. Erv hates the interactional stuff. Look at him." Web turns to watch Erv fumble with a box of pencils. "He's miserable," he says, gleefully.

She sits and considers Erv. This additional information changes how he looks to her. She watches his eyes shift. His furtive glances at his watch. And when he lifts his wrist, she can see a dark ring under his arm. She sees sweat on his forehead. Maybe his cooling unit is on the fritz.

"Operations and Face Work. Got it." She smiles. "So, what was all that about?"

From the little speaker, Erv announces the next activity, and Web turns the volume knob down again. "That, my dear, was a conformity test."

Now the memory clicks into place. The A-B-C line test is called the Asch Test. Experimenters pay a group of actors to give obviously incorrect answers to questions in order to see if a single unwitting test subject—in this case, her—will dare to contradict the group, or just conform. Why give it here? To see if she'll follow the Set Up's rules against her better judgment, she thinks. She offers Web a noncommittal "Hm."

"Everyone comes early, and we tell them how to answer the third question. Erv tells them it's to prank the person who's late."

"I wasn't late, though," she says.

He waves his hand and turns to her. "We told them to come at twelve and tested some local TV ads on them. We built a confederacy."

"At my expense," she says, remembering that the parking lot was fuller than yesterday.

"Exactly!" Web laughs. "At your expense. Well worth it too. We get better results when we have a bonded group."

"So, is this gig just a big joke and I'm the butt of it?"

She sits back a bit in the chair, and she sees him notice it. "Oh. Don't be sore. You did great! Everyone conforms, Ally. Well, about three-fourths." He looks back through the mirror at the group.

"Look. Mavericks need not apply, okay?" he says with a shrug. He turns the volume knob back up. They listen to Erv talking about brand loyalty for a few minutes.

Web talks over him. "There are seven stages to set up what we do. The first is 'Foundational Work.' That's the prep. Setting the scene. Erv built this space—soundproof walls, doors, the two-way mirror." Ally follows his eyes around the room. She notices a back door.

"The second stage is the 'Taste.' We gathered the participants and gave them each $70 to do a focus group."

Ally looks at the projection screen, and the wall of icons has returned. She hears Erv discussing each brand.

"But," she says, "while you're asking them whether they can identify corporate logos . . . what you're actually doing is building brand recognition for the corporations themselves?"

"Right," he says. "We didn't pick randos. We targeted people with on- and offline social networks that could fill a college stadium."

Ally shakes her head. "Diabolical."

"Just business," Web says, unfazed. "The third stage was convincing them that they were happy accomplices in a minor conspiracy."

"You brought them in on a joke played on me. Being distracted by one ruse, to get them to buy another."

"Right. That's the 'Build-Up.'" He continues, and Ally doesn't stop him. "We're now in the 'Pay Off.' We give them a taste of success. Erv'll call them 'A-Plus Brand Identifiers.'"

She sees him rest the knuckle of his first finger on his top lip, just as he did in the audition when she met him.

"That's bullshit, right?" Ally asks.

At this, Web lowers his voice, as if the focus group could hear him through the mirror. "Of course," he says, "but pay attention." They listen to Erv say, "Since you've been such an amazing group today, I have a thank-you present for everyone." At this, he leans under the table and produces ten gift bags, stuffed with products. She watches the participants spill their swag onto the table. Kiehl's face cream. A nice-looking washcloth. At the bottom, a wearable fitness tracker. Each looks as if they have won the jackpot.

Erv reaches under the table for a second time, producing a stack of clipboards and pens. Web narrates: "Next comes the 'Crisis.' Erv bonded the group, gave them a taste of success, and now they must make a choice. He's got the waiver. Now he's collecting their demographic information and social media deets while dangling merch under their noses."

Then, it all makes sense. "This is the real payoff," she says.

"Bingo. Separating people from their personal information can be a challenge. Not impossible, but costly. This is the penultimate stage. The 'Move.' They might not want to give away all their social media details, but they want the gift bag. They don't have a chance. Honestly, the vict—" He coughs, "—the *audience* would give us their passwords at this point."

"And we conclude with the 'All In,'" Web says, excited again. "Everyone is in the same boat, and happy. Not least of which, Don."

"Everyone?" Ally echoes.

"Well, true. Not you. You got thrown overboard."

Ally watches as Erv collects the forms and dismisses the group, and they filter out to the parking lot. "It's just an old-fashioned con," she says.

Web lights up, proud. "You've got it!"

She watches Erv smile into the mirror at the last person's departure. "Welcome to the world of the Set Up," Web says before correcting himself. "Well, welcome to the world we exploit."

"One question," she says to Web. "Where's my Set Up swag bag?"

After a few minutes, Erv joins them in the interior room, and Web makes the introductions. "Ally, meet Erv; Erv, Ally."

"You really sold me on the grumpy teacher act, Erv."

"You can skip the plucky firecracker act," he responds, staying in character. It's more of a persona than a performance, she realizes.

Before she can respond, Web interrupts. "Okay, okay. We've gotta get you a few tools to help you act IRL." He gives Erv a look. "What Erv's trying to say, if I may, is that you're already acting."

"What do you mean?"

"Everyone's acting. All the time."

"That's rather cynical, no?"

"It's kinda like when you find out that all sushi is frozen, right?" Web says, motioning for Erv to join them at the table. "Interpersonal contact is the best way to change minds, and the Set Up works that angle. Social media does it on the cheap and for mass audiences. We do it in real time. More targeted."

She notices his hands. They move as if he were shuffling cards underwater. She sees him splitting the deck into two stacks, then using his thumb to lift two corners and shuffling them. Spreading out the cards on the table in an arc. Flipping them over before placing them face down again.

". . . and we do it through simple interactions."

Erv picks up from Web: "We do little ruses like this focus group. We're just putting our thumb on the scale of everyday life."

"We'll start you off easy with tactical marketing," Web says.

Erv gets up and walks around the table, and Ally's not sure if he's doing it to stretch his legs or to direct her attention. The banter and physique of both men remind her of old Abbott and Costello clips. "You heard of mystery shoppers?"

"Sure," she says. "The owner at the café hired them once to see how we work when they're not around. The shoppers wrote a report, and we got chewed out a day or two later."

"Exactly," Erv says. "Big chain restaurants and stores do it too. So we do a lot of that. Free food."

"But the promise of the format is really everywhere," Web adds. "In Japan, people rent family members because there's apparently a real loneliness crisis. Men pay someone to be their wife at work functions. Grandmothers rent a grandson to take them to dinner or to go shopping."

Web's on a roll now. "Decades ago, political and economic power required V2 rockets and Panzer III tanks. Now Russia funds companies of online trolls to pretend they're concerned Americans. But you don't need to be a clandestine government agency to deploy soft interactional work. Police hire people to see if underaged girls get carded at bars. Managers of rising country music singers pay fans to attend autograph events to gin up enthusiasm. Companies pay actors to crowd town hall meetings and shout down a ballot initiative. Talk radio's always yowling about 'crisis actors' hired by governments to stage protests or whatever. . . and they're probably not always wrong."

Ally blinks. "Wait. Are crisis actors real?"

Erv shrugs. "The format's flexible. Then there's sex work. What we do isn't particularly different."

She watches Erv wink at Web, Web wince, and both shift in their seats. Gross.

Ally turns to ask Web: "So, the Set Up does all of those things?"

She cannot interpret Web's shrug. Indifference or ignorance? "I haven't done it myself, but like the man said: the format's flexible." Another shrug.

Ally notices that Erv's eyes rest on her as he leans in. Hovering more, almost daring her to ask a more detailed question to be swatted down. She can't place his age. Maybe forty-five. Finally, he emits a little sigh before continuing. "So, one thing you'll need is character development. A few easy roles you can slip into. Okay? Give me a character."

"What? Now?"

Erv doesn't turn away. "Yes, now. Tell me your name, what you do, and why you do it."

"Okay. Okay." She shakes her head, touches her hair. She stalls by putting her sweater over her shoulders. "My name is M-Mary."

"Here's a tip: Americans love to ask what you do. They see it as a shorthand for who a person is. If you're an investment banker, we think it tells us something. If you're a bank teller, it's supposed to tell us something else. So, M-Mary what do you do for a living?"

He sits down again and gestures with his open palm.

"Ah, I'm a dance instructor."

"Clunky delivery and unoriginal," Web says with a smile but raises his eyebrows enough to encourage her to continue.

"Yeah, but I promise you, it's not like that. I didn't want to be a dancer," Ally starts. She straightens her back. "I was a tomboy. My sister was the dancer in the family. I was the second child, dragged along to all her performances. An afterthought."

She places her hands on the table, activating her left one to punctuate what she says with four percussive pats on the table. "So much so I was constantly looking for ways to siphon attention from her. Kat was seven and getting a little bratty, and one day, she didn't want to go to dance class. I had watched her enough to say, 'I can do that.'"

Erv interrupts with a grunt. "Artless," he says, leaning back. "And not just because you're cribbing from *A Chorus Line*. Have five or six background stories and weave in some facts with *non*-Broadway-based fiction to make it easier. And believable."

Ally knows she can't look defeated. She raises her eyebrows as if to appreciate the notes.

"Don't mind Erv," Web says, attempting to temper Erv's edges. "His theater geekdom outpaces his patience." Erv rolls his eyes but relaxes his body. "Sketch out four or five characters. A few stories. Nothing flashy. Detailed enough to be believable but dull enough to be forgettable. Absolutely no accents. Limited affectations. Don't be a Picasso, be hotel room art."

"You need to be average," Erv says. "That should be easy enough for you."

"Thanks," she says. That stings, but he probably has a point. Apparently, she was unremarkable to talent scouts, so maybe she's perfect for this. "We're just a couple of average-looking fools here," she says, going for a touch of sadness.

"Forgettable," Erv says. Satisfied, he rises and asks, "You have the phone we left you last night?"

She grabs her bag. "My Up Phone? Yeah."

"'Up Phone?' Cute. Okay, kiddo," Erv says.

"Can't I use my own phone?"

"Nope. Use this one," Erv says. "Exclusively." She watches Erv wake up his phone but cannot see what he taps out as he continues. "All communication is through WhatsApp, and you get paid through the CashStache app."

"It makes a cute little 'cha-ching!' sound," Web adds.

Erv continues his overview: "PicSnapR's a social media photo app. You'll take a selfie at every gig. It's how we push brands, but selfies also serve as accountability for when you're doing your job."

"Peak Gen Z," Ally says.

"Exactly," Erv says. "Just like breathing. Your account is @SUAlly. We've already set you up with five thousand followers and a few dozen posts."

Before she can think of another question, her new phone lights up with a WhatsApp notification. "TEST."

Erv continues, "Link it to your bank account, ASAP."

"When do I get paid?"

"After lunch," Erv says. "Your first real gig is tomorrow. You'll get a text in the morning."

"Good," Web says. "Now that you're all set, let's get something to eat." He stands and picks up a nice leather shoulder bag she hadn't noticed before. Ally considers telling him she already ate, but she collects her belongings, including the new phone, and follows him.

7

WEB

Web watches Ally hesitate as he opens the door to Jimmy's Wok 'n' Roll. "What's the matter? Not into Chinese-slash-Japanese food?"

"No, I like-slash-love it."

"I'm slash-Korean, not Chinese-slash-Japanese, I'm not offended."

"At what? Your own joke?" she says. "I just . . . Never mind."

She returns a wave to the lucky cat figurine at the doorway and walks in.

Web orders beef noodle soup from the left side of the menu, and she gets a "Gritty Roll" from the right side. If you ask Web, one of the bonuses of this gig is how, when they move offices—which is often—there's always a new little neighborhood ecosystem to explore, including new food. Web has been enjoying this little family place for the past couple weeks. To himself, he calls the owners Papa and Mama Jimmy.

Mama Jimmy asks Ally, "Left side, now right side?" and Web sees Ally shake her head. Confused, he tries to smooth it over by taking his wallet out to show that he'll pay. Mama Jimmy rolls her eyes. They get their red plastic trays, fill their fountain drinks, and find a booth. He pours two waters from the machine too. "Gotta hydrate, Ally," he says. "Fountain drinks don't count."

He's sure he's giving her too much info at once. Alice had two weeks of prep work before their first gig. Ally has to be ready tomorrow. He wonders why there's a rush.

Once they settle in, Ally says, "Nature abhors a vacuum, and I just fill awkward spaces with talking. You don't need to teach me how to fast talk."

"Well, it's more like 'slow talking,'" Web starts. "Short stories, not long ones. You're not going undercover with the mob."

"But it is undercover?" she says, popping a roll into her mouth.

"In a way. We're not convincing anyone to bring their own bag of ice to a dank hotel room so we can remove their kidney in a bathtub. But sometimes you need a minor story or two."

"Define *minor*," Ally says as she picks at her food.

"I sometimes imagine it like carrying around a different wallet. For most people, their wallet is like a copy of their personality. Take Erv. He has a binder clip with a driver's license and a few bills folded in cash. Straightforward guy. Utilitarian. Not exactly rolling in cash nor going cashless." He tries to modulate his voice, keeping it light.

Ally jumps in, "So, build an identity."

"Yeah. Imagine a few ID cards, maybe a picture of your family. How many credit cards does your character have? More than three might mean you move money around to carry zero interest, maybe trying to make ends meet. Or do you have a single picture of your boyfriend? Wife? Kids? Friends? Do you have a card from the fancy organic foods store, or a punch card for the local coffee shop or bookstore. Or a blood donor card or a gym membership?"

He's glad to notice Ally eating a little.

"Building a wallet makes the exercise easier. It's like a mnemonic device. A memory tool. Ancient Romans called the technique a 'memory palace.'"

Ally asks, "And why can't I just be myself?"

As if that's so easy, he thinks.

"You know why casinos use poker chips?" She shakes her head. "So gamblers disassociate the stakes. Losing chips doesn't feel like losing real, hard-earned money. Same with the identity wallet. A fake identity makes it easier to disassociate from the work, and easy to move on. High impact, low emotional investment." He takes another sip of soup. "So let's try it. Come up with a character, but start describing who they are with what's in their identity wallet."

Web sees her pull a curl of blonde hair behind her ear, revealing a patch of sunburn in her scalp.

"Okay," she says, looking up to the menu board, thinking. "My name's Eliza. I gave my parents eleven wonderful years and then more than enough misery for small-town Georgia church people to handle."

Too much. He'll have to help her reel it in. "Where's your accent, Liza?"

"E-liza, please. You're one smart tea cake, ain't cha?" she says in an overwrought Southern drawl. He winces at the overwrought affectation, and she returns to her baseline, the General American/ Eastern Standard accent that all British actors aim for in the business. "If you're patient, I'll tell you what happened. Anyway, the last straw came in the shape of my mother's Klonopin bottle. The next day they sent me to Last Chance Camp. It was my parents' last resort."

"Sounds rough, E-liza," Web plays along, though he knows he probably shouldn't.

"It wasn't. They didn't have the balls to send me to a real scared straight program. But they did the whole cutting off the hair and ID bracelet thing. I played it stubborn. In mandatory therapy sessions, I railed and screamed. I said I wanted to hurt my parents. I told them I wanted to run away. Full of piss and vinegar, and I wanted to spray it everywhere."

Web asks, again, "Okay, but where is your accent?"

"Nice of you to ask twice," she says. She makes serious eye contact before placing sushi into her mouth. He knows she's buying herself time again, but he doesn't mind. A fine tactic.

"All the while they taught me to be more mannered, more practiced. More civil. My teacher, Henry, goaded me. He called my accent 'low,' and hammered the raising out of me. That's why I don't speak in a dirt-bound, pickup truck accent."

She continues, "One weekend, they had a party where I had to act the part of a polite middle-class member of society. If people couldn't pin my accent, I got computer time. If I'm honest, I can't even do a convincing Southern accent anymore, I just try to mimic Reese Witherspoon."

At that, she sits back in the booth. *Scene.*

"Twice as much as you need, but I'm into it," Web says, lying. "What's in the identity wallet?"

"An ID from the juvie residential facility, a tress from my intake haircut, and a card with enunciation exercises on it," she says.

"Enunciation exercises?"

"Amidst the mists and fiercest frosts . . ."

"Oh, okay. Remember: the idea is to put people at ease, not to dazzle them."

"What if I slip up?"

"People usually ignore disidentifiers."

"And those are . . ."

"Cues that don't gibe. Erv told me this. 'When bodies are naked, glances are clothed.'" He thinks about how few people reacted to her walking around in her garment bag dress but continues down his hopscotch path.

"So, everything's a game," Ally states.

"Isn't it?"

"Everyone's an actor," she says. "Now everything's a game."

Web thinks for a minute. She's on the right track, but it's new to her. He realizes he had never needed to be taught any of this.

"Okay," he says, laying his hands flat on the table. "In Japan and China, it's common to pick up your bowl and slurp your noodles. In Korea, you don't. Koreans also use a spoon for rice, while in Japan and China, you use chopsticks," he says. "Soup is soup, rice is rice. But how you eat them depends . . ."

". . . on where you are," Ally finishes.

He remembers his mother's chopsticks, kept in the back of the silverware drawer. The long, polished metal fascinated him. They had an embossed flower at the top to keep them from slipping in the crook of your hand. He would bring them out when setting the table, and his mother would replace them with forks. "Americans don't use chopsticks," she'd admonish him. He'd practice eating with them when she wasn't home. And she wasn't home a lot.

Ally fills in the space while he's adrift in thought. "Is it your mom or your dad who's Korean?"

"My mom."

Born Bak Kyeung-hee, her business name was Mia. She came to Vegas because she heard about the success of the Kim Sisters—Korean performers who performed American songs for the US military and were hired to perform in a "China Doll Revue" at the Thunderbird Hotel. Long before K-Pop, the Kims dominated the city for over a decade, even performing on The Ed Sullivan Show two dozen times.

His mom's first role as "the Asian" was at a topless club, but within a year, a regular had offered her a job as a server at a casino. The hotel paid for training classes, and she moved up to the blackjack tables.

The Flamingo hired her when a wave of Asian customers arrived in the eighties. Then, they had to hire more Korean dealers because her tables were always full.

"Tokens aren't just for slot machines," she told him. From her work atop and behind the tables, Mia learned a lot about how Americans act. He was just one in a long line who learned how to act. How to switch. And he didn't really have to think about it most of the time.

"Does your mom live in town?" Ally asks, snapping him back onto his own track.

"No," he says flatly.

He was seventeen when she left. No note. Just one cleaned-out dresser drawer. It wasn't six months later that his father said, "I'm going to go get her. I'll be back." He handed Web a roll of two thousand dollars and left six months' paid rent—none of which promised a swift return. It was enough for Web to finish high school, but when the landlord came around for the third time, he had to move on. Web packed an Adidas bag with a few changes of clothes and a pair of his mom's chopsticks. He made it his BOB, his "bug-out bag," a term he learned from his father.

Web didn't bother locking the door, leaving the rest for the eviction company to put to the curb. He figured he would get an apartment in town and keep working to save enough money to go to UNLV someday. Maybe study history. Maybe he was biding time. He was resigned to living in the moment, but "the moment" was now stretching into years. The Set Up effectively hijacks most future planning.

"My folks left a few years ago," he says. Before Ally could follow up, he continues, "My ma wanted me to act American but think Korean." Because she hadn't planned on sticking around, he adds in his head.

"Act American?" Ally asks.

"Is it the *acting* part or the *American* part that you're balking at?"

"I was just wondering why your mother saw Korean thinking and American acting as incongruous," Ally says.

"It's not like any culture has a lock on hidden rules. There are rules and then there are rules. Just like spoons and rice." He takes a bite and lets Ally dwell on that.

"Hidden rules depend on context. How does that help me?"

"Imagining what other people think of as the rules, not what you do, helps you in the interaction game. It requires an understanding of the other's perspective. The Germans call it *verstehen*. My ma called it *nunchi*. Heard of either?"

"Not once," Ally said.

"It's like . . . You remember how Erv was riding you in front of the focus group? He was doing something un-Korean. He wasn't allowing you to save face."

"He shamed me."

"Right, saving face is a big deal in Confucian societies. The word in Korean is *Chemyon*. My ma would've considered Erv catastrophically rude. Nunchi is reading the room. If you listen and observe, you can save face for others, and for yourself."

"Chemyon. Nunchi," she echoes.

"Reading people is the most important part of what we do, Ally. Nunchi is essential for *kibun*—preserving someone's sense of self."

"I didn't know I'd be taking a language class. Aren't we all selfish?"

"More of a culture class? And yes and no. We're selfish, and we're kinda not. It—"

Ally cuts in. "Depends on where you are," she finishes.

"Here's my trick. Most people lose their critical faculties when someone is attending to their emotional needs."

Ally considers it. "Blinded by the like," she says.

"Blinded by the like. Sure," he echoes in agreement, doing that thing you do where you repeat what the other person says to build a connection. What's it called? Mirroring? Or echoing? He can't remember the word for it.

Time to get moving.

"Let's go to the comic shop," he says.

"Really?"

"Can't a Black man enjoy comic books?"

"I thought you were a slash."

"Careful," he says. "I get to make the race jokes."

"It's just . . . I'm not a fan."

"Hm. Well, second-degree nerdism isn't contagious. Humor me." As they walk out, Web waves over his shoulder: "Thanks, Mama Jimmy!"

As they walk down to the ComixXchange, Web pulls a case out of his bag and puts a pair of glasses on.

When Ally throws him a raised eyebrow, he says, "They're false lenses."

They walk in and a "shhhewt" sound—the little hydraulic noise from *Star Trek*—announces their presence. Framed comic covers, TMNT posters, and Green Lantern T-shirts ring the walls. Vintage comics are in the back, newer ones in racks in the front. Superhero comics to the right, "local legend" authors and nonsuperhero graphic novels to the left. Colorful speech bubbles announce different sections. "Recommended Reading!" There's a cozy reading nook of couches near the register.

Web picks up a volume of *Sandman* and continues the conversation. "I get it. I used to think comics were just for children and creepy old dudes. Goofy, righteous heroes and zero-dimensional evildoers. Garish colors. But then someone passed me a copy of this."

He hands the graphic novel to her. The cover has a partial image of a man's face set behind a kind of grate. Smooth, egg-shaped stones fill the rest of the holes. "It turns out, graphic novels are far more than I expected. They're super complex. Weird and fucked up characters. Fewer capes, more darkness."

"*Persepolis*, *Pyongyang*, *Jimmy Corrigan*," the cashier adds. Web smiles. "Right. Right."

Web says, "You're an actress, so you probably could think about it this way: it's like prestige TV."

"Like the difference between *Friends* and *The Sopranos*?"

"Yes!" Web nods. "Similar quantum leap in quality and storytelling in comics decades ago. People are missing out."

"When they realize it," the guy behind the counter says, "I'll be rich!"

Ally keeps looking at the book in her hands. "So, what's the *Sopranos* of comic books?"

"Arguably . . ." he moves to another section and picks out *Maus*. "This one."

She takes it in her hands and says, "Okay, I'll get it."

"Okay, so let's unpack what I did right there," he says, taking the book out of her hands.

"What right where?"

"I persuaded you into a sale."

He watches Ally's hands drop a few inches. "Explain," she says through a smile.

"I used a trick called 'Feel Felt Found.'"

"Feel, felt, found," she repeats.

"Right. In this job, and really in life, we all convince people to do things. But in social work, counseling, anti-racism trainings, used car sales . . . They all use this kind of strategy."

"A good sales technique," Ally says, "relies on persuasion."

"Good sales technique is the ability to create a problem that someone didn't know they had and offer a solution back to them for a reasonable price." Web says. "You start by saying you understand how someone *feels*, and that others *felt* similarly, but then you *found* something that changed your mind."

"You told me you used to feel that comic books were for kids—but then you realized that there was a difference between comics and graphic novels . . ."

"Yup," Web says. He's built her up; now it's time for the crisis. He sighs, a little dramatically. "Look, Ally. You're picking things up. And I hate to . . ." he thinks more about how to play her. "But . . . I can't say you're ready. In two weeks, sure. Maybe three."

At this, she bounces twice on her heels. "Nooo," she says. She touches his arm. "I'm ready. I can do it. I can act. I can nunchi the shit outta this." She smiles again.

"This work takes work. It's not something—no offense—that anyone can just pick up."

"I'm super sticky." She pleads and then, adding a layer, says, "I need to keep this job, Web."

He sighs again, trying not to overdo it, and looks into her eyes. "You sure?"

"Yes. Definitely." Web nods and stacks *Maus* atop the *Sandman* volume.

"I was really going to buy that," she says.

"Oh, I know," he says, pulling a $100 bill out of his pocket. "I'm going to get you *The Invisibles*, too."

Erv is waiting for them outside the store.

With a nod to the brown bag in Ally's hand, Erv guesses: "*The Incredibles*?"

"*Invisibles*," Ally says. "And *Maus* and *Sandman*."

Erv gives a neutral nod.

"Okay." She looks at both of them. "Well, thanks for a morning filled with super-agent training and comi—, um, graphic novels!" She waves and heads to her car.

As she walks away, Web watches Erv scan her from head to toe. He knows Erv's not taking her in, he's sizing her up for clothing. Web texts the Set Up: "Green light." They both watch Ally pause to take and post a selfie, and as she reaches her car, Web hears a 'ka-ching' from her direction. He watches her look at her phone again, then turn around to give them a thumbs-up. Web waves back.

In a low register, Erv asks: "Did you give her the 'Choice'?"

"In and in," Web says. "You don't think she'll make it, do you?"

He watches Erv watch Ally drive away. "No," Erv says. "I really don't."

WEDNESDAY

8

MARSHALL

He arrives two minutes before class starts and starts talking as soon as he's through the door. "Remember: when you're early, you're—"

He stops when he sees another printout of an old *Record* article on the lectern. "Who . . . Did anyone see . . . ?" He trails off when he looks out to a cloud bank of faces. "Any?" He sees some curiosity and bewilderment. He picks up two stapled pages and scans the headline and byline: "Hope for the Unseen" by Marshall Grant.

Marshall holds on to the printout and tries to recover. "Okay. Remember we will have a special guest on Monday. We're interviewing City Manager Elías Losado. So I want you to send me your three questions by Sunday night. Each question must have one news item and a justification for the question. I'll ask the four or five best in the interview."

He watches a few of them take notes.

Marshall has known Losado's chief of staff, Ava Reyes, for years. When they were both on the lower rungs of their respective ladders, they went on a few dates before she broke it off. These days, they just trade occasional professional favors.

"Keep in mind, I'm calling in a favor to make this happen. Be nice. Never burn a contact." Never share the history of that relationship, either.

A few students chuckle. The value of a contact has been a common theme in this class. He pauses and returns to the article, rereading the text. "Someone is going through my old work."

Marshall looks up from the page. "This article is from September 28, 1998. The rescue mission on Bonanza opened a new shelter, serving women and their children, and they sent me to cover it." He waves the printout in the air before opening it to the second page. The focal point is Katie Morera, a new arrival at the shelter, and the story was about the city's limited affordable housing.

He had almost convinced himself that the first archival missive was a lark, a bit of flattery perhaps.

This second article, however, makes a trend. Somebody is taking the time to revisit his work. But who? And why?

He shakes his head and returns to the moment.

"On Monday, we talked about the journalistic storytelling trick of placing people within capital-B Big, capital-I Issues. We write people as people, but they're a news item because they stand for something else. The city needs to be told in micro."

He asks questions to get students to recap yesterday's class, imagining what it must feel like when a trapeze artist flings herself into the air, waiting for her partner to clasp her wrists—waiting with soundless air trapped in his lungs. When he's at his best, in these pauses he's thinking two moves ahead.

Teaching is show business, after all.

In that moment, however, he catches the eye of one older audience member, staring at him without a notebook or computer. It's not altogether surprising to see an older student, nor one without a notebook. But he isn't expecting to see DA Investigator Tracy McCall beaming a shit-eating grin from the fifteenth row. She's leaning back in a dark gray pantsuit, light blue blouse under the jacket.

A student's voice breaks his stare. The smack of contact, hand grasping outstretched hand, from the front left: "How do you reconcile portraying the humanity in people but also using them to tell your own story?"

Marshall turns to make eye contact with the student, a woman in a middle row. "Do you see that as a problem?" he asks her.

She continues, "Isn't that stealing a piece of their humanity? Particularly when you see journalists strike at people's most vulnerable and unexpectedly public moments?"

"True," Marshall nods. He speaks to his shoes as to not appear too confrontational. "People lose their anonymity, but we grant them a voice too. We place them within a greater context of meaning." The student's eyebrow remains arched. "In this case, she is trapped in a context of housing policy and real estate law, not just her own choice."

"Well, it's better than listing someone as John Doe," the student says. He takes it as a slight snipe. "But doesn't that deny her agency? Strip her of her choices?"

Sensitive to the gendered dynamic of the accusation, Marshall doesn't let it show he's a little wounded. "Offering context doesn't rob

Ms. Morera of her humanity. It amplifies her circumstances, rather than diminishing them."

Thankfully, the student doesn't have a response for that.

He walks up to the lectern, spinning quickly to add some drama. "Erring on the side of shining a light on the powerful and giving voice to the disenfranchised, here I talk about how Ms. Morera was evicted on a ticky-tacky violation because the landlord wanted to increase the rent—a practice that continues today, by the way." He makes eye contact with Tracy. "Local law enforcement doesn't do much with these kinds of infractions." Her smile folds into a tight line at the taunt.

He hears another question, from a student in the far back, D+/F range of seats. "What about the vehicular manslaughter story? Whose side were you on? What light did you shine?"

His stomach lurches. He wants to move forward, not back. His coffee breakfast sloshes as the rest of his body remains still. He maps out the path to the nearest bathroom, but it settles.

"Well, didn't I? I'm sorry I didn't catch who said that." Marshall walks up the aisle toward the questioner but stops only a few rows up, checking his tone. Trying to soften it, he says, "But yes, I did an okay job there."

He is slow to anger in class, not so much because he's temperamentally mild-mannered but more because teaching requires mutual entrainment. Anger, he knows, brings negative teaching evaluations. Being as muted as possible, almost mild enough that his lectures could be sold as organic baby food, keeps students relaxed. Cowardly, perhaps. But there aren't that many options for a sunsetting journalist.

Marshall returns the paper to the lectern and scans his class notes, hoping to slip into his planned lecture. Avoiding eye contact, he says, "I don't know if I want someone revisiting the city's history, as seen through my younger self." He hears a murmur from the class before he moves to a discussion of quotations and attributions in reporting. Broad and bland. Nice and safe. Baby food.

Three students linger after the lecture for some clarifying questions on the final assignment. He feels Tracy hovering and remembers to put the printout in his bag.

With the last question answered, Tracy walks out of the building with him.

"Good to see you in action. It astonished me at how few of them were online shopping, although I saw one student watching a zombie movie."

Marshall chuckles. "I hope you're not here to evaluate my teaching."

"What's up with the news clippings? A fan?"

"Or an antagonist. I haven't a clue." Might as well get to it. "Speaking of clues. You got something for me?"

Tracy slows her gait and veers to a shaded bench. Marshall would prefer to talk in his office's AC but submits to her nonverbal request and sits next to her. He gives her "what's up?" eyebrows.

"I looked back at the Fremont story and the statements I collected. Your lady friend says she saw the distracted driver clip the kid. Bad luck all around."

"All this I know," Marshall says.

"Right. Your girlfriend told you."

Ignoring the barb, Marshall asks, "Did it go to court?"

"Driver practically begged for blame. Ten percent of all traffic deaths are pedestrians, so that's common enough. Someone asking for charges? Uncommon." She pulls a metal water bottle out of her bag and takes a healthy gulp. "Since it was both the actions of the pedestrian and 'reckless disregard of substantial risk' on the driver's part, it never amounted to a criminal case."

"What happened to the driver?"

"Federal guidelines on involuntary vehicular manslaughter are about a year, but it was state. Considering the mitigating circumstances and lack of a record, he received a misdemeanor, six months and a three thousand dollar fine. Not heavy."

"Not light, either," says Marshall. "So, where's the mystery?"

"I concur that it's not really a case for Miss Marple. But here's something you don't know," she says. Marshall quickly pulls his notebook out of his bag. "Why don't you join the modern age and get a smartphone, Mar? You could be tapping out notes."

"You know I have app-phobia," he says.

"Fear of apps isn't a real thing, but learned helplessness is." Tracy shakes her head, getting herself back on course. "Anyway, I investigated the John Doe. No ID, no family to contact."

"Okay," Marshall says.

"After your article ran, we got a call at the station. A kid recognized the description of an old roommate in your article and came in to ID the body. Cal Rothman."

"I must've got his name from you after because I put it in my notebook later."

"Seems right. He told me the victim was from Pennsylvania. Not on good terms with the family. This guy lived in a complex called . . ." She scans her phone and says, ". . . Ogden Villas."

Marshall calls up the downtown map in his mind. "A few blocks from the accident."

"Maybe a half mile. He was picking up day-labor work with the undocs on Charleston. Kept to himself. But get this," she says, and Marshall looks up from his notebook. "Roommate told me their last conversation was an argument over some fundamentalist group. Called themselves the Third Family."

He shakes his head, shrugs. "Never heard of 'em."

"Me neither. The roomie says Rothman just didn't come home one day, leaving him with the lease. Roomie figured he fell in with the Family group." She continues, "So I looked them up. They were a Unificationist Church."

That surprises Marshall. "Moonies?"

"That would be the unofficial term. I checked in on them."

"Who did you speak to?"

"Mostly a guy named Joshua . . . Kollis," she says. He writes the name down. "Not a welcoming lot, but that didn't stop me from looking around during Bible study. He said they hadn't seen Rothman in weeks. There was no sign he'd lived there, but it looked more hostel than church. Apparently, they were detached from the Moonie mothership. Kollis said their branch was 'independent.'"

"Like a splinter sect?"

"Infidelity, befitting our local customs," she says.

Marshall scribbles the details. "You didn't pursue it further?"

"We didn't have the resources to investigate noncrimes, Mar."

"Hm. So, a drifter kid falls in with an off-brand cult, hides in a hotel under a fake name for a few nights, and then winds up headbutting a Cali tourist's Buick Regal."

"Sounds right."

"I guess I'll check out these Unificationists."

"Mar . . ." she takes another sip of water. "You know 'The Aristocrats'?"

"The raunchy comedian joke?" Marshall doesn't follow the sudden turn.

"Vegas cops play a similar game but more morbid. They share old stories about bodies and bags of money buried out in the dunes. Cops all swear they know someone who knows where the bodies are. One person will tell a story about a hole found out by Sloan or something; another will talk about the made guy who was found rolled up in a carpet with both ends duct-taped shut and put in a shallow grave. You remember that line from *Casino*: 'There are a lot of holes in the high desert, and every one solved a problem.'"

Marshall's been out there, on long drives to where the roads get all watery at the horizon. Mountains, salt flats, and ancient lines of railroads gone nowhere running in between. Ghost towns like Electrolite. No, Rhyolite.

"Have you heard of Bobby Berlin?"

He shakes his head.

"Bobby Berlin was a millionaire gambler. Not mob but mob-adjacent, right? People talked. He was in the transportation business. Trucking. Four-car-garage type of house. Matching wife. It was in '95, now that I think of it, because that was my first year on the force. They found his body an hour south of the city, near Lake Mojave. Bones burned, a fractured skull."

"Shit."

"Yup. At this point in the story, the cop will string you along. They'll throw out hypotheses. Any decent cop should be able to give you three plausible reasons for why they found a dead body, even if it includes a joke about poor career choices or 'lead poisoning.' Pissed off the wrong guy on a real estate deal? Crossing some crime family?"

"Perhaps," Marshall guesses, "unsavory things happen when looking for an exit plan?"

She nods. "But the question was: 'Exit outta what?'"

"The mob, no?"

"Little Bobby wasn't trying to get out of a mobbed-up business arrangement. It looked like a hit for sure, but it was his marriage. Turns out he was trying to leave his wife for a dancer at the Crazy Horse Saloon, and she wasn't having it."

Marshall thinks about it. "You're saying the mob didn't dump as many bodies in the desert as we're led to believe?"

"I'm saying things are sometimes exactly what they seem, and most times, the past is better left alone. Some holes really do solve problems."

Marshall deflates, taking in the warning. "Thanks, Trace."

"Anytime," she says, getting up.

Marshall realizes his office hours are already half over. If any students came to see him, they're long gone. The hallway is dark and quiet. After unlocking his office, he keeps the shades drawn low and the lights off.

He fires up his office desktop, hoping to find inspiration by sheer chance. Tracy's information is pinging around in his head. Something doesn't feel right.

Maybe Tracy has her own agenda. Was she holding back? Does she want him to stop looking into the case because she might have missed something?

He wants answers. First, he finds Ogden Villas on Google Maps and then he pulls his “Sidewalk Calamity” article out of his bag to find the intersection near where Cal was hit: Carson and Sixth. He calculates the distance: 0.8 miles. Then he does a little searching to locate the Unification Church. Nothing on the map. He finds the address from an old local blog post: 940 East Ogden. All in the same one-mile radius.

Second, Marshall searches the university website for someone who might be willing to talk with him about Moonies. A professor of sociology, Dr. Renée Lévesque, lists “sociology of religion” as an area of expertise on her faculty webpage, and he sends her an email.

Third—a long shot—Marshall looks through his class roster, scrolling through the faces. There’s no one named Rothman. No one named Morera, Kollis, or even Berlin for that matter. He recognizes a few faces from the first rows of class. Most of his students could be there every day or never, for all he knows. One of them is up to something. Or not. Their campus ID card faces stare back at him, unblinking and mute.

He hears a “ping” and toggles back to his campus inbox. The message is from his toothache of a department chair, Len Dorris: “Stopped by your office hours and didn’t see you. We need to talk.” It’s summer; nothing could be of great urgency. He’ll get to it later.

There are also two emails from students asking where he was for his office hours. Scroll, scroll, scroll.

There's an email from a noncampus address, with the subject line "FINAL ROUGH DRAFT," and he clicks on it. One of his students is working on their final, sharing it early even, and he appreciates the gumption. But the text makes little sense. There's a kind of thick description he looks for. But he can't make sense of it. No paragraph or page breaks, even missing punctuation. A description of food, a restaurant. And comic books. Marshall looks at the email address: "Phoebeepbeep@gmail.com." That doesn't ring any bells.

Marshall sits back. When the list of puzzles is getting longer, he's at the beginning of a story, not the end of it. But more importantly, he realizes a story didn't just slip through his fingers: there were a lot of threads he didn't think to unravel.

You straight up dropped the ball, he tells himself. *You fucking idiot.*

9

ALLY

Ally sees Erv's sulky face sticking out the window of the white cargo van. It's three minutes after one. "Late again," he says with a smirk. "Get in." He activates the sliding door, which beeps twice and slides open with a "sjjjjooop-click."

Ally climbs in. Web, in the passenger seat, says, "We almost left."

"I know, I know," she says, putting her bag and the two empty totes she was told to bring on the floor of the van.

The sliding door beeps again and slowly closes behind her.

"Next time you won't be in trouble, Ally. You'll just never hear from us again," Web says.

"Got it," she says.

Erv pulls out from the curb and heads to Eastern Avenue, and she guesses they are going to the Taj M'all again. Erv takes a corner a little too tightly. She thinks of Erv's driving approach as that of a wannabe alpha dog—nosing his way to the front of a pack of cars. Automotive swagger. Impatiently maneuvering to be first at a red light that would've been waiting for him regardless.

After a few minutes, Web turns around to watch her tapping on her phone. She asks, "How did you get this job?"

Web says, "I'm glad you could join us on such short notice."

"My manager has a fully developed sixth sense for loosening allegiances," she says. Ally would prefer keeping her job at Chroma for many reasons, including keeping shifts with Phoebe. But she's missed two shifts now, and Dana will probably put her on the schedule less often or on low-tip shifts.

"This is a big week, which is a little irregular. It's tough to juggle gigs, I know. Hustling is its own job. Try to hold on to your barista job. You'll make good money with us—but the work is infrequent, so you need to keep hustling."

"What do you two do?" Ally asks.

Erv says, "He works at Mad—"

"A twenty-four-hour fitness place," Web jumps in. Erv chuckles and redirects his attention to the road. "Night shift," Web adds.

Ally waits for Erv to answer, but it's clear the conversation has reached its end. When she looks up again, Erv's turning into a Rita's Comidas on Sahara. The building is recognizable as a one-time Taco Bell; like a hermit crab, the smaller local chain moved in when the bigger chain moved to a more attractive location. After barreling over a few speed bumps without slowing, Erv parks.

"Today's a busy day. Three performances," Web says. "A wandelprobe first."

"A wandel-*what*?"

"Wandelprobe. A walk-through rehearsal of a performance."

"Saturday we'll be doing a dinner," says Erv. "Your dress rehearsal today is for us to see what you can do for lunch."

"Wait," Ally says, putting her phone in her lap. "What?"

"What 'What?' You don't like Chinese food. Now you don't like tacos?"

"No, it's . . ." she says as she looks at the front entrance, frustrated. The Taco Bell architecture offers a kind of reverse authenticity, perhaps—a symbolically sufficient curbside "Mexican-ness." "I guess I was more of an In-N-Out kid."

Erv presses a button, and the sliding door opens. *Beep beep. Sjjjjooop-click.*

"Wandel yourself some tacos," Web says with a chuckle. She steps out of the van; Erv and Web make no move to exit. "Your mission is to take a picture of yourself in the kitchen and post it to PicSnapR. If you're successful, you'll get paid for it. Don't cheat. You can't, like, tell the cashier you're getting paid to do it and slip her a hundred bucks."

Right, Ally thinks. *As if I even have a hundred bucks to slip her.*

Ally grabs her bag, and the van door clicks shut. She hears them laugh through the glass.

Ally walks under three palm trees and an awning and steps inside the Rita's. Soft norteño music drifts from above, and there's a queue. Good: that gives her some time to think.

If nothing else, Ally knows how a line works. At Chroma, she has a set of scripted jokes that elicit a decent number of tips. She's faced customers while they zombie-gaze at their phones.

A mirror behind the registers reflects twenty red booths, half in use. Most of the clientele are Anglo. Almost everyone is eating. Two groups are either waiting for food or are done. She sees the traffic on Sahara blur past. Ally watches it all, every edge and line of it, expand and contract with her breathing. Instinctively, she pulls out her phone. She finds the note-taking app again, and her thumbs funnel nervous energy into threads of words. "Three registers. Two are in operation @ 1:16pm. Cashier is . . ." But she stops. Her task isn't note-taking but to get into the kitchen. Easy peasy, Martin Scorsese.

Seeing the heels of the person in front of her move, she takes a step forward without looking up. She hears voices around her, but the voice in her head is clearer. How can she get past the cashier? Force? Should she pretend to be a secret shopper? Would that be cheating? Should she pretend to be a health inspector? Could she pretend to be another store manager?

"I said, welcome to Rita's Comidas. How can I help you today?" the cashier says with a somewhat accented irritation.

Ally looks up. "Oh, hi. Sorry. Sorry." She lowers her phone and looks at the name tag on the cashier's chest. "Sorry, Teresa. Fish tacos and a large watermelon agua fresca," and then, after too long a pause, Ally says, "please. For here." As she pulls her wallet out of her bag, her fingers brush against the plastic wrapper of a granola bar, and this gives her an idea. She blurts out, "Oh. Are there any peanuts in the restaurant? A peanut would kill me."

Teresa's fingers pause and her face gets serious. "No. No, ma'am. We use peanuts in mole, but we don't serve that at this branch." She waits to see if she will have to cancel the order.

Ally thinks about verstehen. Empathy. Nunchi. Read the room.

What, Ally wonders, does Teresa need here? Reassuring she won't be difficult? "Okay. Okay," she says, beaming sunshine without teeth. "Thanks so much, love," and hands her cash. Teresa's shoulders and face relax, happy that the exchange is reaching its expected conclusion.

"Here's your receipt. Number 79. Thank you." Teresa's eyes shift to the next customer over Ally's shoulder, her perfunctory smile returning.

"Gracias," Ally says as she blunders with the receipt. Ugh. Why did she say that? But Teresa is already asking the next customer how she can help them today.

Ally finds a table, sits down, and collects herself. She watches the line dwindle, and when she's mustered enough will, she returns to the counter. She clicks the rainbow vortex icon to open the PicSnapR app on her phone. Teresa finishes up with a customer, flicks her eyes toward Ally, and Ally recognizes a flash of annoyance. Only bad news comes from a customer's second visit to a counter. Teresa purses her lips for an instant and tilts her head up with a nod to show she's ready to engage with Ally.

"Can I . . . can I see your kitchen?" Ally asks.

"Eh, no, ma'am," Teresa says. "That would be a health code violation."

"Look, I should believe you, but as I said, I have a severe allergy and would just feel much more comfortable if I could just see if there's peanut oil around."

"Ma'am," Teresa says, "I could lose my job letting every customer inspect the kitchen." She is, impressively, keeping a smile on her face. Ally admires the craftsmanship.

Strengthening her resolve, Ally raises her voice and takes a step to the side of the counter. "And I could lose my life." Then, softer, she adds, "I won't tell anyone."

She hears the door open behind her and sees Teresa's eyes flick over her shoulder. In the mirror, Ally sees Web walk in. She can't let him distract her. Focus.

The new customer tugs at Teresa's attention, and Ally presses for advantage. She feels another pull—a kind of urge to comport with everyday etiquette. That firm internal monologue telling her to avoid causing discomfort. What about Teresa's kibun? How can Ally help her save face?

"Love, I hate to put you on the spot." At this, Ally scans the room, avoiding direct eye contact with Web but also confirming that he's only a few feet behind her. "That sign, there? 'Please let us know if you have any allergies prior to your order?' That's about me. You had your food handler training, right? I work in food service and had it too. You remember the eight food allergens? Milk, eggs, fish, etcetera? I'm the peanut one. I'll be quick."

Ally sees resolve in Teresa's face too. "What would your boss do if you let your customers tour your kitchen?"

Good point. Ally goes hard and quiet, surprising herself: "I understand you can lose your job, but I can try to get you fired if you *don't* let me in the back."

She doesn't know how she'd react to a customer who said this to her, and her shoulders tighten. She tucks her discomfort away to unpack later. For a second, Ally wonders if Teresa is in on it. Is there a game here? Did Erv come in earlier and make her some kind of confederate? Is this like the focus group?

Reality swings for a moment before Teresa breaks her gaze to look at Web again. Ally sees Teresa give her a slight nod toward the kitchen, and she slips behind the counter as Teresa says, "Welcome to Rita's Comidas . . ."

In the back, four men are at their workstations. Two at a grill. One at the prep counter, chopping onions. Another, further back, working at a sink. The prep cook looks up.

"This isn't the bathroom?" Ally adds, "El baño?" He shoos her away with a hand and returns to his knife work.

Ally retreats a few feet, takes a quick selfie with the line cooks in the background, and returns to the front of the house.

As Ally walks back past the counter Teresa says, "Wait . . . Miss . . ." Ally can see the front door; it's so close.

"MISS."

She stops and turns to see Teresa with her tray of food. "Number 79?"

"Thank you," Ally says sheepishly, avoiding further eye contact. She registers Web's presence and heads to a table. He's waiting for a to-go order.

She flips through her phone while she consumes her plate of fish tacos. She goes back to the PicSnapR app and posts the selfie with #TacoWednesday? and #nopeanuts.

When she's done, Ally clicks on a few people to follow on PicSnapR. She searches for and finds @SUWeb and @SUErv. Their pages offer dozens of pictures, mostly taken in and around the city.

They are universally unexceptional. Web has a few of himself—accountability shots, she guesses—and she pauses to look at them more closely. She sees one of him at Red Rock Canyon, the swirled layers of stone hanging above his head. Another seems to be at the downtown soul festival.

WhatsApp pings: "Leave in five." Ally looks up and doesn't see Web.

The feeling of being observed fades but not completely: Ally feels some internal critic watching her. Is this the acting career she wants? Is making people uncomfortable worth it? She thinks about the money. She redirects her energy on typing some notes and sends them in an email.

After four minutes, she busses her tray and walks out with the rest of her agua fresca.

When she gets in the van, Web and Erv are eating tacos, white paper bags on their laps.

"Splendid. Harder than you guessed?" Web asks. Ally doesn't say anything, so he continues. "People say you see someone for who they really are in severe situations, but I think people can only shine in the harrowing, soul-jarring crucible of everyday life."

Is this what you think everyday life is? Ally wonders. *Forcing people to do things they don't want to do?*

"You did the thing, kiddo," Erv adds.

He takes Ally aback. "Is that— Is that praise?"

"It is Erv's closest approximation to it, yes." Web responds. Ally allows herself a moment of pride. She doesn't know whether she likes or loves the feeling.

Erv starts up the van and backs out. They all hear a scraping sound. "Christ on a cracker. Check if it's okay," he grumbles.

Ally isn't sure if he means her, but the sliding door beeps open.

Erv has clipped the back bumper of the car parked in the adjacent spot. Ally rests her agua fresca on the hot-plate asphalt to examine a red smudge from the car's paint on the van's black bumper and a charcoal-colored streak on the car from the van. An exchange of contact information in tint. Erv hangs out the window.

"It's okay," she says. "Scratches, no dents."

"Get in," Erv says.

"Shouldn't we . . . ?"

"Get in," Erv says again, rolling up his window.

As they pull away, Ally realizes she left her watermelon juice on the pavement. Before she can mention it, she hears a little "ka-ching" emanate from her bag. Checking her phone, she sees she just made $100. With $100 from yesterday's training/comic book excursion, she's already a third of the way to this month's rent.

After ten minutes of driving, they arrive at the offices on Desert Inn. Web tells Ally to bring her bags in, and Erv stays in the van. The conference table and chairs are gone from the first room, and there's a row of open boxes in the middle of the room. They're full of clothes.

"What's this?" Ally asks.

"You said we needed to work on sizing women up," Web jokes. "It's props. Every actor needs a wardrobe, and you, frankly, need some nicer clothes. No offense."

"None taken," she says with flat indifference.

"Take as much as you can fit in your bags. There should be a range of stuff here. Get a variety. You'll need something a little flashy for tomorrow night and something more formal for the dinner on Saturday. Not too showy, though."

Intrigued at the prospect of other performances, she's already on her knees, digging through the box closest to her. Thinking of Phoebe's jokes about Herbalife, Ally asks, "Is this coming out of my paycheck?"

"It's free," he says, waving his arms. "Think of it this way: pinnacle brands send crates of clothes to famous musicians and influencers in the hopes they'll wear them on Instagram. Why not you?"

"So, I'm Solange?"

"Give or take a few million followers," he says.

"Hey, you're the ones who gave me an account with *only* five thousand followers. Is there a Saint Laurent box?"

"You're being paid to be an influencer, but just an in-person, regular one. No Saint Laurent. More like Lululemon and Everlane this season."

She looks at Web, realizing that he's probably been wearing merch all along as well. That would explain all the Lululemon.

"The shoes are over there," Web says, pointing to a set of boxes. "Skirts and pants over here. You'll figure it out. When you're done, be in shorts or leggings under a skirt for our next performance. Not a dress. Nice, not formal. Middle. We're gonna do some tactical marketing on the Strip."

He opens the door and says, "But try things on, fill the bags." He sees her glance at the two-way mirror.

"We'll be in the van," he says. "Both doors lock themselves."

Ally hears the click of the door behind her and wonders where to start. Madewell jeans. Lulu leggings. A box with old-school Adidas. Belts. Erv did a good job. Everything's mostly her size, and in some cases, there are a few different sizes.

Ally usually gets her clothes secondhand at the Buffalo Exchange; even there, most of these clothes are beyond her usual price point. As she touches the fabric of a blouse—so soft!—something touches her in return. She feels a symbolic thread dangling from each piece, invisible but undeniable. She wonders what she'll owe for what's being given.

Ally picks a few simple tops that are flattering and classy. The label inside says Cuyana—not a brand she's familiar with. She tries on a cream-colored batwing tee. Her fingers touch the hem of her top, and she stops to look at the mirror before she pulls it over her head. She considers her reflection. She listens and hears nothing other than the cold air move through the vent. Maybe a hum from the traffic.

She walks to the inner door, watches her image walk between the boxes. She scans her reflection to see if mirror Ally will stop her. No sign comes. She exhales slowly and turns the knob.

It's locked.

10

WEB

The marks bump helter-skelter through the pale horde of tourists gawking at the high casino facades. The woman's wearing a tank with two Greek letters, and her hair—so blonde it's almost white—attractively frames her blue-sky eyes. The man is in flip-flops and a muscle shirt, flaunting three black bands of faux tribal tattoos on his right forearm. Both are so powdery white they almost make Web want to sneeze. They're perfect. He lifts his eyebrows and points his chin in their direction, signaling Ally, who needs no further instruction.

"So sorry. Can you help us?" she asks, extending her smartphone without waiting for a response.

Web must admit, Ally is getting a nice response—much less suspicion than he would usually garner, even if he were holding a Primetime Emmy in his other hand. She's wearing a soft, patterned skirt, a cute lilac striped, boat neck top, and new Adidas, and over the course of her last few interactions, she's developed a little one-foot drag-and-lean as she approaches her marks. It's endearing and unthreatening. Catlike. She couldn't look more middle of the road if he'd dressed her up in two yellow lines. She's landed four of five targets thus far. He's pleased.

This is the kind of gig Web has come to think of as a classic Set Up setup: approaching tourists in a targeted demographic—in this case, eighteen-to-twenty-four-year-olds, or "the Red Bull demo," to put the PicSnapR app in front of their eyeballs. One hundred photos, $100 for the afternoon. There are a few easy tricks, which Web showed Ally before they hit the Strip: Use the phone as a landing party, then enter the target's zone of attention, apologizing for not yet launching the app. Say something like, "Sorry, it's right here," while displaying the candy-colored whirl icon before handing the phone over and gushing, "It's sooo easy," or, "I love this thing sooo much." Web knew Ally had her role down when she started improvising. "I can't wait to show those bitches about my time in Vegas, amiright?"

Everyone's already taking pictures nonstop, anyway. It's the new nervous system linking the body's dopamine reward pathways with the blurred- and blissed-out exterior environment. The sidewalks on the Strip used to line up Mormon-straight to the curb, but now they jut and curve to "design" people—bodies bouncing from one casino to the next—into slow and steady flows. This coercive architecture, happily, creates little nooks for Web and Ally to do their work.

"I'm so sorry, can you take our picture?" Ally asks the couple. The woman shrinks back a little, and the guy seems flustered. "We really . . ." he says, bumbling, gesturing down the sidewalk to an open-air beer garden.

Ally focuses on the sorority girl. "Just a quick pic," she pleads. "Help a sister out."

The Delta Gamma glances over quickly at the boyfriend and then relents. "Sure," she says. "Of course." Ally's at five out of six.

Web has a second gig nested into the first, another job, parallel to Ally's, and he's nailing it too.

With a few practiced thumb swipes, keeping his phone hip-level, he snaps a photo of the couple while Ally fumbles with her phone. When Web noticed the girlfriend step back in a half-sulk at Ally's intrusion, it only confirmed he had his gal. The sulk could be because Delta Gamma's preoccupied about the money they're blowing on this trip. Maybe she's annoyed at Ally's intrusion. Or maybe she doesn't want the attention because she's cheating on her boyfriend.

Ally loads PicSnapR and hands her phone over to Delta Gamma.

Ally and Web position themselves to have the replica Eiffel Tower behind them. He feels Ally give his midsection a brief squeeze. Who, he wonders, is the audience for that touch? He smiles a smile for everyone involved. The Delta Gamma counts. Three, two . . . one.

She takes a few pictures, verticals and horizontals. Web can tell she thinks of herself as something of an amateur documentarian. Most people do. Ally talks up various social media features as Web huddles with her in a performative review of the mini-photoshoot.

"This app always makes us look so cute," Ally says, singsonging the last word and keeping the couple tied to the interaction for a few seconds longer.

Web knows this kind of ruse exists in a legal gray zone. He doesn't fancy himself a law expert, but guerrilla advertising in public spaces did strike him as problematic, so on a quiet afternoon, he looked it up. The Federal Trade Commission's website on commercial practices states that corporations must disclose payments between the seller of an advertised product and its endorsement. He read the fine print until his eyes went woozy, but once the money started flowing through his phone, his discomfort faded. The CashStache app, with its little green mustache icon, would fire off a "cha-ching!" sound to notify him money deposited into his account after every job, and the more he heard that sound, the more certain he was that those legal issues were someone else's problem.

"We're just asking a favor," he told Ally in the van on the way to the Strip. "We even hand them our phones."

"A sign of trust," Ally nodded. "Like the 'In and In!'" she added, her spine straightening at the opportunity to prove she'd memorized the steps of the con.

"Exactly," Web said, with mentorly pride. "Same concept. We're not selling the app. No money exchanged."

He's long suspected that they're working in synergy with other corporate strategies stalking the dozens of annual events and conventions that invade Vegas. The National Finals Rodeo, or an electronics convention. Or booze, or fashion, or concrete, or automotive parts. A Fashion Auto Parts Convention, or Boozy Electronics Expo. He doesn't really care. Along with secret shopping, focused marketing has been the steadiest of their gigs.

The Strip's whole strategy is stimulation overload. Dueling piano men playing "Piano Man." Adidas/Vans/Converse shoes sales. Spiraling lights and bright tubes of alcohol. Tribute bands and has-been-celebrity-digging-through-their-back-catalog residencies. The Strip House (a "Sexy Steakhouse on the Strip"—the rare Olympic triple axel of puns). Music blaring from every doorway, along with chilly air. Cultural turbulence.

On the other hand, the Set Up's strategy is tactical. Amid the mayhem, they're left to work in expressions and gestures. In the in-between.

"There's always a company desperate for product placement," he told Ally. Sometimes he's displaying a tailored suit as a semi-interactional performance art mannequin at a conference. Sometimes he's wearing new tech.

And, he reflects, sometimes he's looking for philandering partners. His job is just the ground game. Strategy and logistics happen on the other side of his phone. Husband Job, Girlfriend Job, whatever. It all boils down to the same relationship: between him and his money.

A few minutes later, he feels a vibration in his pocket and a "cha-ching!" from the CashStache app.

Ally's proven she's gotten the hang of the gig, and they'll meet their quota quicker if they split up. "Remember to hydrate," Web says, with concern imitating breeziness. She pulls a water bottle out of her bag and jiggles it for his benefit, acting in return.

"See you at the van in two hours," he says, and then mimics the Set Up: "Confirm?"

"Confirm!" Ally responds with a half-assed salute. And then the crowd's undertow swallows her whole, a sea of "She's the Crazy One" bachelorette party, Dunder Mifflin, and American Flag souvenir tees crushing a lone surfer.

Web looks up at the T-Mobile hockey arena to see the lines shimmershake from the heat. A suitable backdrop, he thinks. He pulls out his phone and looks for his next mark.

It's an unusually full day of work. After they regroup at the van, Erv drives them to a warehouse on East Sunset, out by the airport's cargo center. He opens a double-wide storage unit to reveal eight scooters: two pearl white, two sky blue, two olive green, and two ruby red. Around the scooters are more boxes, rolls of cloth, other oddities. There are three bicycles on hooks. Web's not sure what's in the boxes. They're in constant flux. Out of sight, he knows, fresh boxes arrive, and old boxes leave. Erv keeps the inventory.

It looks like the prop room for a theater company because, well, it is.

Erv explains the gig: they're to park the Vespas in front of select restaurants before the dinner hour begins. Web can't help but laugh. What is it about white people and Vespas, he wonders.

Ally asks, "Is this, like, a marketing campaign for Vespas, or for the restaurants?"

"Maybe both? Etcetera," Erv says in a flat tone. "Take a picture of yourself at each location, with the scooter in the background. And be careful. I spent an hour waxing them up."

Despite himself, Web admires the fifties-sleek style and candy-colored gloss. The Vespas resemble cute little retro robots. Would they make him want to eat at a restaurant? Probably not. But then, he's probably not the target audience.

Web finds helmets for himself and Ally, and they head to Henderson on their first run on the white scooters, with Erv trailing them most of the way in the van. At Lake Mead Parkway, Ally and Erv turn left while Web heads a little farther south, parks in front of a sushi place and then waits for them to pick him up. They loop back for the sky blue scooters, and then the green.

When they pick Ally up from her third drop, she's waiting in the shade. After hopping in the van, she asks, "Why an office building?" She says it in a way that seems rhetorical, but Web feels she wants a response.

He scans the sign on the front. There are three businesses: Joseph Family Dentistry, Oakwood Corporate Housing, and In-Hwa Group. The dentist's office has a little image of a tooth, with what looks like multicolored dental floss spun around it. The In-Hwa icon is a blue 'I' in front of a black 'H.'

"No idea," Web responds.

She asks, "Do patients take nitrous-fueled rides home on Vespas?"

"Clearly," he says.

Web hears Ally sing a line he recognizes from *Little Shop of Horrors*, reaching a decent falsetto.

On the final ride, Web welcomes the solitude. Riding a scooter is more visceral than driving in the van. It's like playing a sport instead of watching it.

Waiting for Erv and Ally at the last drop site, he sits outside an Argentinian restaurant, near the valet station. The valet offers the Nod, with no need for further comment.

The dinnertime clientele pass his line of sight, and he sees a few noticing the scooter, parked near the entrance. He takes in their clothes. Most of the men are wearing crisp, striped button-downs. A lot of blue. He smells the asado on the woodfire grills and hears the snickering sound of misters nearby.

He surveys the sunset over the mesa-like casinos and the Spring Mountains Range. The sky's color approaches the apocalypse-red hue of the Vespa. He turns to see the pale orb in the purpling-bruise slice of the sky.

"When we see a full moon," his mother would always remind him, "we're only really seeing half."

One of the only fragments of his mother's background that remained in his childhood was a porcelain moon jar. He remembers how his eyes would trace along a seam that was visible only when the light hit the milky white orb just right. His mother once told him the line was from fusing two unequal hemispheres. "They aren't supposed to match," she would tell him. She'd describe how assembling dissimilar pieces conflicted with the Confucian ideal of harmony. "Imperfections," his mother would say, "make us human."

He thinks about the imperfections of his particular parental halves, and then his reverie is interrupted by a dry, throat-clearing "eh hm." Web looks to his right at a man with keys in his hand. "Shouldn't you be standing?"

Web looks at the thirty-something white couple. They're a little older than he is, or maybe just dressed as if they are. He clocks the Dries Van Noten print of the man's shirt under a bright blue linen suit jacket, and she's wearing a Van Noten wrap with matching color accents. There's a silver Tesla pulled to the curb. The valet station is empty; he must be parking another car. Looking down at his Lululemon stretch khakis and short-sleeve polo shirt, Web realizes he's not *not* dressed like a valet. He freezes, considering various responses. Tell the guy not all Black men are valets? Let it pass?

"I—" Web starts, but the man tosses his fob in the air without waiting for the reply. Web watches the couple walk into the restaurant and fantasizes about taking a quick joyride. He read somewhere that Teslas have some zip for an all-electric vehicle. Something about fewer moving parts. He wonders how far he could get before the battery died. Two hundred miles? Three hundred? Where would he go? LA? He imagines starting a fresh life, grabbing his bug-out bag and never coming back. The car might get him there. Would it even be stealing?

Web catches the valet's eye as he returns to his post. He's smiling, having watched the exchange from afar. Web tosses the key fob to him and they both nod again. No questions asked, no answers needed.

Mercifully, the white cargo van pulls behind the silver Tesla, and Erv slides open the door, letting Web climb in.

"Boys," Ally says as the door closes, "maybe I can buy myself one of those scooters with all the money we're gonna make."

Web smiles, but the corners of his mouth drop as he turns away from her, remembering what Erv said about her being a temp.

"Who's ready for dinner?" Erv asks from the front. "I could eat a scooter."

"You think they have Amarillo Roadhouses in Texas?" Web asks, walking up to the wooden doors.

"Are there Mexican restaurants in Guadalajara?" Erv asks.

"Yeah, but do you know what they call them there?" Web asks, thoroughly disappointed at the precipitous downgrade from the Argentine steakhouse to this chain. "Restaurants."

Erv says, "Before 1848, this *was* Mexico . . ."

Web feels Ally wordlessly trail them from the van to the heavy wooden doors.

The hostess seats them at the front window, and he makes Erv slide over so Ally can have her own side of the booth. He can tell Erv gets uncomfortable about their seating arrangement when Ally excuses herself to go to the bathroom.

Web reckons he'd be impressed but not surprised if Ally were to slip out the back, order an Uber, and vanish with the few hundred dollars she's made. But she returns quickly.

In fact, she seems to have collected a few thoughts while away. He sees a resolve in her face.

He waits as the server arrives, introducing herself as Sam with a curt howdy and a light accent that's probably a put-on and that makes him think of Ally's fake Georgia accent.

Erv quickly orders for everyone. A ribeye, medium, for himself; chicken fried steak for Web; and a potato—"free range," whatever that means—and house salad for Ally. An unsweetened iced tea, a draft beer, and a Coke.

"Um," Ally starts, but Web realizes what Erv's doing and puts his hand up to Ally behind his sticky menu, out of Sam's line of vision. She sees it and settles back. He can see in her face that she's thinking it through.

When Sam completes her pleasantries and fades into the faux woodwork, Ally starts up. "What the hell?"

Web sighs and answers in a low voice, "I think we're secret shopping." He focuses on the local news on the TV behind the bar, hoping to avoid further conversation while Erv stares into space.

Ally sighs, "A heads-up would've been nice."

"It would have been nice, Erv," Web says to his partner, who only smirks in response.

Ally's unamused. "You guys are real cute with your show-and-tell," she says. "Does it make you feel like you're in control, even though you have, what, 10 percent of the picture? Five?"

"How do you know what we know?" Erv asks.

"And how do you know what we don't?" Web adds.

"You told me yourselves: Etcetera," she counters.

Erv starts with, "If you're the kind of person who thinks she needs answers for everything . . ." Web holds up his hand as Sam returns with their drinks.

Erv rears toward the server. "I didn't order a Coke. I want a Dr. Pepper instead."

Web watches Ally, who remains still, eyes down.

"Oh, I—" Sam says, reaching for her ticket. Web watches the light in her eyes fade a little.

"Never mind what's in your little notebook," Erv says, and she pulls her hand away from her apron. "Bring me a Dr. Pepper."

Ally adjusts her position as Sam looks over the group. "I'll be right back," she says before disappearing again.

"You don't have to be mean," Ally says.

"You don't know what I have to do," Erv responds.

"I know you're gonna get a loogie in your side of creamed corn," she says. "Are either of you untroubled by the ethics of doing these performances?"

"Why would we be?" Erv spits back. "We're just acting."

Web can't see Erv's face without turning his head, but he can hear the usual rough edge in his voice sharpening into a blade.

"Maybe because people like Sam don't know they've bought tickets to your little one-act."

"Our," Erv says.

"What?" she asks.

"*Our* little one-act, you mean."

Web watches Ally's shoulders dip again, slowly. He says, "This is all something of a gray area . . ."

"Sure. *Our* one-act," she says. "But you both seem all too comfortable in the gray."

Web is certain that secret shopping is the firmest legal ground they've stepped on today.

"Don't be a Pollyanna, Ally," Erv responds. Then he says, "Polly*ally*," in a way that's supposed to break the tension.

Alice and Web used to pepper each other with mini-theories about how the city worked. Web would come up with some speculation about a casino's over-oxygenated air being infused with corporate-secret combinations of lavender and peanut butter to produce maximum docility. She would counter with detailed explanations of unlucky numbers in different cultures. Eight in India, nine in Japan. He added that four was bad luck in Korean, since it sounds similar to the word for death. "Bad juju," she said. "The devil's bounce," he replied. "The whammy," she'd say. Everything was fodder. Web wonders, now, how much Erv resented the way this ongoing banter excluded him.

Sam brings their food, and Web watches Ally's face rise to offer a wide smile before mouthing a "thank you" to their server. She's trying to communicate that she has a different agenda than her gruff counterparts. The server's eyes sweep the table before she departs with a stiff smile.

For a minute it appears Erv has lost his appetite, either for food or conversation, but eventually he cuts into his steak.

Ally puts her cutlery down instead of eating, and Web can almost hear Erv's eyes rolling beside him.

"Do you ever get competing text messages?"

"What?" Web mumbles. The breading around his steak crackles under his knife as he thinks about his side mission on the Strip earlier.

"Nonanswer noted. I noticed Web was just as surprised as me that we're working as secret shoppers right now."

Web's impressed but doesn't give away much.

"It's called a job, Ally," Web says. "You want our server to question whether she should bring us our meal?"

"Save your pedanticism. Do you guys just run around town doing whatever your phone tells you to?"

Web puts another piece of steak in his mouth, feeling the pepper work on his palate. He finds a hint of Tabasco hidden in the breading. He swallows. "Maybe you don't know a good thing when you see it. We get paid plenty for our discretion."

"Digital money doesn't paper over your absence of curiosity."

Web hears a sigh from Erv and notices that he's resting his wrists on the table. He's looking at Ally without responding, just watching her side of the exchange.

"What is it you think we should be curious about?" Web asks.

"Like," she says, working around the leafy edges of her salad, "how do the scooters get back to the warehouse?" Web takes a long drink of iced tea, and Erv turns to look out the window.

"What about it?" Web asks.

He can sense she's gathering a head of steam. "My guess is there's another team that picks them up at the end of the night. There's someone else doing all the same jobs we do all over the city, only in reverse. Like a Night Shift 'Void' Team that unravels our jobs—returning the scooters and repairing the broken and interrupted interactions we've sown across the valley."

Web has never considered this. He realizes, just as quickly, that Erv almost certainly has. Erv might have a poker face, but he doesn't have a very good poker body. He is getting annoyed.

"Enough," he grunts, putting down his fork and knife. He draws his shoulders in and leans forward to Ally. "I do it, okay? The money usually solves these problems," he says. "Did you get your payment for the scooter job?"

"Oh," Ally says, still looking at Erv. "Uh. Let me see."

He watches as she taps in her passcode and swipes at the screen. "Y-Yeah," she blurts. "Got it." And then, "Wow."

Web sees her face ease a little more. Ally sits back in full retreat, into the phone. Erv wins, but he throws a final taunt for good measure: "Using the word *pedanticism* is pedantic."

After a few minutes, Erv yells for the check from Sam, who zips in from behind them, as if expecting the call.

"I'm not done," Ally says.

"Talk less next time," Erv says.

Web looks at the table, embarrassed by the waste. Half his steak, Ally's whole potato, and most of her salad. It reminds him of the waves of food left over at casinos, the Styrofoam boxes his parents used to bring home.

"We should get this to go," Web says.

"No," Erv responds, putting his broody face on as he gets up. "Leave it."

THURSDAY

11

MARSHALL

"The good news, folks, is that we're almost two-thirds through our summer session."

Marshall looks around the lecture hall to assess the enthusiasm. There are a few claps. Excitement between instructors and students tends to be asymmetrical, but in this case, he's somewhat relieved too.

"So, let's get started," he says. "I was planning to talk about *The Death and Life of American Journalism*, but our mystery student has given us another prompt," he says, waving the article he found on the lectern when he arrived a half hour early for class. Whoever is leaving these articles is a real early bird. "It's about the anniversary of a landmark housing case, and—interestingly—it's from back when Monday's guest, City Manager Elías Losado, emerged onto the political stage."

Is this all related to Losado's planned class visit on Monday? A good article to pull into class discussion. Marshall just wishes he knew whether he's pulling or the one getting pulled.

Marshall scans the article to find the quote from Losado, who was a city councilor at the time. The anniversary was a chance to build stronger protections for renters. He remembers Losado walking a careful line between advocating for renters and not upsetting property owners.

He cycles back to the discrimination case and walks through how he wrote it up, mostly focusing on how to make the anniversary of a historical event a proper "news peg" for a piece. "We say journalism is the rough draft of history," he says. "But an anniversary is an opportunity to write a decent second draft."

He reads his description of the Oakwood complex aloud to the class to talk about mise-en-scène. He riffs on redlining and then reads a paragraph describing what the apartment complex looked like in 2009, contrasting how it looked ten years prior, under severe neglect.

"I try to consume as many details as possible to ensure I have a massive amount of information to work with but also to help readers feel as if they are there. Sometimes what's important isn't obvious at first. That stuff is for *CSI: Las Vegas*. Or maybe I'm slow. But some of my best writing has come from analyzing my notes well after the fires were out, after I switched off my cassette recorder. It's called 'exhausting a scene.'

"In fact, that would be a great assignment for this weekend," he says. He registers a murmur of annoyance emanating from the class. "Yes, besides the questions for Losado."

No backtracking now. "Go to a location," Marshall continues. "Take out a notebook and write everything you see. Drain a place. This isn't an essay, it's a recording. One thousand words won't be enough to come close to it but should give you a sense of the exercise."

A student speaks up. "Will you grade this?" And another one says, "It's not in the syllabus."

Marshall finally can make eye contact with the second one: a young woman, in her late twenties, with the icy look of someone retaking the class after misjudging it as a lark the first time around. Before he responds, she continues, "You cannot just drop an assignment on us. Some of us work and have families and need to plan our workload." Her eyes harden but also flit around to see if she has support from any classmates.

Marshall sees a few nods of agreement. He's unwilling to mount too much of a defense and considers offering extra credit. "Well, that's true," he says. "Okay, okay. Fine." Marshall registers a little relief from his TAs, pleased they don't have to grade an unplanned avalanche of papers. He shoves the article in his bag and moves on to other topics.

Following the last of the students up and out the doors, he sees a shadow standing still in the doorway. He sure is getting a lot of visitors this week. He recognizes the outline of his department chair, Len Dorris.

"You're hard to track down," he says when Marshall meets him at the doors.

A few feet down the aisle's incline, Marshall's at more than a positional disadvantage. Higher up, and backlit by the windows to the courtyard, Dr. Dorris looks more authoritative than usual.

Marshall tries for lightness. "Well, being elusive is a critical part of being a—"

"It isn't a compliment," Dorris says. He is the kind of person who makes jokes like "spreadsheets are my love language." Most of their interactions are over email, and Marshall realizes he would have preferred it that way in this moment.

"Let's walk to your office hours. I wouldn't want you to miss this important—and contractually obligated—part of your job. Again."

"What's with the visit, Len?" Marshall asks as they weave through the rush of students between classes.

"Well, I've received complaints." Marshall winces.

"Threatening students with their grades for asking questions? That's more than a no-no, Marshall. I went to your office hours, even sent you an email, but I haven't heard from you. So here I am."

He doesn't have much to say to any of it. Marshall tries an apology. "I'm sorry, Len. I'm working on something."

"We're all working on something. Some of us figure out which is the side hustle and which is the main gig."

"Sure. Easy math when you've got a tenure-track job. My hustles gotta coexist."

Dorris blinks and eases up. "Look. I hired you because you're a working journalist. You've got cred. The students know that, and I know it. But that doesn't give you carte blanche. You need to recalibrate. Let's finish this class on good terms?"

"Good terms. Yes. You won't hear another complaint."

"I appreciate the confidence," Dorris says, turning to walk away.

Back in his office, chastened and alone, he lets the firehose of email wash over his eyes. He finds the email from Dorris with the subject heading: "Urgent." Well, there's no point in opening it now.

Another email from Phoebeepbeep@gmail.com comes in. It's an enormous block of text-speak without paragraph breaks. More descriptions of places and people. A Mexican restaurant. He catches the phrase, "The city needs to be told in micro . . ." a phrase he said in class yesterday. He looks for a clue that might connect to the two articles that appeared this week. The writing looks like Phoebeepbeep is "exhausting a scene," but the email is from yesterday.

His phone rings, startling him out of his thoughts.

The voice on the other end starts, "Can you proofread my post on Rate My Professor? 'Professor Grant is like Sesame Street: Informative, yet . . .'"

"Not today, Tracy," Marshall groans. "Can I help you?"

"Help me? Cute. You know what students say about you on that website? You have a chili pepper."

"How would you feel about a 'Rate Your Cop' website?"

"Alright."

"'Officer Borer is consistently unprepared for routine traffic stops . . .' It's a great idea, really. Internal Affairs would love it. Instead of chili peppers, you can have pepper spray. 'Officer Dickins, two cans.'"

"Har, har. Go close your door." He does as he's told.

Tracy says, "I blew the vehicular homicide case."

"What do you mean, you blew it?"

"I mean, I was young. I didn't follow through either." It sounds as if she's speaking from her car. Muffled yet loud. "I should've given the Moonies a second look, Mar. I'm making it up to you."

"How?"

"You didn't get these from me," she says, prompting him to grab a pen and his stack of yellow sticky notes. She offers four sets of phone numbers and addresses. "Three are unlisted. I looked up the current contact info of everyone around the scene back in '95. Four still live here."

"Why are you giving me these contacts?" Marshall asks.

"I don't know," Tracy concludes. "Maybe you want to see what they remember about that day. The third one, your old girlfriend, was a touch harder to find because she's not on a lease or deed. Be careful, old friend."

At that, the line goes dead.

He returns the receiver back on its old dial pad and looks at the list of numbers. What new light could possibly be shed from revisiting decades-old memories?

He dials the first two numbers and hangs up before leaving messages. He stops at the third number, which might as well have been written in pink neon. Instead, he calls his real estate agent.

A creaky voice speaks on the other end. "Hola?"

"Oh, shit. Did I wake you?" Marshall checks the time on his computer. 12:30 p.m.

The voice brightens up. "Nah, I'm messing with you. How you doin', Mar?"

Marshall rolls his eyes. "I'm perfect, Ernie. Are you at the office or on the road?"

"The former, and soon the latter. Meet in person?"

"Yeah. That would be good," Marshall says.

"I can always find a spot on my calendar for you."

"I'd like you to look at a downtown lot with me. Half an hour. Pick me up at the *Record*'s parking lot?"

"Then and there," Ernesto says, hanging up.

Marshall scrolls through his emails before his eyes fall back on the third number on the sticky note. He calls it.

A gasp escapes his lips at the "Hello?" he hears on the other end of the line. Her voice sounds the same.

"Brenda? It's Marshall. Grant," he says. After a millisecond of a pause, he adds, "From *The Record*."

"I only know one Marshall, Marshall," the voice responds. "Long time. You aren't calling in an official capacity, are you?"

"Ah, no."

"A social call then?"

"Well, no."

"So, after all this time you're calling me 'from *The Record*,' and you're calling for neither official nor personal reasons?"

Over the years, Marshall has imagined how this call would go. He didn't imagine it much worse than this, though it was a fair facsimile of their banter. "It's 'official' in a spiritual rather than a technical sense. Look, something's come up. Can we talk?"

"We are talking."

"In person? Tomorrow?"

After a long pause, she says, "Can't tomorrow. Saturday?"

Marshall smiles into the phone. "Great. Yes. Thank you. Atomic?" He adds quickly, "It's not a date."

"You want to meet at our old bar for this 'not a date' date?"

Back then he knew it was unethical to date a source, and her barbs remind him of that old sting of emotions. At the time, he was new to everything. The job. The city. It was a heady mix.

"Four? That's a universally accepted nondate hour," he offers.

"In more of a spiritual sense than a technical one," she says.

"The Atomic's a shadow of its former self," he says. "Like me."

After enough of a pause to make him consider asking if she's still there, Brenda says, "This town despises antiques, but I'm not immune to their charms. Saturday. Atomic at four," and she hangs up.

He hangs up and stares at the old flip phone, considering how he's an antique, just like it is. Maybe just out of touch.

He looks at the fourth number on his sticky note but doesn't call it. Instead, he does a web search for "Brenda Dentner." Nothing. No social media. No employment record. He tries an image search but doesn't see anyone who looks like the woman he dated on and off for over a decade. He adds "Las Vegas" to the search. It doesn't change the results.

Marshall looks at the clock. He should leave now to be on time for his meeting with Ernesto, but he still has another thirty minutes of office hours. He listens for footsteps coming down the hallway, only hearing silence. Dorris won't come back, will he?

Fingers crossed.

The compound at Tenth and Ogden is boarded up, ringed by a high, spiked wall and "No Trespassing" signs every eight feet. Standing on the sidewalk, Marshall and Ernie can see the roofs of a tight knot of buildings inside. There's a main building made with stone and a chimney, and two newer structures. Three unkempt acacia trees sprawl themselves upward. At the wall's base, an empty beer can sits next to an abandoned prepackaged sandwich, plastic and egg salad melting into each other. A white lamppost peeks over the wall, its ornamental head loose. It's a sad tableau.

Marshall feels the dry wind pull the moisture from his mouth. "What do you want to know, M.?" Ernie asks.

"You tell me. What do I want to know, Ernie?" Marshall takes his notebook out.

Ernesto Espejo has been Marshall's land guy for a decade. Not his realtor—Marshall is a dedicated renter—but his go-to for stories about neighborhoods and properties. Ernie boasts that he has a story for every downtown lot, and in Marshall's experience, he under-promises and over-delivers.

"Well, I mean, I know there was some kinda Hare Krishna group or something here. Lots of traffic. Always new people around."

"Not Hare Krishna. Moonies."

"Hm. Let's see," Ernie says, looking at his phone. A few more clicks. "Lot 9, Block 8. Residential. Appraised at about 870K. Multi-unit building. Looks like a teardown."

"Yeah?"

"From the looks of it, the value of the land exceeds the value of the buildings left on top of it."

"We're talking about this walled-off area?"

"Yeah," Ernie says, stopping. "Three plots divide the block. Two smaller ones—this one and that empty one on this side—and the big one that's the parking lot that empties to Fremont."

Ernie leads them to the side to appraise the block further, giving a clear sight line to the parking lot. An old marquee, repurposed at the southern end of the lot, reads: "A furniture store keeps calling me, but I just wanted one night stand." Just beyond, on Fremont Street, Marshall sees the Atomic and distractedly thinks of Brenda.

Ernie continues to interpret what he's finding on his phone. "Both of the small lots on the block are owned by the same company. In-Hwa Group." Marshall wishes he could look over the wall, but even if he could get over it, there's probably nothing to see. "There's a lot of this kind of piecing together lots around here. The buildings are shit but the lot is fire. Tearing it all down doubles the value. Looks like they could get one-point-five for both. Maybe even two mil," Ernesto says.

Marshall looks around. From the seventies through the nineties, this rough-scrabble knot of downtown hotels around Fremont Street—Binion's Horseshoe, the Lady Luck, the Four Queens—was surrounded by a ring of "grind joints," gambling dens devoid of pizazz, just slots and a lot of hard faces at the tables. The area was left behind decades ago, when fancier places along the Strip started popping up. But after all this time, people are making moves around here once again. He looks around, sees graffiti on a wall. Not the usual tags, though. Art.

Ownership moves underfoot, like tectonic plates slowly grinding together, without notice. "Seems ready for development, no?" Marshall guesses.

"Here? Yeah. Maybe. It's kinda in the middle—where the downtown meets neighborhoods. Maybe not prime. Prime-adjacent. That's always a target: Places on the come-up. You know, Las Vegas has no patience for anything to emerge organically. We use brute force."

After everything he's learned about casino development in researching his book, Marshall can't disagree. Thirty, forty years ago, middle-income folks were already out in the suburbs. City planners came in, dubbed the area an arts district, zoned a new concert hall, an outlet mall, then the late Tony Hsieh and Zappos came in. "It was the mob and Mormons," Marshall adds, "now it's MBAs?"

"It's how the West was won, man. There will always be a politician looking to solve a problem with a stretch of pavement."

"Human nature abhors a vacant lot," Marshall says as they walk back to Ernesto's car. "What ward is this? Five?"

"This is a little notch of Ward Three. Weird quirk."

"Three? So, Losado's old ward?"

Ernesto doesn't need to look up this kind of information on his phone. "Yup. Lots of Latinos. Remember, this was Mexico first, man," he says with a laugh, starting the car. "These days, you want to get something done in town, the Latino community in Ward Three might not be the first stop on a politician's charm tour, but it's up there." They've wandered into Ernie's protective zone. "Five thousand people migrate here every month. More Latinos than not. The only ones who seem to notice are the Mormons and telemarketers."

"You have anything on Losado?" Marshall asks, hoping to sound casual.

"A player, but good at it. *Con ganas.* Good for us. Why?"

"Curious. I'm interviewing him for my class on Monday. Is there a background I should investigate?

"C'mon vato, doesn't everyone? Ay, why? Don't mess with Landslide Losado." Ernesto pulls from the curb.

"You know him personally, yeah?"

Ernie's smile evaporates. "What? You think all of us Brown people know each other?"

Marshall pauses. "I mean, Ernie, I—"

Ernie laughs. "Hey, I'm messing with you. Yeah, I know him a little. Just as a volunteer though. Garden variety community organizing. Look, if you want dirt—"

Marshall waves his hands and changes course. He says, "No, no. I just—" before stopping himself.

"He's well-connected," Ernie says. "Well-liked."

Everyone likes to have their own hand on their steering wheel, and Marshall can tell Ernie's starting to bristle at being maneuvered. He backs off a little.

"Okay." Marshall changes course again. "Do you know if Mexicans are into the Unification Church?"

"We love church," Ernie grins. He thinks more. "I can't say I've met a Universalist though."

"Unification, not universalist," Marshall corrects, but Ernie shakes his head. "You ever hear of the Third Family?"

Ernesto pulls into the parking lot at the paper and says, "No, no. I can't say." He thinks about it some more before asking, "Like the mob? That kind of family?"

"No," Marshall says. But then considers. "I don't think so."

"You think you've got a story here?"

"No," he says again. "At least, I don't think so. Thanks for the tour."

12

ALLY

Ally hasn't spent much time in the Container Park; she's always figured it's not her scene. But as she and Web walk through the early-evening crowds, she can see the appeal. Working spaces for start-ups and hip office spaces on the second and third floors of the glass and corrugated steel shipping containers. At ground level, there's oversized checkers and a super-sized play structure—a literal playground for adults. The heavy smell of weed drifts by on a light breeze.

There's a sophisticated ice cream place. There's a spot "serving real Mexican food by real Mexicans" and another offering hipster hot dogs. There's even a branch of a local soul food place called The Second Choice.

All Ally sees are theater sets, costumes, and props. A city block in miniature. It's no different from the casinos. She looks up and sees one of those second-generation globe cameras. Sticker graffiti at eye level reads, "One nation, under observation."

On a stage in front of a plastic lawn, there's a band playing swaggering versions of dusty standards. A sign reads, "TONIGHT: Ethyl Mormon & the I Don't Think So's."

"This next one's another cover," the singer says, tucking a zither under her arm, "unless you haven't heard it before." She exudes a fifties waitress vibe, plus ink. Her rhythm section is proficient, no-nonsense, and undistracting, with ties, vests, and rolled sleeves. They could all step right from this stage into bartending shifts at an artisan cocktail lounge.

Ally remembers she's got work to do and slips her hand into Web's, nuzzling a little into his shoulder as they walk. She surprises herself with how easily she plays the part. She feels his hand relax. They find the Fallout Bar and head inside.

Web tells the hostess they'll sit at the bar. Ally sees three tables pushed together with a "RESERVED" table tent, and Web gravitates to the two empty stools nearby. "The bachelor will have his back to the wall to face the bar," he says.

"You know that how?"

"Alpha male."

She scans the room as if absent-mindedly and orders a club soda with lime, something she thinks will look like alcohol. Web gets a local beer. Ally sizes up the room. Around one hundred customers. She counts ten servers on the floor, three bartenders. One barback, methodically digging grime out of his fingernails. She turns to Web.

"You think I can do this?"

"Only if you want to get paid." He takes a sip of his beer.

Ally squirms on her stool and smooths her new Cuyana silk skirt. This isn't how she was hoping to spend the night. She had to cancel a dinner date with Phoebe, a bit of emotional gymnastics that landed poorly with her girlfriend . . . especially when she left the apartment all dressed up and in makeup. As Web put it, they're on the cheat beat. A Girlfriend Job. A mission to derail a bachelor party. Someone—presumably the target's fiancée—is paying them to make sure the bachelor doesn't end up at the strip bar down the road.

"Here they are," Web says as a group of men walks in to the beat of flip-flops and loud back claps.

Ally shoots a glance over her shoulder and finds the man of honor. Howie. A pretty nondescript white dude. In the picture Erv showed her earlier, he was holding a red Solo cup, mugging for the camera, smirking. She's relieved that he isn't wearing a tiara or an "I'M OFF THE MARKET, BITCHES" T-shirt. Why she's invested in the character that underlies his bro vibes, she can't say. She switches from curiosity to analysis.

The group settles in at their tables, with Howie in the middle of the pack.

Ally smells Web's aftershave as he leans in to speak in a low voice. "Okay. In about five minutes, after they place their order but before they get their drinks, we're going to get in a fight. Loud enough for them to hear it."

"You really think this is going to work?"

"If you do it right, it will. Guys love to play the hero, especially in front of other guys. And Howie's the center of attention tonight. He swoops in, and you convince him to stay while his boys go to the strip club."

"And if he doesn't make a move?"

"Improvise."

She realizes this isn't just taking selfies on the sidewalk. Perhaps reading her unease, Web says, "You look great, by the way. He'll come over." His obvious use of nunchi makes her feel both soothed and managed.

"He looks dim," Web concludes. Ally hopes so. She's not exactly confident about her ability to flirt with any man, let alone the kind of guy Howie seems to be.

Behind them, she hears the group sing along as "Wagon Wheel" plays over the sound system—a kind of bro version of "The

Internationale." Ally glances over her shoulder, hoping to survey the group. As she does, Howie meets her eye. She blinks twice and turns back to Web. "He just caught me looking at him."

"Good. He's already noticed you. Meet me at the bar at El Cortez when you're done."

She lets that comfort her.

And then he says, loudly, "You know what? Believe what you want!" They stage-whisper themselves through an argument, punctuated by a loud "eert" sound as Web pushes his barstool back and stalks toward the restrooms. Ally lowers her head for a few minutes, only coming up for a sip of her club soda, trying to manifest an initial interaction with Howie.

She turns around and catches his eye again. She fakes a yawn and sees his mouth take in a copycat gulp of air. Good: he's paying attention. Ally finishes her drink, recalling a Psych 101 fun fact that schizophrenics and people on the spectrum don't catch yawns. She considers her next move.

Thirty seconds later, she feels a hand on her upper arm and is violently pulled off her stool. Startled, she pivots to see Web by her side, making a face she hardly recognizes.

"We're going. *Now*," he says, loud.

It takes her a beat to catch up.

"I'm. I'm not going with y-you," she stammers, not fully an act. Her vision narrows, and she can feel attention closing in around her. The bartender stepping over. Too much attention.

"Yes, you are," Web says.

A new voice says, "Hey, hey, now. Let's not have any trouble." Web and Ally both spin to face Howie, towering over them. Ally realizes he's the sort of tall that some women mistake for good-looking, as if he were high enough to hang the moon itself.

"I heard her say, 'no thank you,' bro."

Web finally releases Ally's arm and turns to Howie. "Man, don't 'bro' me. This doesn't concern you . . . bro." Web adds a little bit of physicality to it.

"Maybe it doesn't, maybe it does," he says. In another situation, Ally would have rolled her eyes.

"Sit down," Web tells Howie through his teeth before turning back to Ally, but Howie puts his shoulder between the two of them.

"I think you should leave," Howie says. "Alone."

Ally can't see Web's face, but after a moment, his shoulders drop and he backs off. Ally slumps into her stool, and her peripheral vision returns. The bartender moves down the bar, and people return to their conversations. She hears Web take out some aggression on the door for his exit from the stage. What a showman. She's a solo act now.

Howie remains hovering over the stool next to her. "You think he's coming back?" he asks.

"No," she sighs. "I don't think so. Fucker didn't even pay for our drinks."

"Fucker," Howie echoes, looking to the exit. Ally's surprised at how many people will repeat what you say back to you. "Let me buy you another," he says.

"I've already had too much," Ally says with a coy lilt.

"C'mon. One more drink."

She takes a deep breath to center herself and to lend the impression of ambivalence. It works both ways. "Vodka soda," she says.

He snatches the bartender's attention without effort. He orders top shelf. "Belvedere and soda, please. And I'll take the rest of her tab." He turns to her again. "I'm Howie."

"Mona." She always wanted to be a Mona. The Greek root, she once learned, means "solitary." "You from out of town, Howie? Like, on a road trip? No, wait." She makes a show of scanning the group over his shoulder. "Bachelor party."

"Obvious?" he asks, moving around Web's abandoned stool to occupy it.

"Obvious," she says, looking back at the bro pack. "Who's the groom?"

"Me."

"*You?*"

"Obvious?"

"Not so obvious." Why, she wonders, does he smile so much? *I get it, buddy*, she thinks. *You love your life. Enough with the teeth.* She smiles back.

"Why not?"

"You look like a bachelor to me," Ally says, making eye contact before looking back at the sticky amber bar.

"Oh yeah? Maybe Sasha's right."

"Sasha?" Ally asks.

"My fiancée," he says, looking back at his pack. "She says I have a perma-bachelor vibe."

"I'm just stating facts. Like, Vegas is the number one destination for bachelor parties, after all." Trying to keep his attention, she says, "You know, the bachelorettes all go to Nashville. Now, why do you think the dudes come here?"

"I dunno," he says, pursing his lips.

She keeps prodding him to her goal. "Think harder," she says. He does—or at least pretends to—and an embarrassed look washes over his face. She almost feels bad for him.

"The strip clubs?"

"Aw, don't tell me," she prods. His head tilts down, a little. "Of course, y'all are going to a strip club."

"*Gentlemen's* club," he says.

She stifles a laugh. "What? You don't have naked women in . . ."

"Calabasas."

". . . in Calabasas?" Ally says, taking a slow sip from her fresh cocktail without losing eye contact.

She tries to clock a reaction, and she sees him falter. His mask slips. He might be slightly wounded. Remembering what Web taught her, Ally thinks a more rugged gal might interest a So-Cal dude. What's in Mona's wallet? A Colorado driver's license. A Sierra Club membership card. A snowboard and a Subaru. She rolls through Howie's limited offerings, something to pick up on. Calabasas. Driving.

"Did you drive here?"

"Yeah," he says.

"You can't see 'em from the highway, but there are dunes, actual sand dunes out there in the desert."

"We took 15 . . ." he says, trailing off.

She wants to pull him onto her wavelength. "It's not just void. Coming from the Rockies, I just kinda thought the desert was flat, empty space." He's listening, so she continues. "It wasn't until I started hiking out there. Nature finds its niche. Out there, to the south, are these dunes—the kind that you imagine when you think of a desert in the movies, you know? Not Sahara-style dunes, but . . ." She tries to add a little poetry: "You only see the stars where this Christmas tree of a city's concrete fades to dust."

She waits for him to grab onto anything she's laying down to continue the conversation.

"So," he starts. "You're a hiker? We're going climbing tomorrow at Red Rocks."

There we go, she thinks. But if she lets him get too deep into hiking talk, he'll realize she has the orienteering skill of a Brownie. Let's switch gears.

"Talking to me isn't breaking your bro code?"

"I'm no bro," he says, and in the mirror behind the bar, she catches him scanning her skirt. Ew.

"Sure, you aren't," she says, acting more invested. "Athletic? Yeah, I can be." She squirms on her stool—cutely, she hopes—and tries to disassociate, just as Web taught her. Be a poker chip.

She rests her hand on his bicep, looking back at the dude pack, which is humming with what approximates conversation. One or two look up at her, checking in, before cracking a quiet joke. "No Bro" Howie looks back at them with a swift nod and a smile.

"I should probably . . ." he says.

She realizes she might have to do some convincing after all. She remembers the first "F" is "felt." "I felt like I would be getting married soon, too." Then, she remembers, there is "found." "But when I found pictures that Debbie texted him—"

"Debbie?" Howie says, turning back to her.

"I know. 'Debbie,'" Ally says with an eye roll. "They met in the mornings, when I was working my shift at the café, or at school. He asked me out tonight to apologize, but . . . I don't think he's really sorry." How, she wonders, is this going to play out? She looks around. Is she going to go through with this?

"Ouch," he says, turning back to his group.

Ally tries to command his attention. *Focus, dude.* She continues, "And it's not the cheating per se, you know? Can . . . Can I really trust anyone again?"

She aims for a little drama, not too much.

"I've found trust to be a fragile thing, you know? Any asshole can break it. But I guess, whatever was once bound up in that trust—" and here she makes what she hopes are high-wattage, meaningful eyes at him, "—is set free."

Ew, she thinks. Can't just go straight for an offer of spending the night together, though. Ally sits up a bit, and she can't tell whether it's Mona or Ally who is finding her resolve. She deals out a few additional seconds of eye contact. And then Ally sees a woman hovering behind Howie, a little too close. She's blonde, with a cute hipster haircut Ally recognizes as similar to her own, though this woman is a little older, with a delicate bicep tattoo peeking out from her roughly cut Bikini Kill T-shirt. Ally has the same shirt, the band name above an old record player, white on black. Ally's not sure whose attention she's trying to catch: the bartender's or Howie's. She's close and cute enough to gain some from both.

Howie pivots to make room, and Ally senses some lost ground. Ally leans into Howie, but she can see he's distracted by the other blonde. Ally touches his forearm again, this time with a slight pull. She feels his muscles tighten.

"Tell me what you do, love," she says. She feels grateful the bar lighting will conceal the flush she feels blooming over her face.

"I'm a songwriter."

"Ain't your people with the bachelorette parties in Nashville?"

"Maybe. But no, you can have a decent side career writing jingles in LA."

Okay, she admits she wasn't exactly expecting this. "Jingles, eh?"

"Don't knock it. It's hard work. But I'm also a singer-songwriter solo artist."

"Like, folk music?"

He laughs. "Actually, I'm working on a concept album. The central idea is songs that are riffs off novels. I'm calling it 'Book Covers.'"

Unsure of how to proceed, she just says, "That's cute," and watches his face slacken a little. She remembers it's her job to puff him up, not deflate him. "No, no," she says. "That's . . . very cute. An example, please."

Ally maintains eye contact with Howie but registers the hovering hipster woman as she finally nods at the bartender to show she's ready to order. Ally hears the woman order two beers.

He looks around as if to demonstrate that this is not his audience and says, "I'm not gonna sing you a song, Ramona."

"Mona, silly," she says. "Just tell me about a song."

"Ah. Okay. There's one called 'Bachelor's Delight.'"

"Perma-Bachelor's Delight?"

"Fairly cute, but no." He pauses, seeming to think about how to describe it. "It's about a guy who thinks he's in charge of a relationship. He feels he makes the important decisions—job, house, etcetera—and gets everything his way. But later in life, he realizes he lost control of the wheel. He was trying to gaslight his wife into a happy marriage, but it turns out somewhere along the way, it turned around: his wife had been steering the ship all along."

"Okay, so what book is that based on?"

"Well, it's a repurposing of Melville's *Benito Cereno.*" Impressed, Ally's thrown off. Maybe she's got him wrong.

"Never read it. Repurposing how?"

"The book's about Delano, the captain of a whaleboat—the boat's named *Bachelor's Delight*—that comes across another vessel, a slave ship whose Spanish captain, Cereno, tells Delano the Spanish crew died from a fever and only he and the slaves survived. Delano doesn't really think much is amiss, although he finds it curious how the slaves seemed to be running the ship. It's only when Cereno abandons his own ship to join Delano that he realizes there has been a mutiny."

Ally's somewhat taken. Maybe not zero interest. "Hold up. What is a guy who reads backbench Melville novels doing with a bachelor party in Vegas?" She takes another sip of her drink.

"Well, *Cereno* is kinda a classic in the sense that Melville doesn't reveal the whole truth of the story until the end. So, you know, you shouldn't trust everything you read. Or see."

"I believe they call that an unreliable narrator," Ally says. She mulls over Howie's metaphors. "I think it's all this booze, but the wife is the slave crew, then? That's—"

"Problematic, for sure," Howie begins, but she can see that he doesn't have a counterargument. Instead, he adds, "Maybe you've had too much, ace."

Who's gaslighting now? she wonders. "I can hold my own, thanks. It sounds like the husband should, um, jump ship, right?"

"I'm not . . . I'm not sure what you mean," he says.

Finally receiving her two beers, the blonde in the Bikini Kill top awkwardly turns around, commanding Howie's attention once again and triggering a little more desperation in Ally. Flirting, it seems, won't be enough to seal this deal. Mona needs to be more assertive.

She touches his arm again, pulling him in a little. "Forget the high seas, and let's go to the desert together. You and me," she says, surprising herself. She doesn't think she's ever so deliberately ratcheted up her own anxiety scale. Even if effective, she wonders what she would do with him in the middle of the desert. She pushes. "Look. We're in this outrageous locale and it's all artificial. Fake boobs, fake lakes, fake canals, and palm trees trucked in from god knows where." Then, looking in his blue eyes while nodding the direction of the door, she says, "Let's jump ship."

"Leave my friends?"

"Yeah." She nudges his arm with her elbow. "I think they'll understand. I don't think you're a gentlemen's club kinda guy anyway."

She watches the lights change colors on his face as he thinks about it. He takes a long drink of beer. Finally, he says, "I couldn't ditch them. They came all this way . . ." He nods to the bartender and makes an "I'm signing the check" gesture with his fingers and points to both her drinks and his.

Ally feels the loss coming—but loss of what, exactly? Money? Confidence? Self-image?

She tilts her neck. He looks at her lips and rests his arm on the back of her stool, which she registers as interest. Ally feels a rift, a cleaving in herself. She leans forward and pauses, thinking of Phoebe. But then she remembers that it's just acting. It's a role. Mona. A poker chip. Actors kiss in movies. Her breath flutters right before their lips meet. It's affecting. He tastes like hops. For a moment, she has the sensation of tumbling backward.

13

WEB

"Hey, hon," the low familiar voice says.

Web looks up from contemplating three hearts on the poker machine built into the bar. "Hey yourself. How's your night shaping up, Nyah?"

"Like a pear. A lineup of losers at the sucker's rodeo."

"Maker's Mark. Three cubes. Please."

El Cortez is Web's go-to for downtime on Fremont. Something about the Spanish Colonial hacienda vibes of the old building, the dicey mob history, and the easygoing staff does it for him. Past the bright mint green canopy and fifties "Coffee Shop & Bar / Free Parking" sign, the place is dark and unfussy. Too unlovely not to love. Clean bathrooms. Short bars designed to nudge people to the slots and discourage chitchat. Busy enough to not be entirely depressing, but not busy enough to choke everyone on cigarette smoke—just enough to cling to his clothes in a way that reminds him of how his folks smelled when they came home from work.

Plus, while NASA-trained engineers apportion the cocktails on the Strip, bartenders like Nyah at places like the El Cortez are generous. They're not in your face about it either.

Web reviews his performance at the bar. He hates to play the angry Black man, but it works, and it's not his fault that it does.

He goes for a flush, tapping the red buttons hard, taking out a little aggression on the machine. Nyah returns with a bourbon on ice and leaves with a knowing smile. He absentmindedly watches the reels windmill around. Keeping his hands visible is a burden. Managing expectations is exhausting.

Tap tap tap. Three Jacks.

He enjoys Nyah's attention but prefers to move around unnoticed. He reaches for his false glasses and realizes he left them in his apartment. Muscle memory at work.

He bought the nonprescription glasses for a gig at a bicycle industry convention up in Reno and found they worked even better than he'd expected. They were a kind of veil. Like pulling out a graphic novel at a café. Like wearing an MIT T-shirt. The opposite of what he just pulled with that Howie dude.

Tap tap. Zip.

The Set Up forces him to enter all kinds of uneasy spaces. Before this gig, self-policing exacted a psychological toll. Now he's honing his stagecraft, code-switching, and writing his own scripts. Crafting his own deceptions.

Tap tap tap. Three tens, pair of deuces. Full house. Modest bells ring, and he recoils as if the electronic merriment were a punishment. He'd almost prefer losing.

Time passes, and he's up $225. Nyah replaces his empty glass with a fresh drink, unprompted, ice clinking.

"You working tonight, handsome?" She scans the room in case anyone needs her, before leaning against the bar.

"Yeah. I'm— I'm on an extended five."

"Why aren't I lucky enough to have our breaks match up?"

"My pops always said to save the luck for the leprechauns," he says.

Web knows he's susceptible to anyone who calls him handsome, or hon, or both. He doesn't need the affirmation, but he appreciates the attempt at easygoing manipulation. Game sees game, etcetera.

"You see," she says, "my pops told me, 'Luck favors the prepared mind.'"

Web's about to respond when Ally breathlessly clasps the back of the stool next to him.

"Woo. What a rush!" she whispers into his ear.

As Ally sits, Nyah wordlessly heads to the other side of the bar.

"Where's Erv?" Ally says.

"Where's Howie?"

"He's still at Fallout. But he thinks he's gonna meet me at the Four Queens in, I'd say, forty-five minutes," she says with a grin.

"You just left him there? Are you 100 percent? You need to be 100 percent," Web says.

"Relax, Web, relax," she says, her grin failing. "I nailed it." Nyah returns to address Ally.

"What can I get for you?"

Web senses a chill and says, "Nyah, this is my friend, Ally."

"I didn't realize Web had friends," Nyah says while winking without warmth at Ally. "Somehow I thought he was all mine."

"You can have him. I'd much rather have a soda with lime," Ally says. Nyah chuckles and leaves. Ally turns to Web again. "I did it, Web," she says. "I did it."

He looks at her face, lit up from the digital screen in the bar. Her eyes look like spinning reels. Web senses her body humming.

"You sure?" he asks. "You're not just gambling with your own money, you know. We're in this too."

"I know."

He turns in his stool, and his line of inquiry. "Assuming the client is his fiancée," he says, "she paid us to keep him from going to a strip club—presumably because she doesn't want him to leer at another woman's body. And so, let me get this straight, you planned to ensnare him in a casual hookup instead?"

"Yuppers," she says. "And it's a *gentlemen's* club, Web. Not a strip club. That's demeaning." She rolls her eyes with a grin.

"So, either way, the client finds out her fiancée is . . . ?"

"What? A dirtbag? Trust me: It won't be news."

"What's won't be news?"

"That he's a dude, dude."

Nyah brings Ally her drink, hovers for a moment, then leaves.

Ally takes a sip. "I put his name on the reservation so he could get a key to the room at the front desk," Ally says. "He'll cool out in the hotel room for a while. Hoping I'll arrive. When he realizes I'm not coming, maybe he'll order room service or some porn on the TV to spite me, but it'll be worth it. He'll wait long enough to not lose face in front of his friends. They'll meet up later."

"A honeypot. What happened to being squeamish about manipulating people?"

"Which way do you want it, Web? Enthusiastic or squeamish?"

"Do you think it's fair to set him up like that?" Why, he wonders, is he pressing her on this?

Her jaw drops. "Did I nod off during your exhaustive lesson on fairness? That's lit-er-ally the name of the business, Web."

He pushes onward. "Hold up. He's just a dude being a dude because of the opportunity you presented him, right?"

"You're asking if I believe his personality changes based on the fictional prospect of a one-night stand in a tacky hotel?"

"Yes," Web says. "People adapt to the available options, Ally."

"No, Web," Ally says. "People are consistent. Consistently awful. Especially men. There might be a choice, but it only produces a very narrow bandwidth of outcomes."

He dials himself back and leans into his stool. He sees her read his body language, but now it's her turn to push. "I presented him with two options: a night of simulated sex at a 'gentleman's club' with his bro pack, or the promise of actual sex. Like you've been telling me: We're all playing roles, and they shape our motivations. Even if I don't know who this Howie guy is, he's still *the bachelor* at *a bachelor party*. It's practically fate. Gross, gross fate."

"Your promises of 'real sex' were . . . what, Ally?"

She shoots him a "give me a break" look, the corner of her mouth pulled up to her cheek, displaying a dimple you could lose a marble in. "An act," she says with effort.

Web looks at her and bites his lip. He sees a little more resolve in her. He relaxes, seeking a truce. It's not as if he's going to send her back to the bar to finish the job. "Well," he says. "I guess we'll see. In the meantime, Erv should be on Mr. Howie's movements."

"Mr. Russell," she says.

"What's that?"

"I had to get his name for the reservation. Howie Russell," she says, rummaging through her bag for her phone.

"Potato, po-tah-to. Scenario, scen-are-io," he says.

He watches Ally contemplate her phone. She types something. Is she taking notes? Texting? Who? Etcetera.

He hears a "whoosh," and whatever she sent is off. He imagines the message trekking off into a hidden universe of cables and cell towers. She rests her phone in front of her, and he gauges the distance. Web considers the apps tracking their locations, likes, and swipes. Selling data to the tech start-ups right around the corner. Or in California. Or Shenzhen.

Ally turns to him, hoping for a new topic. "Where are you from, anyway?"

He makes a dramatic sigh, as if to say, "Here we go."

"Most folks come from somewhere else, but I was born and raised on the Westside." He sees Nyah enter the conversational orbit and brings her in, using her as an unwitting accomplice. "Nyah, how long have you lived here?"

"Since pre-K. You?"

"Third gen. My father's parents came from the South. They lived in this neighborhood first, to work near the casinos."

Nyah's voice gets lower, and says, "Nobody told them Vegas was called the 'Mississippi of the West'?"

"They figured it out," Web gives a bitter laugh. Web knew stories. Like, for example, that Sammy Davis Jr. would say he had no skin color for the twenty minutes he was on stage with Deano and Sinatra, but he went right back to being Black as soon as he stepped into the wings. While his fellow performers gambled and drank at the bar, Sammy left through the kitchen door along with the trash.

Nyah adds, "Black folk were 10 percent of the population. The Westside had barbershops, salons, restaurants, groceries, and clubs all along Jackson Street."

"Why'd they move to West Las Vegas?" Ally asked.

Web and Nyah exchange a glance. He says, "It was more of a push." No different from other cities—African Americans and their businesses clustered, catering to the clientele that was often unwelcome across town. Business licenses and mortgages were easier for addresses on the Westside, and white folks blocked Black folks from good jobs. There was even a law forbidding Black dealers.

He turns to Ally. "Hear of the Moulin Rouge?" She shakes her head. "You?" Nyah shakes her head as well.

"The Moulin Rouge opened in '55. It was supposed to be desegregated, a place for Black performers who performed on the Strip but weren't allowed to stay in the hotels. They even had an all-Black cast of showgirls. My grandfather worked the late, late shift. There were 3:00 a.m. shows! After the Strip closed for the night, everyone would come to the Rouge for these elaborate shows and a speakeasy-style hang. It was a place that leaned into Blackness, too. The lighter showgirls had to wear darker pancake makeup! My grandpops remembered the skin tone had to be #31.

"It closed after only a few months, despite getting national attention. An NAACP lawsuit in the seventies finally forced the major casinos to open all jobs to African Americans. My grandpops and then my father being two of them."

Ally sits back and picks up her phone. "Am I boring you, Ally?"

"No, no," Ally says, sitting back up and placing her phone down in the same spot. "I wanted to make a note to myself to study up on this more. Promise."

Web watches Nyah busy her hands on some glassware. A pro bartender move, learned from years of bobbing through conversations of all kinds.

Ally puts both hands up. "I like hearing about your family. I understand why you're connected to this place."

Web feels more of an apprehension than a connection. As if his parents will reach out to the present and grasp his throat at any moment. Like a kid overcome with dread at the idea that his appendix—a hidden and dangerous piece of himself—might suddenly rupture. It's been years since he stopped expecting his pops to step through a door or to catch his mother walking by a window. He still instinctively looks for them. But his parents are just some ghost organs, ready to explode.

"Well," he says, "They weren't high-priced New York therapists, but they had good jobs that gave me a good childhood." It comes out more testily than he intended.

A customer gives Nyah a little wave, and Ally and Web sip their drinks in silence. Web knows he doesn't need to be prickly. Careers in and through the military and in the service industry offer enough transferable life skills to satisfy a thousand course credits of history and culture. Both his parents got degrees of a sort. What they're using them for now he can only guess.

Ally silently heads to the bathroom. She takes her bag, but Web notices she leaves her phone sitting next to his.

Web casually casts his eyes around. Ally's gone and Nyah's chatting at the other end of the bar. He picks up the cell as if it were his own.

He looks at the image on the lock screen. It's a picture of Ally and her roommate, not the wavy pink and red default wallpaper he and Erv have on their phones. Odd. It's possible Ally could've changed the lock screen on her work phone, but why? He then punches in the passcode Erv gave her: 230537. The keypad shakes and gives a "Try Again" prompt. He tries again. Shake. "Try Again." Three more attempts before he's locked out, and Erv sets up the phones to erase all the data after ten attempts. Web tries the reverse of the passcode: 735032. Shake. "Try Again." He gives up.

Either Erv set a different password (unlikely) or Ally somehow circumvented the phone's controls (improbable). Erv's particular, and she wasn't hired to be a hacker. Would Ally have a Set Up protocol he wasn't apprised of? Is she on a different job than he is, and if so, why?

It's not one puzzle but two: not only what's up with the phone itself, but what to do about it. Should he ask Ally? Tell Erv or the Set Up? Or just keep it to himself?

His phone vibrates on the bar, and he quickly returns Ally's phone and picks up his own. He reads the text from the Set Up and captures Nyah's attention for the check. As Ally returns, her phone's notification comes in, thirty seconds after his.

"He never went to the hotel," Web says, looking down at the little black screen of his phone. He guesses what the job would have paid. $300? $400? What would a fiancée be willing to pay to keep her future husband from a strip club? What's that worth?

"What?" she asks. She says it in a way indicating she knows exactly what he means.

"Erv watched him go to the strip club," he says.

"But . . . I—" Ally starts.

"But fucking nothing," he cuts her off. "You blew it. Erv's going to be outside, and if you think *I'm* heated about not getting paid, I assure you, he'll be hotter."

He puts $50 on the bar and waves to let Nyah know it's hers. Completely forgetting his $247 of winnings in the poker machine, he stalks out of the bar without looking back.

FRIDAY

14

MARSHALL

It relieves him somewhat to find the sociology department just as desolate as the journalism hallways. He walks toward the sound of a keyboard clicking furiously, emanating from the only open office door.

Dr. Renée Lévesque's gold wire glasses sit in a frame of brown bangs and locks and a white blouse buttoned to the neck. She's a little younger than Marshall, and tenured.

Her desk showcases a picture of her and two dogs, a laptop, an inch-and-a-half-thick stack of paper with more red editing marks than black ink. She's outfitted her office with her own light fixtures and painted the walls a warm yellow rather than industrial eggshell. His eyes gravitate to two blocks of books with her name on the spines: *Opiate of the State* and *The Sacred Kaleidoscope*. A little knot of jealousy hardens in his gut.

“Marshall Grant,” she says, briskly. “Come in. I looked you up,” she says, nodding at her monitor. “I read the recent piece about the new tech park. Didn’t know you were on campus.”

“I’m just a lecturer. It’s an open relationship,” Marshall says, though he knows he’s lucky Len Dorris called to offer a low-paying adjunct instructor job—perfect for a disgraced but experienced journalist—after Marshall lost his job after breaking a story about corruption at city hall. The same article, as it happens, that had been waiting for him on the podium before this morning’s class.

Back in 2015, Marshall got a tip about a corruption story and met a man in a parking garage with a folder of documents that looked legit—a stack of certificates of occupancy to real estate developers, along with a matching set of files disclosing donations to several nonprofit organizations tied to half the city council, including Elías Losado. Someone asking for favors is common enough, but someone getting them is another kettle of fish. More evidence, produced via email, provided details. He checked the names, the nonprofits. He put out feelers and got enough pushback to sense that he was onto something. The editors signed off on the work, and it ran on the front page: “Pay to Play City Hall.”

But then, after the article was published, financial disclosures that hadn’t been forthcoming prior suddenly emerged, dissolving details he’d found rock-solid only days earlier. Marshall’s contact vanished. An inspector general from the Department of Justice was brought in to clear the councilors of wrongdoing. It was a mess. The paper ran a retraction and an internal ethics inquiry. Marshall was the symbolic sacrifice.

"How's that relationship working?" Lévesque leaned back in her chair, ever so slightly.

"We've kept out of each other's business. Until recently. I reached out to you because I'm working on a different story." He wonders if that really is what he's doing. What story? "I'm curious, Renée—"

"Please. René was my father's name," she says with a smile. "Call me Dr. Lévesque."

He has a wish for a sinkhole to suddenly swallow the building whole. "Dr. Lévesque. Yes. Sorry. Thank you. I'm curious . . ."

As he pulls his notebook and pen from his satchel, she cuts him off again. "Is this on background? Happy to chat, but I've spent too much time teaching journalists things they should study themselves only to go without attribution." She doesn't appear annoyed, although he would understand if she were. "It wouldn't be too much for you to mention my latest book, would it?"

"Fair enough," he says. "To be honest, I'm not sure if I'm either in the early stages of something or chasing long-dead news."

Lévesque sits back. "Okay," she says with a sigh. "Your email mentioned Unificationists."

"Yes. It's not polite to call it a cult, but—"

"NRM," she says.

"NRM?"

"New Religious Movements. Recent, peripheral religious groups. It's not my specific focus, and I don't know much about them in this area, but I am aware of their history in my home in Quebec."

It reminds Marshall of his own hometown. Awakenings, it seems, are always looking for a place to land. "Why is that?" he asks.

"My pet theory is because of the Catholic Church's outsized role in La Belle Province. Canada has a pretty laissez-faire attitude to religion. Since NRMs are oppositional, and because Canadian schools, interestingly, don't explicitly teach how to think critically about religion, Québécois are more . . . gullible? The woods are full of funny sparrows."

"Funny how?"

"It's a phrase. Not funny. Odd. In the sixties there was a guy named Jean-Gaston Tremblay. A self-proclaimed pope who led a splinter group called Apôtres de l'amour infini. The Apostles of Infinite Love. He wanted to build a new Vatican two hours north of Montreal. Then, in the seventies, there was a group supposedly led by the reincarnation of the Virgin Mary."

She turns to her computer and loads a PowerPoint deck in a few clicks. He sees several symbols as she flicks through. A heart with arching wings, skull and crossbones, a pinwheel shape around a black sun.

She rests on an image of a two-headed eagle with a "T" and an "S" on a crest. "This is from another one. The Order of the Solar Temple. A New Age-y, UFO group." She turns back to him to say, "I do a deep dive into the sacred symbols in class. The students love it."

"What draws people to these cul— I mean, NRMs?"

"Well, if you go far back enough, in the Middle Ages, trade groups needed to protect their valuable skills and pass them from one trusted member to the next. Masons turned into Masonic Orders. Today, they're a benign humanitarian service and friendship-oriented group—think of an Elks Lodge or a Rotary Club, although with dwindling membership. They still attend to social and psychological needs."

"Ren- Sorry. Dr. Lévesque. You're saying the Moonies are one of these benign groups?"

"No, I'm not." She looks at her computer, this time to check the clock. "You must forgive me. I can never tell what's too much prologue. As Marx said, 'The tradition of all dead generations weighs like a nightmare on the brains of the living.'"

She pauses, looking at Marshall, and he gets the sense that she's looking through him somewhat.

"'Moonie,'" she continues, "is a pejorative term drawn from the name of the church's founder, Sun Myung Moon—Korea's first billionaire. Officially, they're the Unification Church. They believe Jesus was a 'Second Adam' and Moon was a third, sent to save the world."

Marshall writes fast. As Lévesque talks, he sees her look at his notes with a quizzical eye. He doubts she can read them, even if they weren't upside down. Illegibility is an unintended consequence of bad handwriting—an old physician's trick.

Lévesque continues with the story, how Moon, equally divinely anointed and business-savvy, came to the US on a mission to "subjugate" Americans. The group bought the *Washington Times* to gain political influence, reaching their peak in the late nineties. Then, in 1999, one of Moon's sons, Philip, fell from a seventeenth-floor window in Reno. Moon died in 2012, and the church fractured in a power struggle among his widow and ten of his adult children.

"What about the branch here?" Marshall asks.

"Unclear," she says, looking at a news article on her computer. "After Moon's death, the Vegas group split from the larger church. The Unification enclave here called themselves the Third Coming or Third Family. There's always been more attention paid to Mormons and Scientologists in this town, so when a middling sect of the Moonies rebranded themselves, it didn't exactly make the news."

"Can you tell me anything about them? This 'Third Family'?"

She exhales in a way that makes him feel bad for asking. "I figured you'd ask, so I called an interviewee. They told me it's a bunch of true believers. They had a two-building commune-type compound downtown in the nineties."

"I stopped by yesterday. It's boarded up. Did he know where they are now?"

"She," Lévesque pauses before continuing, "did."

"Sorry. She knows where they are?"

"Yes. Said they moved to Laughlin."

She passes him an address on a yellow Post-it note, and he tucks it into his notebook. "Ah," he says, cursing himself silently for not yet having looked for them outside the city.

"That's what I've got," she concludes. "Now, I've also got two articles to review and a date with two yellow Labs. If you won't tell me what this is for, I'll—"

"Okay," Marshall sits back in the chair. "I wrote an article a long time ago. A kid was possibly on the run from this splinter group, then got himself run over by a Buick. I missed the part of the story where he lived at the Third Family compound."

"On the run?"

"Or not. Unclear." He reimagines Cal jumping into traffic. A few bucks in his pocket and a gold necklace in his hand. "This kid was a bit of a loner. Troubled background."

"That fits the type."

"Is it possible they brainwashed this kid?"

Lévesque adjusts herself in her swivel chair and purses her lips. He's testing her patience. "As much as students love to talk about it, brainwashing isn't a thing, sociologically," she sighs. "People are malleable in some ways, not in others. Only 10 percent of cult members stay after a few years. Brainwashing makes good TV, but it's more like there's a kind of entraining. That 10 percent is wrapped up into the fabric of the group."

"People get deprogrammed, though, right?"

"I mean, it's a concept. Not a scientifically proven concept," she says. "Compared with supposed brainwashing, deprogramming sounds worse: coercion, kidnapping, physical restraints."

"Don't you have to be 'programmed' to get 'deprogrammed'?"

"Right, but if we look at those who leave the Unification Church or Scientology, it's those who went through *de*programming who were more likely to believe they were programmed. Those who left on their own accord didn't think they were brainwashed at all."

Marshall asks, "Moonies would've attracted a kid like this?"

"Like I said, he fits the type. NRMs prey on disaffected outcasts. They get a high from what sociologists adorably call the 'love bomb'—the full and fast investment, the deep embrace, all cast with near-divine purpose that NRMs can give them. Where else can you get that?"

"You make it sound like a reasonable choice," Marshall says.

"I very much mean to," Lévesque says. "Behavior can appear irrational when it's robbed of its context."

"You're saying these people aren't all that crazy, then?"

"Emphatically. Think of it this way: Many organizations entrain us . . . with their lingo, or fashion, or rules of etiquette, or rituals. Monasteries, Boy Scouts, the military, prisons, small liberal arts colleges. NRMs and cults just do it differently. There's similarity wrapped in difference."

Marshall says, "Are these groups prone to violence?"

"Violent? Sure. More than anyone else? Don't quote me on it," she says.

"Did any of the groups in Quebec break the law?"

She pauses to sip from a mug that says "Instant Sociologist: Just Add Coffee." "Oh, certainly. I can think of one group, the Ant Hill Kids. They had a charismatic leader and the telltale signs of a doomsday cult. Living on a commune. Multiple wives. Psychological and physical abuse. The leader was convicted for murdering a group member."

"So all this goes on without anyone knowing?" Marshall asks.

"You'd think that NRMs want to keep a low profile, but it's actually the opposite. Publicity's a way to solidify a kind of 'us against them' sentiment and attract new members. New congregants, new money. There are other avenues for legitimacy and money."

"Like what? Drugs?"

"Some go legit," she says. "The Unification church has dozens—probably hundreds—of business and nonprofit fronts and affiliations. They've diversified." That renders Marshall silent. She sits back and concludes, "My advice? You should follow the money, not the morals."

15

WEB

The trick to tailing is knowing where your target is going before you begin. Then, it's easy. Drive close in heavy traffic, distant in light. Know the roads beforehand. Use public parking. In the city, cars move at a more urgent clip, and four-lane roads make it easier to pass a slowpoke. There is a greater risk of slow drivers in idle suburban areas.

Unless they've robbed a bank or are on a TV show, ordinary people are far too busy singing with the radio, texting, avoiding speed bumps, or just being immersed in their own bullshit to notice a tail. The biggest risk, Web knows, is that someone *else* might notice him. In Nevada, stalking is a misdemeanor for a first offense, and he would like to avoid explaining to the police why a Black man is following a white woman.

Fortunately—but also unfortunately—at the moment, Web doesn't have a white woman to tail. He's parked, sitting in a bubble of cool air, in stasis. Right now, his biggest challenge is bladder control.

He's been parked to the west of Ally's apartment complex since 8:04 a.m., after watching the opening shift lumber into Café Chroma and confirming Ally wasn't part of the crew. If she's left her apartment, he would have seen her. And he hasn't.

His phone vibrates with a text. "Pick up package at Tropicana reception Name: Kellan Nelson Deliver to front desk at Cromwell by 6:00 p.m. under the same name Confirm."

He confirms and checks the time. 10:47 a.m. In his time working for the Set Up, he's followed dozens of people, cataloging their routines and texting his notes to god knows who and for heaven knows what purposes. Occasionally, he sends pictures or videos. Today is the first time he's tailing someone on his own accord, and so far, it's been a bust.

Erv lit into Ally like a flamethrower for not closing the Girlfriend Job last night. "All you needed is a rack worth a second look," he said crassly. She told him to get fucked, but Web could tell she was wounded.

Erv saved some fire to singe Web too. "How much money are you willing to lose? And for what?" The only way to convince Erv not to make a case for cutting her loose entirely was to bet on it. Now, he has $100 that the Set Up calls her back, and another $900 riding on Ally's making it a week. But Web's not here to secure his bet. He doesn't want her to lose the job.

He curses himself for not bringing the most important equipment for stalking someone: a decent book. He scans social media, watches the sunlight blanch the pavement, guesses the airlines for the planes rising from Harry Reid International Airport.

At noon, his hunger breaks his resolve. Some private investigator, he thinks. Even a second-class Boy Scout—or a Boy Scout, Second Class—would've packed a granola bar. To distract himself, Web drives around the back and walks through the complex to see if he can peek into Ally's apartment. Blinds drawn, lights off. He supposes he could knock on her door but decides it would only spook her. So he circles back to his car.

He's missing something. He thinks about the home screen image on Ally's phone and his inability to unlock it. He puzzles over the emerging mosaic of who Ally says she is—an aspiring actress, from New York, only been in town for a few months—and what he suspects. He's just not sure he's seeing the whole picture. No need to tell Erv anything yet.

He drives the three blocks to Café Chroma, easing over each speed bump to not draw any attention from a bored cop. Finding a spot out back, he looks through the picnic table-sized glass windows and sees Ally putting on a black server apron as if she's starting her shift, and he can't figure out how he missed her. Where has she been?

He can't stay in the van for hours. He has things to do.

He drives to the Tropicana hotel's registration desk to pick up the package for Kellan Nelson—a square black tote with a zipper running three-fourths of the way around its top and a small strap. Like an insulated lunch box. After the pickup, Web finds a parking spot a little north of Chroma on Maryland Parkway, on the university side of the street.

Web decides to do some research from a proper computer and not his phone. He tucks the black tote at the foot of the passenger seat and heads to the Lied Library.

Once in the six-story atrium, he finds the nearest computer. Despite the arching ceiling, the place smells of toner, dead wood, and despairing late-teenage celibacy. He opens a browser, searches for "Ally Parks," and gets two dozen pages of hits. He narrows his search. "Ally Parks" and "New York." Nothing. He's a little surprised at a high schooler's light online footprint. The Set Up surely researched her. He looks for combinations of "Allyson," "Allison," "Parks," "Psychologist," "Manhattan."

Well, it's not like he's never come up empty while searching for someone online. He considers typing in his parents' names for the billionth time but stops himself. He stares at the cursor. A blinking digital eyeball, opening and closing. Opening and closing.

Web breaks the stare, sits back, and surveys the nave-like cavern. The soft lighting and quiet conspire to make him sleepy. He wonders how students can study here. It's like an anti-casino. He stares at a pair of students a few tables away and their large textbooks, wondering what they're studying. Physics? He looks at their In-N-Out takeout bags. In summer, it's easier to sneak in lunch.

He turns back to the computer. In-N-Out. When they pulled up to Rita's Comidas, he remembers Ally saying: "I was more of an In-N-Out kid." He does a search. There are no In-N-Outs east of the Mississippi.

He opens another browser window and types "Allyson Parks" and "California," then "Los Angeles." This gets some hits. He clicks on images and finds a thumbnail image of what looks like a younger Ally. Different hair, fuller face. But her. He clicks on the image. The link opens to an article in the *San Gabriel Valley Tribune* about a performance of *Little Shop of Horrors* at Mark Keppel High School. He finds Allyson Parks's name as the actress playing the role of Audrey I. He searches for the school. It's in Monterey Park, a suburb of LA. Ally said she went to LA after high school.

She said parts of her story were real. As far as he can tell, at the very least she lied about where she's from. He smiles at being fooled by her New York psychoanalyst parents' shtick. Well, after all, what does he know about how people live on the Upper West Side?

As he's about to log off, he looks at the UNLV homepage. He locates the campus directory, searches for and finds Ally. A theatre and journalism double major. He realizes she's been acting far more—and far more effectively—than he suspected.

From over the espresso machine, Ally half whispers, "*What are you doing here*?"

"Can't a guy get an iced coffee?" he says, trying to keep the conversation light.

"A guy? Yes. You? No. I'm working. Go." She bangs spent espresso into the knock box.

He moves to the pickup station at the side of the machine. "Look, Ally—"

She flicks on the espresso grinder and stares at him as the noise fills their shared space.

When the grinder cuts out, Web asks, "Have you heard from them today?"

She toggles the grinder twice, taps the filter basket on the counter, gently wipes grind off the rim, tamps down the espresso twice, takes a towel and lightly wipes underneath the overhang of the espresso machine, and loads the filter basket with a flick of the wrist. She presses a red button, then shakes her head no.

She bends to the under-counter fridge, takes a container out, pours milk into a metal pitcher, and returns the container.

Web says, "Do you—"

She places the pitcher under a steam wand and turns a knob, emitting a scream of air forced through milk, and stares blankly at him again. She might even be enjoying herself. He watches Ally tilt the pitcher and listens to the milk change pitch from a squeal to a grumble.

When it quiets, he asks, "Do you want to live in that apartment forever?" He watches as she pours the espresso into a mug and then, keeping the cup at an angle, lets the steamed milk pool and lift the espresso before leveling the mug. She shakes her wrist a little, making a leaf design. "Do you want—"

"Emily! Your drink is at the bar. Emily!" Only then does she turn to him. "What?"

He continues, "Do you want to work on latte art for the next ten years?"

She stares at him. He thinks his iced coffee order is next.

"You could do worse than working with us while you finish your double major." He pauses, wondering if she'd recognize the comment as bait. "You could go back home to LA with a nice bit of coin."

He interprets a flicker of surprise before she turns to her next ticket. He's prodding her, hoping she'll disclose something, though he's not exactly sure what he wants her to say. Does she have some plan, or is she just putting one foot in front of the other like everyone else?

She hands him a sixteen-ounce iced coffee, and he takes a long, bitter swig from the cup's brim.

"It doesn't matter," she says, returning to her half-whisper voice. "They aren't getting back to me." At that, she asks her coworker to take over the barista station, and he watches her head into the back. After a few minutes without seeing her return to the espresso machine, he leaves.

An hour later, from a block away, he watches her leave the café in her work apron and sit down on a concrete berm out front. He sees a man follow her. His back is turned, and Web can't see his face, but he watches as Ally looks up at him and smiles. She knows him. Maybe a customer. They talk. When Web catches the man's profile, he sees that it's the bachelor, Howie. Why is Ally meeting her mark from last night? Did they plan to meet? Could she have blown the Girlfriend Job deliberately?

He looks down to the black tote. He has thirty minutes to get it to the desk at the Cromwell. An urge to open the package strikes him. He's never done this, though as far as he knows, there's no rule against it. He looks at Ally and Howie still talking and reaches down and grabs the tote. He takes a breath and unzips it.

Inside is a disposable ice pack and two twelve-ounce water bottles with green caps. Nothing else. No note, or money, or anything. All these years, he's never once opened a package or breached an imagined ethical line and it's just . . . water? Is this some kind of fucking joke?

He looks up at Ally one last time, checks his mirrors, signals, and pulls a U-turn on Maryland to make a left on Flamingo.

16

ALLY

"I missed you last night," he says.

Howie's voice startles her, fucking up the heart nestled in leaves she's creating with milk foam. "Aren't you supposed to be hanging from a zip line?" she says. "Or getting pantsed by a slot machine somewhere?"

"Cute. It was rock climbing."

She tries to play it cool. "How'd you find me?"

"You said you served coffee to students. That narrowed it down a bit. You lied about working the morning shift, though." Ally takes a moment to berate herself for not being inventive enough in her identity wallet. This is why you make things up. She feels an additional surge of embarrassment that Howie might notice how the woman at the bar last night had inspired her to dig out her old black-and-white Bikini Kill tee this morning. Maybe he won't notice.

Last night, she sent a WhatsApp text to the Set Up ("I'm so sorry. I'll do better") and she received zippo in return. To expend her nervous energy, she tapped out a detailed description of the bachelor party on her phone.

"I thought it was odd when they said no one worked here by the name of Mona."

She looks down at a ticket. Iced mocha. She grabs a cup and some ice. Finishes it up and turns to her manager: "Dana, I'm gonna take five."

"You already took—"

"Cover me, please?" Ally begs. Dana would've been a great nun in another life, albeit a heavily tattooed one. She shows her indifference to worldly things by never differentiating Ally from Phoebe while still soundlessly judging their relationship and shirking pleasantries enough to avoid tips. Ally pops in the back and grabs her bag without waiting for Dana's response.

Howie follows her out the door. "Sorry," she says with a shrug, sitting down on the edge of a planter. She wonders what her responsibilities are in the moment. Is the gig over? Keep up the game? "Look, my relationship . . . It's a steaming mess."

"I figured," he says with a smile.

She notices his face falter a bit. Perhaps, she thinks, he is reading her present disappointment over screwing up the Girlfriend Job as guilt over lying to him, for which she feels only a tinge of regret. Of course, lying to him wasn't the worst of it. She thinks of the kiss again, and how he was almost sweet about it. Ally sensed a touch of innocence to it but perhaps only thinks that because she's grateful he didn't get all handsy. She feels her face flush.

"I'm Ally," she says, sticking out her hand.

"I'm still Howie," he says, accepting it.

She's having a hard time reading him. Under the average-dude coating, she sees there's a bit more to him. "What did you mean when you said you missed me?"

"I felt obliged to the guys, so we went to the club. After half an hour, I told them I was getting a private lap dance and slipped out the back and went to the hotel. I watched a movie after I realized you weren't going to show."

She recognizes that he's waiting for a response, but Ally isn't sure how to process the information. She wasn't a failure after all. She had him. It's a consolation prize that doesn't pay the bills.

She says she's sorry, and she means it.

"Don't be. My luck is improving," he says. "I suppose I can't take you out for a cup of coffee."

"No, you cannot. And we don't serve Red Bull and Hennessy, I'm afraid," Ally says looking over to the white Set Up van parked one block away. She sees it pull away and make a U-turn.

"But that doesn't mean we have to say goodbye." She jumps up. "Your car's nearby?"

"Yeah, I'm the black Hyundai over there."

Ally had spotted the van parked down the road earlier, on her first break, and walked over, hoping to confront either Web or Erv. It was empty, but the red scratch on the front bumper from Erv's taqueria fender bender confirmed her suspicions. She wasn't surprised when Web showed up in her queue for a coffee.

Moving toward the Hyundai, Ally says, "Great. Let's test that famous passion for adventure, shall we?"

"Sure," he says, striding to catch up with her. "I'm open to trying new things."

"Stellar," she says, as they pull away from the curb. "This sounds so dumb, but . . . follow that van?"

"No problem," he smiles. "I figure I owe you."

"How's that?"

"Because I ordered room service on your card," he says. "A lot of it."

"Fair."

They both laugh, and Ally allows herself to be a little relieved at the break in tension.

"So we're following your boyfriend, aren't we?"

She's not sure that it's Web driving, but she suspects it. "He's not—" Ally starts before biting her tongue. "It's—"

"It's a steaming mess, I get it," Howie says. "You think he's cheating on you."

She thinks about it for a moment. "I don't think I really know him at all," she says, honestly.

The van turns onto Las Vegas Boulevard. Howie's doing a surprisingly good job. He's pacing two cars behind without being trapped at lights.

She looks around the interior of his car. There aren't any personal effects, not even a straw wrapper in the cupholder. He and his boys don't make a mess on a Vegas road trip, she guesses. It's like the car is a reflection of Howie's unremarkable surface. This guy is practically Mormon, she thinks. Compared to Erv's opacity and Web's mosaic self, Howie is a warm, if dim, light. Not altogether unpleasant to be around. Comforting as a rerun. She thinks of Web's kaleidoscopic pieces, coming off each scene, moving in and out of light. Why did he stop by the café? To warn her? What was that about LA?

She wants to talk but bites her lip. If acting naturally is so easy, then why does it demand an act? Ally runs through some training that Web and Erv dumped on her. Understated emotions. Hotel art.

She winds back the reel. She's got this. "You said Melville isn't honest with the reader. Are you an unreliable narrator?"

“Am I— What?” he asks, eyes still on the road.

“As the narrator in the song. Are you singing as a reliable narrator, or are you like Melville, deliberately holding back information from the listener?”

Whether it was the daylight or the fact that she’s conscripted him on a mission not of his choosing, Howie doesn’t seem as game to chat about his music as he had been the night before. “I— I—” he stumbles and refocuses on driving. They see the van turn in at a hotel called the Cromwell.

“Shit. A garage. Let another car go ahead.” She lowers the seat down. “If someone gets out, I’ll follow him. Wait nearby, yes?”

“Con . . . firmative,” he says.

“That’s not how words work,” she says under her breath.

In the garage, they watch Web park the van and head to the casino entrance. Ally jumps out, phone in hand, to follow.

Ally tries to mimic Howie’s trailing in the car, and Web appears to be unaware of her presence ten paces behind. She makes a few half-attempts to duck behind slot machines or a corner—quickly, and without a need. She watches as he delivers a small black tote to the front desk. From behind a column, she watches the receptionist laugh at a joke. As he turns, Ally pivots around the column and buries her head in her phone.

When she gets back into the Hyundai, Howie has the car running. He says, “Unless that was a quick hookup, I’m guessing he didn’t meet anyone.”

“No, he dropped something off,” she says.

“What?”

“Some bag.”

"You still want to follow him?" She sees something behind his face flicker, like a faltering bulb in a marquee. He's unsure. But the lights aren't all out. She can still read the sign.

"Yes, please," she says. "I'll . . . I'll make it up to you."

This seems to convince him, although she worries about what it might mean later. They trail the van along the Strip for twenty minutes.

As the light on Sahara turns green, a man stumbles into the street with a three-foot-tall margarita in hand. Howie hits the brakes.

"C'mon," he says. "Move!"

Ally watches the van continue up the Strip. *We'll lose him*, she thinks. Howie asks her, "What's the protocol here?"

Howie doesn't wait for the man to get to the median, only to clear the lane.

"Go!" Ally says, unnecessarily. The tires squeal enough to capture the drunk's attention, and before they drive on, she sees a glimmer in the man's face as he realizes that he is, in fact, standing in the middle of one of the busiest streets in America.

Howie catches up to Web, and Ally's heart rate slows. She's impressed.

"So," Howie says without taking his eyes off the road, "I looked at your tab when I paid it. You were only drinking club sodas."

"I—" she starts.

He looks back at the road and makes a left.

"Wait! What are you doing?"

"Didn't he go this way?" Howie asks, pointing with his chin. "NoNoNo," Ally says. "Turn around. Turn!"

"It's one-way."

"Turn on Fourth."

Howie obeys, slowly. She doesn't see the van. "Park. Just park," she says.

"Maybe we should—"

She shushes him. "Just wait." Ally launches a map on the phone, searching for something nearby that might be Web's destination. Casinos. A pawnshop. Nothing sets off a bell. But if he wasn't headed for something downtown, he would've hopped on the I-15 to avoid traffic. He was going somewhere around here.

Then she sees it. Mademoiselle's.

She remembers Erv saying Web works at a place with a name that started with "Mad." What if he doesn't work at a gym but at Mademoiselle's Gentlemen's Club? Same place Howie had his bachelor party. An awfully strange coincidence.

They're only two blocks away, and Ally directs Howie to the location, telling him to pull over across the street.

"Well, I don't know what to say about this," Howie says. "C'mon, let's get some dinner. I'll buy."

Ally scans the lot for the van. Maybe it's in the back.

"I don't think he's coming out," Howie says.

"Just wait," she says.

But after ten quiet minutes, Ally unbuckles her seat belt. "No way," he says. "I'm not going in. Again."

"Cool. I didn't ask you to," she says, closing the passenger door as she sees him mouth the word, "But . . ."

As she approaches the door, Ally flashes a wide smile at the bouncer. It's only when she looks down and sees her café apron around her waist that she remembers she just walked right out of her job. Too late to worry now, she thinks. She loosens the apron in a quick move and stuffs it into her bag.

"Hold it," the bouncer says, lowering his arm into Ally's path. It looks more like a leg. His neck is thick enough to look like he's wearing an inflatable airplane neck pillow.

"Yes?"

"We might play Beyoncé in here, but no single ladies," he tells her.

"That's a rule?" Ally knots her face into a pout.

"Yes, ma'am. Women must have an escort." He points to a laminated sign, entitled "Dress Code," with plenty of fine print.

She considers using the same moves that she used on Teresa at the taco place. "Can I just pop in and check it out?"

A black SUV pulls up and unloads a pack of five middle-aged men, and they command the bouncer's attention.

"You need an escort. Step aside," he says, waving the guys in. Ally watches him slip the driver several folded bills.

"Sure. I left mine in the car," she mumbles before retreating.

Thankfully, Howie is still there. He rolls down the window as she walks up. "They wouldn't let me go—"

He cuts her off. "No single ladies. I tried to tell you."

She reads him with an up-and-down look. He's got a casual but nice button-down shirt, sleeves cuffed, and chinos on. He should pass the dress code. Wearing all black from her barista job, she thinks she should be okay. Or at least, that wasn't the bouncer's primary concern. Ally asks, "Is there a dark corner we can sit in?"

Howie produces his prominent teeth. "I think there is," he says.

The bouncer nods as they walk to the door, as if they hadn't just had a conversation. Howie leads her to a booth with a low table.

She slides across from him, her back to the room, and looks around through the mirror behind his head. He says, "So, to recap. Last night you thought I wasn't 'a gentlemen's club kinda guy,' and today—"

"I've convinced you to come here. Yes. It's different."

"—to spy on your boyfriend."

"Yes," Ally says. She has no other answer. They both look around the room. "Do you see him?"

"Don't think so," Howie says.

It's a large room. A long central stage with two others on the far walls. The lights and bodies move quickly, and the pink and purple circles offer partial views. There's a general but inexact coordination between the women on the stages and the thumping music. Strobe lights bounce off shiny chrome, both horizontal railings and vertical poles. It's still early, but it's dark inside. She judges the place to be at a third of its capacity, with four women dancing. She assesses the groups of men in the booths, looking for Web, until a voice surprises her in its proximity, "Can I get you two a drink?"

Ally doesn't look at the server before answering, "No, thank you."

The server leans forward into Ally's line of sight. Big hair. A long black dress with a slit that seems to go up to her lowest rib. A sultry, Scarlett Johannson voice. "It's a two-drink minimum."

"One minute?" Howie says. He makes a show of perusing the drinks menu.

"Sure," she says. "My name is Reyna."

"Thanks, Reyna," Howie says. He catches Ally's attention. "Ally? Are we staying? I don't want to pay $50 for watered-down drinks just to chaperone another confrontation with your boyfriend as he folds singles into G-strings."

"He's not—" she starts, and then through a reflection in a mirror, she spots Web in the DJ booth. He's about forty feet away, the brim of his All Money In cap pulled low. He's wearing a tight black tee, not the polo he was wearing at the coffee shop, and he seems fully engrossed in his work.

A dancer moves to a section of a stage that breaks Ally's view of Web. The dancer flips up the pole, holds herself up with the crook of her knee, and reaches her arms out to either side. The woman lifts her body up and twists her wrist to slowly rotate her entire body 360 degrees, with one leg horizontal and the other bent back around the pole. Ally can't look away, admitting to herself that she's a little turned on. The stripper looks at Ally and, before she can turn away, winks.

This, Ally thinks, is not the kind of fitness she had in mind when Web said he worked at a twenty-four-hour gym.

Howie picks up his phone and works it over with his thumbs. He says, "I'm going to text the guys and tell them . . ." but he fades right back out of her awareness again.

Of all the skin joints in all the towns, in all the world, she wonders, why are we all here? Is Web playing some sick game with her? Or is someone else?

"*Ally*?" Howie says in a way that makes her confident it's the second or third time he's said it. She realizes that both the waitress and Howie are staring at her. "Are. We. Staying?" he asks.

"I've seen enough." The look on his face shows that Howie has not, but he follows her anyway.

17

MARSHALL

Back when he was a full-time reporter and stuck on a piece, Marshall used to head for the desert. Lengthy cruises out to where the roads go all wavy and the ghost towns decompose in the sun used to clarify his tangled thoughts.

At the southern tip of the state, Laughlin is an hour-and-a-half drive south of the Hoover Dam and along the Colorado River. Everything around Laughlin seems just a paler shade of bleached. As if the wind has peeled away everything down to the whitest Coconino Sandstone. The setting sun paints it all a warm pink.

After engineering some nerve, he arrives at the address Lévesque gave him. He finds a ten-foot solid black front gate and a mute adobe wall. If this is a church, it doesn't look like one. The compound looks older than the surrounding buildings. If they were smart, the Unificationists bought this land for cheap in the nineties, then divided and sold plots to developers. He'll check out the property histories.

He doesn't know what he expected. Men dressed in crimson robes and creepy *Eyes Wide Shut* masks? Gregorian chants spilling over the walls? Like everyone, he enjoys the great Southwestern game of extrapolating what a house looks like from what you can see above a wall. In this case, the rooftops and second floors look like a dense warren of small homes. Similar to the old location, but six, maybe seven times larger. Conducting their business behind high walls doesn't make these folks all that unique. Good fences make good neighbors, supposedly.

On an intercom box, there's a brass plaque that reads "Southern Kingdom" and, below that, a call button. Marshall leans out his window and presses the button.

He hears the whir of an AC unit somewhere and nothing else. No signs of life. He presses the button again.

"Hello?" he calls out. "Hello?"

After two minutes, a deep voice crackles through: "No visitors."

"I'm a reporter."

"No visitors. No reporters. We've recorded your license plate. Do not come back."

"I just have a few questions. Could I speak with someone?" After another minute of silence, he offers a meek "Hello?"

He rolls up his window and parks his car a few houses down the block. He looks back at the rough outline map he printed in his office. He cannot see the two pools, but he identifies the rectangles on the map as nine two-story buildings from their rooflines. Mute windows. Not much else to see.

With one last look at the gate, he flicks on his directional to head home. Checking in his rearview mirror, he sees a dark sedan parked in front of the compound that wasn't there before. He waits a few minutes, but there's no movement. Might as well head home. He pulls out and looks in the rearview to see the sedan do the same. He stops, and the sedan stops too. Drive or not?

He gets to the interstate, and the car mirrors his turns, lane changes, and speed. Marshall doesn't think to turn on the stereo or AC. The heat does its work on his pores.

After five minutes of aimless driving, he decides to pull into a park. He gets out, finds a bench, and looks over the Colorado to

Arizona on the other shore, waiting and hopeful. The sedan follows him and parks a respectful distance away. No one leaves the car; no mystery man joins him to share the view or have a conversation.

At a loss for what to do, he pulls out the notebook with his notes from the crash scene, flips to notes he didn't share with the class. The driver wasn't drunk, and the jogger's report established that the pedestrian stumbled into the street too quickly for the distracted driver to react. No stop sign. No light. There was some sense the driver wouldn't be charged with vehicular manslaughter. A tragic accident. Or suicide. The whole thing wouldn't have merited much attention if Marshall hadn't written about it. He figured he wrapped the story in a neat bow, more of an ending than anyone could've made, and moved on.

Now that knot seems to have been illusory. He didn't discover the roommate. He didn't figure out what Cal was doing before he turned up dead. No idea about Cal's family. No clue about this group. Tracy did more work on it than he had, but not much more. He doesn't know why she passed along contact information for the witnesses, including his ex's phone and address. He can't tell if she is trying to push him to find more answers or scare him off the story altogether.

Inhaling the dry desert air, he feels full of disappointment, but on the exhale, he feels a little seed blossoming in his chest. He isn't sure what it is, but there's *something* going on here, and he needs to find out what it is. And then another, more pragmatic part of his brain wakes up, with another, more pragmatic set of questions: *Is there a story here?* Article, he thinks. Maybe even a book.

Saying a prayer, begging for someone from the group to approach him, he realizes he'd even welcome some kind of threat. But neither comes. After a half hour, the sedan pulls away.

18

ALLY

Back in the car, Ally collects her thoughts. She notices that Howie is driving toward Chroma.

She sees the sign for Desert Inn Road. “Wait. Turn around,” she says, breaking the silence.

“Not again,” he says.

“Pull a U and make a right,” she says. When he does, she says, “One last stop.”

She guides him to the Taj M’all.

“C’mon Ally. Enough with this. Let’s get dinner. I’m starving.”

“Pull around back,” she says, before adding, “Please.” Without comment, he does what she requests. Ally looks down the length of the backside of the mall. There are two loading docks and three dumpsters at about the midway point. Nothing else. It’s desolate. Howie puts the Hyundai in park.

He leans toward her, and Ally realizes that he might have the mistaken impression that she wants to find a place where they can be alone. She opens the car door and gets out. He looks at her and exhales a slow, exasperated breath. “What are we doing, Ally?”

Bending down to speak with him, she says, “You can go.”

“Is this a weird mating ritual?”

Zero percent interested in keeping the conversation going, Ally turns to the building.

From behind her, he asks, “Are you some kind of detective?” She thinks, *I’m no detective*, still holding on to the thought there might be a clue she is missing. *But I might be a journalist.*

Ally walks to the door that should align with the front entrance to the Set Up. It's a plain metal gray with a deadbolt and a small gold number: 37. Along the back wall, some suites have windows, including this one. She tries the knob. It's locked. She looks in the window, but it is midnight dark inside. The darkest place in town, she thinks. She feels the window frame and attempts to lift it. It budges, just a little.

She hears Howie again. "Ally, c'mon."

She turns around, about to attempt to convince him to get out and help her pry open the window, but then she hears a vehicle coming down the alley. She makes for Howie's car, but there's no place to hide. A white cargo van emerges, and its headlights blind Ally. How did Web know?

But when the driver steps out of the car, it's Erv, not Web.

"Ally, get in the van," he says.

"Erv, I—"

"Don't you think you've pulled enough shit?" Erv snaps.

Howie steps out of the car and approaches them. The two men stop about seven feet from each other, with Ally in between. Feeling chivalrous, or maybe just stupid, Howie says, "Ally, who is this?"

"None of your concern," Erv says.

Staring down Erv, Howie says, "Ally, get in the car."

"Stay out of it, frat boy," Erv says.

"Are you trying to wind me up, little man?"

Ally sees Howie's hand ball up. Erv is older, but she figures he'd give Howie a challenge. Not that she wants things to come to that.

"One of these paths leads to a decent future for you," Erv addresses Ally, keeping his eyes on Howie. "The other one does not. Let's not get Mr. Russell involved any further."

"How does this guy—" Howie starts.

Bang. Even Erv seems startled when the door to Jimmy's opens and a cook comes out to carry two trash bags to the dumpster. It's too far away to see the person's face, but Ally watches the red ember of a cigarette float in the dark. On the return to the restaurant, the figure pauses, as if to consider the trio. After another few seconds, the door closes and they're alone again.

Ally turns to him. "Go back to your boys, Howie. Thanks for the company." She grabs her bag from the seat of his rental and says, "Good luck with your album." After a beat, he offers an uncertain nod.

She gets into the passenger seat of the van. Through the glass, she gives a meek wave to Howie as Erv pulls away.

"What the hell, Erv?"

"There is no need to spy on people's private lives," he tells her. "Maybe try to do the job you're supposed to do, rather than fuck up things that aren't your job?"

She rides in silence. She steals a look at Erv's face as he drives. The lights dancing over his brooding features give her the impression of a rock, smooth and unperturbed, at the bottom of a lake.

"Like you said before. Some people set up the con, and the others get conned." Erv says. A black sedan pulls in front of them, and he gives a long, almost soulful blow on the horn. She looks around and sees they're on Vegas Valley Drive, heading east. Well past the turn to her apartment complex. It's a road she's been on before. When she first arrived to town, looking for an apartment, she used to pick one of the main thoroughfares and see how far out she could drive, watching the CVSs and strip malls become sparser and the road thin into the desert. "And then, there are those who're taken off the board," Erv finishes the thought. "It's uncomplicated. Show me someone with pure ethics and I'll show you a bum on the street."

Ally pulls her shoulders back as if to fight but straightens back up instead, not that Erv notices as he continues.

"I don't care what you were doing today. Etcetera. But you need to tell me, right now, if you're gonna play by the rules, Ally."

She looks forward. She feels the night getting darker. She looks through the windshield, into the nothing.

"I'll play by the rules, Erv. I don't understand them, but I'll play by them." She looks at him as he looks straight ahead.

"I hope, for your sake, you do," he says. "Me? I don't give two shits in either direction."

As if she's said what he wanted to hear, he makes an immediate turn on Cabana, back to Flamingo, and then back to her street. When they get to her complex, she gets out without a word.

"You switched to late shifts now?" one of the Neon Witches yells from the pool area. "You and your girlfriend should come relax in the hot tub," another says. The other two chuckle in response.

The witches weren't the only ones who noticed a change in her. She'd all but forgotten Phoebe's anger over Ally both canceling date night *and* getting dressed up to go out. *I might blow both Girlfriend Jobs*, she thinks.

"Toil and trouble, boys," she says, waving as she walks by.

Once home, she lets Beep talk about her day. Ally senses no willingness on Phoebe's part to close the distance between them.

She gets the courage to casually look at the phone, and not receiving messages seems to be the theme of her evening.

Ally throws the device on the stack of graphic novels by her bedside and presses up against her girlfriend. Beep offers resistance, but not for long. When Ally closes her eyes, there's a swirl of color, and she tries to push away images of Howie, but Web takes his place. And then the dancer appears, her body splattered in purples, blues, and pinks. After a little prompting, Ally and Phoebe intertwine like the shifting fingers of two hands.

SATURDAY

19

MARSHALL

If the campus library is as bustling as a morgue on summer weekdays, on the weekends, it is a crypt. It suits Marshall's mood. As he walks in the automatic doors, he sees that even the staff is MIA. If two or three chairs were overturned, maybe a table, it would have a zombie flick ambiance. No one minds that he strolls in with his Chroma travel mug at 8:00 a.m.

On the drive to campus, he couldn't help but keep looking in the rearview mirror, searching for a blue/black sedan in pursuit. Surely, he thinks, stalking is more of an evening activity. He picks a cubicle on the second floor to keep an eye on the front entry. Not that he knows what would give away someone who is following him. Is there a cult haircut?

He opens his new notebook and his old 1995 notebook to take stock. He writes a series of bullet points:

- What am I missing about the Rothman story?
- Unification Church? "Third Family?"
- Ogden/15th St compound?

After a moment, he leaves a space and adds a fourth line:

- Who is reviewing my old articles?

Might as well start from the top. Marshall flips through the old notebook again to find his notes on the Rothman accident. The name of the driver, in red ink, reaffirming that Tracy provided it after the incident: Randall Carter, from San Pedro, California. He opens a browser, searches, and finds a death notice online easily. Not much information. Age (sixty-two), date of death (May 6, 2008), a code showing he died in Palm Springs. No cause listed. Sixty-two isn't young but not exactly old either. That puts Carter at about forty-nine in '95. Not the bumbling senior that Marshall remembered him being. *Hell*, he thinks. *That's my age now.*

Marshall looks up to see an eighteen-year-old walk through the front doors. Skater-dude type. He turns back to the screen.

The online obituary mentions that Carter served in the US Army and was in Vietnam in '66–'68. Returned home and attended UCLA. Survived by a wife and two children. Instead of flowers, the obit encourages donating to the local Kiwanis chapter. Reminded of his conversation with Lévesque, he takes the etymological off-ramp via an online search. Kiwanis. International service organization founded in Detroit. Algonquin word. Meanings include "fooling around" and "to make oneself known," but the founders of the organization interpreted it as "we build."

He pulls himself back on track. So maybe Randall was a good family guy. Also: member of a fraternal order. He weighs digging into this further and checks the time. It's still too early to call anyone in Los Angeles, and he's unsure what he would even ask. He takes some notes, moves down the list.

Next: Moonies. Unificationists. He flips through his notes from his conversation with Lévesque and does a little more surfing. Marriages. The Moons were the "True Mother and Father." Their mass weddings, called "blessings," were infamous. Trafficking ideas and money around the world. Not as secretive or as powerful as Scientology.

He searches for "Kiwanis" and "Unificationist." Not much. "Randall Carter" and "Unificationist." Nothing of interest. Variations of "Cal Rothman" and "Unificationist." Nada.

Looking over the description of the scene in '95, his eyes rest on his ex-girlfriend's name. He adds "Brenda Dentner" to the series of search combinations. More nothing. Well, it's not like cults keep their membership rolls online.

A couple of young women walk in, talking quietly.

On the third page of results for "Unificationist" and "Las Vegas," he finds a blog post—dubious and in need of any verification, he notes—about the local chapter. An amateur reporter, writing an essay about Las Vegas as a long-standing bastion for esoterics, charismatics, and hucksters, likely because of the informal, pliable legal environment and locals who keep to themselves. There's a link to a story about a case in the eighties of a woman who left the church, claiming they brainwashed her. But when he clicks on the link, it goes to a dead page. He finds more broken links. He clicks on the "About" page, hoping he can find a connection to the website's author, but there's no information on it. The last post was in 2013. Just another cobwebbed nook of the internet.

He's the proverbial gambler chasing his money. Tilting at windmills.

Frustrated, he opens his flip phone and sends a text to his editor at *The Record*.

Four editors have cycled through since Marshall's downfall. With every turnover, the rumors faded, the stigma of his botched assignment mellowing into a mere stain. This latest editor, Vaughn Tutti, is happy to give Marshall assignments when his staff is otherwise occupied.

Marshall 9:05
I have a question

Tutti 9:05
Hard pass

Marshall 9:05
Just information Not an assignment

Tutti 9:06
You know that's worse, right?

Marshall 9:06
I assume it depends on the question

Without a response, he continues.

Marshall 9:09
Is anyone looking into The Third Family?

Tutti 9:09
What's that

Marshall 9:09
Unification Church sect. Used to be downtown. Guy named Joshua Kollis runs it. Property records show he owns land in Laughlin. I guess they moved.

Tutti 9:11
So?

Marshall 9:11
So I wanna know if you have anyone who's done any work on them.

Tutti 9:14
Not that I know of

Marshall doesn't know what else to type, and it takes too long to text on his flip phone anyway, so he stares at the monitor for a few minutes. Then, his phone vibrates out another text:

Tutti 9:18
I'll look into it

Marshall lets out a breath he didn't realize he was holding. Tutti always does what he says he'll do.

Third topic. Development. He flips to his notes from Ernesto. He said the In-Hwa Group owned the downtown site on Ogden

Street. Marshall writes that after the third bullet point. He finds In-Hwa Group easily: a development and real estate corporation. He clicks on the "Our Team" page. There, he sees two cofounders and principals, William Leonard and Oran Kollis, along with a list of twelve support staff. A good-sized operation.

Leonard doesn't ring any bells, but Kollis sure does, though there's nothing illegal about being related to someone. He clicks on the bios of Leonard and Kollis. He reads through the text but doesn't find much other than imposing descriptions of management portfolios, Ivy League degrees, certifications from the appropriate national associations, and affiliations. He hopes Kollis's bio might state it outright: "My father runs a cult in Laughlin, Nevada," but no dice.

As Lévesque told him, these days, everyone's on the level. The mob. The Mormons. The Moonies. Prostitution (although outside the city and county limits). Even pot's legal. There might be plenty of fences, but there's no wrong side anymore. You either have money or you don't.

He watches a woman maybe a decade older than he is walk in and approach the circulation desk to return books.

Marshall shakes his head, surprised by the passage of time. He blew right through lunch. He needs to get home and freshen up before meeting Brenda. He logs off, grabs his travel mug, phone, and notebooks, and leaves.

A block away from Atomic Liquors, Marshall sees an art installation on the facade of an empty building. The shadow from cantilevered letters spells out: "VERY SLOW FOR THOSE WHO WAIT VERY FAST

FOR THOSE WHO ARE SCARED VERY LONG FOR THOSE WHO LAMENT VERY SHORT FOR THOSE WHO CELEBRATE." Art by someone who calls themselves "Daku156." There's a closed-down auto shop, too—good enough for some artsy graffiti, too quirky a site for rehabilitation.

Back in the fifties, this was the sharp northern edge of town, and patrons could sit at Atomic Liquors and watch the mushroom clouds rise from the horizon. There's a photo hanging behind the bar of the view. They would've called Vegas "Fallout City" if not for the westerly winds that blew east to Utah instead of south.

This bar is one of the last bits of genuine history in town—enough of a dive to be one stop on Nic Cage's drunken descent in *Leaving Las Vegas*. The bartender, if asked, will cheerfully tell you how Cage drank himself into vomiting in the bathroom. Since then, the place has expanded threefold and now has the kinds of food, outdoor seating, and shrubbery necessitated by new bougie tastes.

The sign's the same, though. *We love our neon signs*, he thinks. He's ten minutes early, but Brenda's already got a seat at the bar. A power move. Their eyes lock when he walks through the door, and she stands to meet him. He hasn't thought through how to greet her. A handshake? Perhaps reading his hesitation, she leans in for a hug.

"Bren."

"Shally," she says before nodding to the stools. "The bar okay?"

"It's where they hide the booze," he says. She pulls a bulky purse off the stool next to her and swings it around a hook between her knees. Marshall sits, and their shoulders touch briefly.

When the bartender approaches, Brenda orders. "Vodka and a twist of lemon over ice for me, Manhattan in a rocks glass, no rocks, for him," she says. "Your drink hasn't changed, I imagine?"

They both look to Marshall. "It hasn't." He asks the bartender to bring two glasses of water. He looks at the old playing cards and poker chips embedded in lacquer, like fossils in beer-stained amber. No poker machines, however. A mercy, he thinks.

"I suppose it will be interesting to learn if anything else has changed." She smiles.

"Harsh but fair."

Marshall assesses the scene. He smells the smell of stale alcohol. It's busy for a Saturday afternoon. He looks at Brenda's reflection between the bottles behind the bar, capped with their multicolored pourers. There's a little more makeup around her eyes, and her dark hair has some gray mixed in. Beyond her reflection, he sees the properties on Ogden.

"You never left," he says.

"This town is hell, with its only redeeming quality being that it's better than all the other towns."

"It's a place," he offers.

"It's a city for the everyman, Marshall. It's the only place in the country a humble valet can buy a home."

"You were neither humble, nor a valet," he says, pausing, before adding, "You look good." It's not flattery, just the truth.

"Okay, Shally. Let me stop you right there." Her voice is still good-natured but layered with some resolve. "We had a thing. I liked the thing. But it crashed as unexpectedly as it began. What am I doing here? You just wanna catch up?"

"I'm not eager to revisit history," he says.

"All evidence to the contrary. I'm open to some revisiting," she says, looking into his eyes. "What is it you want, then?"

He decides to tell her straight up. "I want to talk about the day we met."

"And that's not revisiting history?"

"Not our history," he tries. In the recall, he feels the melancholy. Initially, she told him she wasn't emotionally available for anything longer than a 5K. "Short loops," she said, to set the pace for their early dates. And indeed, they had a number of lovely but short trips around the track. As promised, she kept her distance. By the end, he couldn't outrun the uneasy ethics of their start line and cut it off.

Laughing, she says, "The day we met *isn't* our history?" He sees her shake her head. "I can't believe I put on a dress for this. Goddammit. Usually, when someone wants to revisit their old flame, they've got other thoughts on their minds, hon."

Their drinks arrive, and she takes a pull after a slight tip of the glass in his direction. "I invested many fifty-minute sessions into putting that day behind me," she says. "Add a few more to put you behind me too. Speaking of the talking cure, how's your mom?"

"At peace," he says.

He sees her wince in the mirror. "I'm sorry to hear that. I liked her a whole bunch," she says.

"Thanks. She liked you too. It's been a while." There was a stretch where he and Brenda would take his mother out for a $3.99 steak dinner. But that was before she got sick.

Marshall cannot find a smooth segue into it and decides to just ask: "Have you ever heard of the Third Family?"

"Whose family?"

"No, *the* Third Family."

"Don't think so. What's that?"

"Some kind of break-off group from the Unificationist Church."

"What's that got to do with the price of whiskey?"

"Not sure. Maybe nothing. They came up as I was looking into Cal's background."

"Cal?" She leans back.

"The kid who got clipped back in '95." He can see her consider a question but decide against it. "Was there anything odd about that day that you remember? Something you never told me? Or the police? Maybe you didn't think it was important at the time, but—"

She cuts him off. "I can't recall, and I don't want to. I have far fonder memories of the days after that, Marshall. For me to keep them fond, I've had to forget what happened to that poor kid." Brenda takes another deep swig. It's large enough that it telegraphs to Marshall she's thinking of leaving. "Look, if this is what you've got, I'm gonna go. I had a long shift today, and I rushed home to get dolled up to meet with you."

"Still waiting tables?" he asks.

"Yup. No shame in that, Marshall."

His turn to wince. He was trying to be curious and attentive, not judgmental. He can't ask questions like a journalist, even if he's one at his core. "Ever come across someone named Kollis?"

"I've never known a Kollis," she says before emptying her glass. "Well, Marshall. I wish I could say it's been a blast."

"Wait." Trying to lighten his tone, he asks, "Can we meet again?"

She stares back, and he registers her disappointment growing like a bruise under her skin. "Sure," she says at last. "But not if we're gonna talk about that kid. I've moved on." She leans in, and for a moment, it seems very familiar. He remembers kissing her. She pivots and kisses his forehead before pulling back to look him square in the face. Resting her hand on his shoulder, he feels her thumb give the slightest caress—possibly to balance herself, perhaps to ease her exit. It is another visceral trigger of memory.

"If you want to look ahead and not backward, call me."

20

ALLY

"Get the fuck out of here," Erv says, laughing.

"I'm serious. How much do you want to bet Ally doesn't live in Las Vegas?"

She's not sure what Web's going on about. "What are you saying?"

Erv's chuckling continues. "No way."

"Way," Web insists. "I'll double down. The airport, the university, and even the 'Welcome Las Vegas' sign aren't in Las Vegas. Ally, you believe me?" he asks from the passenger seat.

"A hundred bucks," Erv says.

There's a joke, and Ally's not in on it. What she can't tell is how concerned she should be. "Keep me out of it," she says from the back. "Where are we headed?"

"Exactly. Where *are* we headed?" Web teases.

"C'mon," Erv says, turning onto Las Vegas Boulevard. "Let me just turn onto *Las Vegas Boulevard* to the Cromwell. Located *in Las Vegas.*"

"You know the hotels on this single corner have a greater occupancy than all of San Francisco?" Web offers up, teasing his bet along.

Through the windshield, Ally watches the hotels tower on either side as the van rides down the fold of an adult pop-up book.

Ally remains unnerved from last night's encounter with Erv, and the as-if-it-never-happened bets and jokes don't help. Questions tug at the edges of her mind. Why was Web staking out Chroma? Was Erv staking *her* out, or Web? She's fairly confident Web didn't see her at the club. Or did he? If not, how did Erv follow her to the office?

It took her time to consider the Set Up's text this morning.

> 7 pm pick up E Rochelle and Caliente Banquet reception for bar mitzvah @ Drai's nightclub at the Cromwell Dress conservatively Confirm.

Eventually, she caved. Confirm. And when they pulled up in formal attire—Erv in a brown suit, Web in black pants, white shirt, and black tie—she was pleased with her selection of a long, dark blue Max Mara shirtdress with a bright orange sash.

Ally was expecting a confrontation, but deep in their wagering, Erv and Web offer not a whiff of acrimony, and she's certainly not going to ask any of her questions. It hasn't been a week, and she's already tired of their cycle of teasing and repairing. She watches Web tap on his phone and then read: "Paradise is an unincorporated township that includes the Harry Reid International Airport—"

"Goddammit," Erv says.

"—the University of Nevada, Las Vegas, the hockey arena, and much of Las Vegas Boulevard," Web finishes and puts down his phone. "One hundred bucks, please."

Erv grumbles, "The Venetian isn't Venice, the Paris hotel isn't Paris, The New York New York isn't New York . . . and I guess Las Vegas isn't even Las Vegas." At the stop light, he pulls a money clip out of his pocket and hands a bill to Web.

"In a way, it never was," Web says, laughing. "The casinos and the mob created Paradise to avoid paying taxes to Las Vegas."

She catches Erv looking at her in the rearview mirror as he says, "You're going to a bar mitzvah for a kid named Yoni. Dad is Oran. Mom, Esther. Got that?"

"Sure," she says. "Yoni, Oran, Esther."

"What's your name for tonight?"

She rummages through her identity kit and, thinking of her dress, says: "Mara." While they ride on, Ally googles for vaguely Jewish-sounding last names. "Mara Lansky," she says.

Erv says, "I'll text that in. Have you done any babysitting?"

"I have to babysit the bar mitzvah boy?"

"Today, Mara," Erv explains, "Yoni becomes a man. But no. Your job is to look after Esther's father. His name is Chess Plotnik. You'll sit next to him at dinner and keep him contained. I'm guessing he's a henwee."

"Henry?" Ally asks.

"HNWI. 'High Net Worth Individual.' Probably a grade A asshole. If you keep him entertained, he won't get cranky. If he's distracted, I guess our clients will be happy."

"Happy clients, happy wallets," Web adds.

"Greeeat. Okay." She looks at the walls of the gated communities as they drive by. "Chess?"

Web says, "A nickname. Your story is that you were Yoni and his sister Shana's babysitter when they were little."

Erv looks at her again in the rearview mirror, "It should help you remember to *babysit* the mark tonight." Ally gets it.

Web continues, "This is kinda a bread-and-butter Set Up gig. Weddings, bar mitzvahs, dinner parties. Lots of interactions. Lots of opportunities to tell stories."

"Asshole babysitting. Got it," she says. "Who's paying for us?"

"Don't know. Don't need to know," Erv says. He passes her an envelope with "YONI" written on it in nice penmanship.

"What's this?" she asks.

"It's a card with $180 in crisp twenties. There'll be a basket at the door. Web'll tend bar as backup." Ally puts the envelope in her matching clutch.

"Ugh. Really?" Web says. "Why are you dressed up then?"

"Know your range. There are no small parts," Erv says. "I'm on standby."

They pull into the Cromwell, the same hotel Ally followed Web to yesterday. Curious, she thinks.

"Drai's is the rooftop club," Erv says. The van pulls to a back door.

As Web steps from the van, he raises his hand to Ally. "You go in the front. I'm taking the Sammy Davis entrance," he says. "I'll see you inside, don't worry."

He makes a face before slipping through a gray service entrance door.

Erv drives to the garage she trailed Web to yesterday. Web must have been doing prep work for tonight, she thinks. She wonders if either of them knows she followed Web here with Howie.

As Erv searches for a spot, Ally gets the lecture she expected. "Don't fuck up. You have one job. Keep him clear of the family."

"Fine. Right," she says.

With his left hand on the wheel, he pulls his phone out and opens to a picture of an older man. "This is Chess," he says. "I can't believe you're being given a second chance. You're a tourist. A student." With Web gone, Erv apparently is in a sharing mood.

Having little to lose, Ally chances opening up a little too. "Fine. I fucked up. But this gig isn't exactly for people who hit the jackpot, Erv. So spare me the seasoned vet and plucky intern routine. How many chances did you get? What failures led you here?" She wonders why he's so mad but also why his anger isn't the only thing he's keeping from Web. Why are they putting her in the field if Erv is so sure she's not up to the task?

"Who did I replace, Erv? Who was she? Was she the one who fucked up or was it you?" She looks to see his face corkscrew a bit but cannot tell if it's because she hit a mark or if he's having trouble finding a parking spot.

"*I* have a job," Erv says. "Come tomorrow, you won't. You aren't half as clever as you think you are. You'll fuck up again. Actually, I *want* you to fuck up. It might even be worth losing another paycheck."

"Christ, Erv. Haven't you ever heard of 'bad dress rehearsal, great opening night'?"

"The only great opening is going to be for your job once this night is over." Pulling into a spot, he opens the van door. "Go to the banquet hall, just off the pool area. Stick to grandpa like white on me."

"You coming?" Ally asks.

"Nope," he pats the wheel to say that he's staying in the van.

The pool on the roof of the Cromwell is another universe from Ally's at the apartment complex. This isn't a place to do laps; it's a water park for adult toddlers, she thinks as she walks through young partiers drinking and being seen to a thumping beat, following the signs to the bar mitzvah reception.

Inside the nightclub, Drai's, a DJ is playing less frenetic dance music from a stage. A pack of teens is already making use of a central dance floor. Compared to the throng outside, everyone here is dressed in their Saturday best. She sees a ring of older guests near the edges of the floor, some of whom appear uneasy at the gaudy display of bubbling teen hormones. Everyone's wearing their happy masks.

There are two tiers of SUV-size leather booths around the room, surrounded on an outer rim by more conventional seating. There are six massive video screens above the DJ. A mirror ball lords over the dance floor, refracting light everywhere. Beyond, a series of themed food stations are bookended by bars. There's a sushi stand and street tacos.

An event like this, on a Saturday night in Las Vegas, must cost a fortune. The AC is working overtime, and she feels a chill even with her shoulders covered.

At the door, there is a guest book and a shopping cart-sized basket, half filled with cards. She puts her card with the others and is waiting to sign the guest book when a man intervenes with a "no need to do that" wave.

He is slight, and his body is articulated by a trim black jacket. Two inches shorter than she is. He scratches his nose and seems to be looking past her, as if he only senses her presence without seeing her. As he raises his hand to his teacup-shaped face, she notices the

French cuff of his shirt, pinned by blue and black cufflinks. This, she thinks, is the kind of person who can throw this kind of party. She immediately feels underdressed and pulls absentmindedly on her orange sash.

"Hello. Mara Lansky, is it?"

"Yes," she responds.

"Excellent." And then, increasing the volume, "I'm Oran." He takes her by the elbow to escort her to the table with name tags. He selects a name tent with "Mara Lansky" written in gold, like all the rest, and hands it to her. She flips it around. Table 32.

That was fast. She told Erv and Web her name no more than ten minutes ago.

Oran steers her through the crowd. It's how her father used to direct her, although by the nape, when she was a preteen. As Oran passes through the mass, he shakes hands with three other people with his other hand. He doesn't stop or introduce her.

Table 32 is already well occupied by name tents. An older woman with a helmet of silver curls nods and makes a thin line with her mouth.

"Mazel tov, Oran," she says.

"I love what you've done to your hair, Cousin Sadie," he tries, but she's already looking elsewhere. No love there, it seems. Content with the exchange, Oran turns to Ally, raises his voice with a little more theater to it.

"Thank you for coming," he says, looking at the other name tents. "Chess is already here . . . somewhere. You'll get along like a house on fire." At that, he weaves back into the crowd.

Ally sees Plotnik's name tent positioned on a plate, with other tents commandeering the spots on either side. She looks at Cousin

Sadie—besides the hair, a garish purple dress with silver sequins and matching purple glasses give the table a lot to look at—to make sure her eyes are elsewhere. Ally sits down to lay claim to her position at the table, moving someone named Karyn to the seat to her right, keeping Plotnik on her left. Ally hopes Karyn doesn't make a fuss.

She looks around at the crowd. Folks chitchat while eavesdropping and scanning the room. Servers weave through with hors d'oeuvres. She sees sushi, bite-sized latkes with lox, and what looks like mini Reubens. She locates Web, twenty feet away and already in place at the bar closest to her table, but not Plotnik. If she has to spend the evening babysitting an asshole, she thinks, at least she should get some good food out of it. But she doesn't want to lose her place at the table. Her heart races a bit as the other seats at the table fill.

Ally hears Cousin Sadie turn down water from the server. "Don't want to rust the pipes. I'll have a Scotch and soda."

After ten minutes, as the crowd shifts toward getting seated, Ally feels a presence at her side. A warm voice says, "Excuse me?"

Ally turns to see an older man. He has a fashionable gray suit, good stitching. A modest wave of well-trained white hair set against a healthy tan, like a decorative flourish around the marquee of his face. Composed, she thinks. He looks very good if he is in his late sixties, and stunningly good if in his late seventies. She realizes he's asking her permission to sit.

"Please," Ally says and scoots her chair to make room.

"I'm Chess. And you are—" He looks at her name tent. "Mara. Hello, Mara." Chess gives a sigh. "Judging by our table position, I'll guess you aren't a blood relation, a politician, or in good standing with the family."

"Hm," Ally says. "Well, I'm no politician. You?"

"I suspect," he says, looking around one last time, "that I am in my third category. I'm Yoni's grandfather."

"Mazel tov," Ally says. "Chess isn't much of a casino game."

"Well, Chesed is my government name, which can mean, among other things, 'loving-kindness.'" He smiles and looks into her eyes. "Speaking of language, it's 'mah-zel,' not 'may-zel.'"

"Ah, I'm sorry. Mazel tov," Ally repeats, wishing her high school drama club had selected *Fiddler on the Roof* instead of *Joseph and the Amazing Technicolor Dreamcoat*. "Congratulations."

"No need to apologize, and thank you. Though I can't say I had much to do with it." Plotnik takes a sip of his water. "So, you're not a politician, and not Jewish."

"I was Yoni and Sheila's babysitter."

"Aha. Very good." Chess nods, clearing his throat. "You weren't at the ceremony this morning?"

Bumpy so far, Ally thinks. "No. I was told I could just come to the party."

Nodding to his name tent, he says, "Don't worry about not being Jewish. Nobody's perfect." He looks around the room. "I'd say one-third of folks here are. My son-in-law, Oran, isn't. He's a different sort of true believer . . ."

Ally doesn't know if Plotnik meant to trail off, but from the sound of it, he doesn't care for his son-in-law. He doesn't mention Oran's wife, his daughter Esther, either. She's getting a feeling for what she's doing here.

Ally thinks about how to turn the conversation to him and away from his family. Kibun. "What do you do?"

Plotnik says, "Lots of things. I would rather learn about you, Mara. Tell me anything." He won't make this night easy, she is realizing. But there's nothing aggressive in his tone, and she sizes him up. High net worth, yes. He doesn't seem to be the grade A asshole Erv promised, though. Maybe a little curt, but he might just be a man who knows there are fewer grains of sand in the hourglass than he wishes and isn't eager to suffer a fool.

"Well, to be honest," she starts, "I'm kind of between things. I thought I would be an actor, but—"

She stops as the music dies down. She's relieved. People crane their necks, and the DJ shouts, "Ladies and gentlemen. It is my honor and privilege to introduce the man of the hour. Everyone, clap your hands for . . . YONI AMITAI KOLLIS!" The room explodes with applause and cheers. Everyone stands, including table 32. Ally watches as Yoni emerges from beside the DJ booth and joins a throng of teens on the dance floor. She can admire the tailoring of his suit even at this distance: the cuffs hitting the wrist and ankle perfectly, the waist drawn in to his broomstick figure. He and his grandfather might share a family tailor. People clap and cheer.

Once the intros die down and the DJ starts up some kid activities, Chess returns to the conversation. "Why did you want to become an actor?"

At the prompt, Ally launches into the Eliza/Juvie story she first attempted with Web at Jimmy's Wok 'n' Roll and has since practiced twice with Beep, adding a few wrinkles to increase the plausibility.

She feels it's really come together as a story. Even Beep, still suspicious of the entire "Drama Squad" endeavor, likes it. Ally has to practically yell into Plotnik's ear to tell it over the music.

Plotnik, however, either misses parts of it or is unimpressed, responding with a noncommittal "Um-hm." He looks over the crowd, commenting, "Cousin Betty is already a bit overserved."

Ally rests her arm on the table, and the gold bangles caught in her three-quarter sleeve jangle together. Maybe he's bored. She looks in the direction Plotnik is looking to see if she can guess who Cousin Betty is before catching Web's eye at the bar. She tries again to pivot the conversation to Plotnik. "So, what do you do, again?" she presses.

At this, he gets a touch animated. "Americans always want to know what you do. Surely there are more interesting things about a person." After a few beats, he says, "Ask me anything else."

She could see how people might misinterpret his avuncular teasing for rudeness, but she doesn't. She leans in and he continues, "Leave the small talk for small minds, Mara."

Ally takes a hot second to think. "How about this: Tell me a story about your last trip."

Before he can answer, a server leans between them. "Red or white?" They both select the latter. But before they can continue, Ally feels another presence.

"Pardon the interruption, but Elena and I just wanted to say hello."

Plotnik turns to look, then stands up. "It's so good to see you," he says. A tall, handsome couple greets him.

Ally stands to move her chair out of the way, but a knot of other people standing close blocks her from moving. She finds herself standing very close with the three of them, forced into what looks like an intimate conversation. They do not seem to mind.

The man coughs, makes a dramatic look around the table.

"On the outs with the family, Chess?"

Plotnik turns to Ally. "Mara, please meet Elena Losado and her less politically savvy husband, Elías. As city manager, he's metamorphosed into the type of politician who no longer needs to ask for votes. That is, until he runs for mayor."

Elena interrupts, "Chesed, we *fully* support the mayor."

And Elías adds, "And you've done quite well under his leadership, Chess." Ally notes an emphasis on the word "quite."

Ally's a little spun at meeting someone she has read about for her class assignment. She wonders what he's doing here before remembering she's the one who is out of place.

As if reading her thoughts, Plotnik turns to Ally to explicitly bring her into the conversation. "No one mistakes Elías as anything other than one of the city's very best climbers," he says, smiling, as he winks at Ally before turning back to the couple. "And no one makes the mistake of knowing who the real strategist is in the family, either." The three of them chuckle good-naturedly, and Ally smiles to play along. Perhaps recognizing her discomfort, Plotnik rests his hand on Ally's arm. "This is Mara. From Georgia, and a onetime caretaker for the children."

"Love the sash," Elena says with a playful tug on its end, a few inches from Ally's hip. It's familiar without breaching etiquette, and Ally is charmed.

"Thank you. Nice to meet you both," Ally says. "Sorry that I can't pretend to guess who is getting the best of whom here."

"It's just as well you don't," Elías says. Returning to Plotnik, he says, "We have some business to attend to at a later date."

"Indeed," Plotnik responds.

"Of course." And then, turning to Ally, "Pleasure to meet you, Mara." They all exchange handshakes. The handsome couple glides on to the next table as Ally and Plotnik return to their seats.

Plotnik seems eager to move on or, at least, uninterested in dwelling. "Where were we?" he asks. "Ah. Traveling." He nods, and she realizes he isn't the type of person to lose a single train of thought. "Ah, that's a better question, isn't it? Did I travel somewhere less known? Under what means did I travel? Will my story reveal that I stayed in a posh hotel or at a hostel?"

She considers saying something, maybe even asking about the Losados, but Plotnik continues. "No, travel is unsatisfactory."

"Why?"

"Economics."

Ally realizes she's focused on his answers and not, as Plotnik is, about the game of questions. She changes course. "If you could live anywhere else in the world, where would it be?"

"A good question, but a tough one for an old man. I suspect my opportunities for relocation are behind me. The only journey I see myself undertaking is to Sheol."

"School?" Ally asks.

"No," he says, smiling gently. "Sheol. Ever heard of it?"

"No."

"According to some, the Torah says that when we die, we all—the wicked and the righteous—go to Sheol, a kind of limbo. The Land of Forgetfulness. There we receive judgment, from ourselves, for our earthly deeds. If we are good, we go to *olam ha-ba*. The next world. My wife passed on seven years ago. We would joke that Sheol would be like a talent show, where anyone on the fence is afforded one last performance. One last chance to tilt the scales." He turns to her and smiles again. "That is how we would say goodbye to each other. 'See you at the talent show.'"

She finds that unbearably sweet. She tries Yiddish again: "Olam ha-ba?"

"It means, literally, 'the world to come.'" He sighs and straightens in his chair. "That," he says, "will be my next journey." He shakes his head and sighs. "An old man talking about death at a celebration. No wonder I'm at table 32."

A salad course materializes, and when the server reaches Plotnik, he asks her name.

"Chanel, sir," she says, bending a bit at the waist.

Looking around, Ally realizes Web wasn't really joking about the Sammy Davis door. Almost all of the servers are, like Chanel, Latina. There are three Black staff: Web at one of the bars and two guys working security. None of the service staff are white.

"Chanel," Plotkin says, "I'm sorry. Can you tell me if the chicken is organic?"

"Let me check for you. In the meantime, arugula or Caesar salad?" They both take the Caesar.

The table settles into eating artfully arranged greens. Ally thinks of all the servers. She thinks of the jocular betting between Web and Erv. "Do you think," she asks Plotnik, "the Caesar salad is from Mexico or Caesars Palace?"

Plotnik chuckles at that, and she feels she's made some ground. "I'll guess the latter," he says, "for the good of my hometown."

"Mexico!" she says, grinning, pleased with herself. "It's named after its inventor, an Italian immigrant with a restaurant in Tijuana." He chuckles, and she takes it as a minor success to outdo a local.

The volume of music creates a barrier to banter, and Ally sees many tables resigning themselves to eating their salad course with minimal chatter. Decent manipulation, she thinks. She takes the time to strategize conversational topics, but none seem, well, organic. She allows herself to be distracted by the fresh greens, the tart undercurrent of the dressing.

Others seem to have less trouble communicating with Plotnik. Over the next twenty minutes or so, a half dozen people carousel by to speak with him. The managing editor of *The Las Vegas Record*: cordial. A member of Friends of the Mojave Desert: flirty. CEO at the Chamber of Commerce: curious. Principal at some law firm: formal. Managing Director of the Arts Center: greedy. Chess is pleasant throughout but never as playful as he was with the city manager and his wife, or with Ally. He points out a few more politicians, and people in the mining industry. With each introduction, she builds an image of Oran's and Chess's family and where they sit in the city's fabric. Unquestionably central. She looks around to see people circulating, shaking hands, slapping each other on the back. Work, it seems, is being done.

Another man approaches and she notices Plotnik look up at him and turn back to his plate. Their hair almost matches in color, although the second man's hair is shoulder-length in contrast to Plotnik's low pompadour.

"Chesed," the man says without much affect.

"Reverend," Chess replies, without looking up.

She watches the man pause for a moment to say a few soft words and then, with a slight head tilt and without a change in expression, walk away.

"Who was that?" she asks.

"The machatunim," he says before clarifying, "The in-laws."

Ally nods.

"I can't tell if this a bar mitzvah or board meeting," she says.

"Usually both. Tonight, you're more likely to meet someone from the Nevada Resort Association than a schoolteacher," he says. He thinks for a moment and continues, "None of these people would think twice about asking me for money, but not one of them would express concern for me over my office being broken into."

She feels he is talking to the room more than to her. "You were robbed?"

"Broken into, not robbed."

"When? Are you okay?"

He shakes his head. "Wednesday night. I'm fine. They made a mess," he tells her.

She doesn't understand but puts her hand on his shoulder, and he responds to the gesture by patting her hand with his own. "Oh, it's okay," he says with a sigh. "Some people make a mess of things, and others clean up."

Ally thinks this room of the local power elite might make the messes others must clean up. "And which are you?"

He considers it, and, almost too quiet for her to hear over the music, he says, "I've been both over the years. Making a mess first. The ruse will be my final move. One last big cleanup."

While he turns his gaze to the dance floor, Ally's mind spins with the lights. *The ruse?*

He seems trapped in a grooved channel of his mind. "Oh, most of these folks will hate it. But I'll pull my last trick before the talent show." Ally can't tell which one of them is losing the thread.

After a moment, he says, "A few of these people will unwittingly play a part, and others will get played."

Ally tries to get him to circle back. "I'm not following, I'm afraid," she says.

"What I cannot figure out, however, is why you're playing me," he says.

At that, her attention snaps back into focus. "I'm sorry?"

"No, I'm sorry," Plotkin says. He sighs. "I'm wondering why you are at this table, in the back of the room, on the lowest rung of the banquet's social hierarchy, chatting with an old man."

"I don't know what you mean."

"You were a good enough babysitter to be invited but not good enough to avoid the status bloodbath of table 32?"

Who is he talking about? What's the Ruse? Who is playing a part, and of what?

"I don't deserve to be in a fancy booth," she says, "I just—"

"Playing dumb works well enough in some contexts, but not with me, Mara. My son-in-law couldn't find sentimentality at a Celine Dion concert. Oran wouldn't waste a seat—even one this far back—on a babysitter who cannot remember the names of his children, even if you could pronounce 'Mazel tov.'"

Shit, Ally thinks. It was Yoni, but was it Sheila or Shana?

"So, if you weren't the babysitter, what were you? I'm too much of a gentleman to ask whether—"

She stops him. "No, no. Nothing like that."

"What is it like, then?" At that, he looks like a teacher who could wait all day for a student to admit they didn't do the reading. She weighs her options. She considers the different stages of the Con, the "feel, felt, found" technique . . . before finally playing the only card she believes she has left. Pity.

"Look, all I know is that I'm supposed to keep you entertained."

"I hate to be indelicate, but are you are a call girl?"

No one else at the table overhears them, but Chanel has returned to refill their waters. A blush comes to Ally's face. Hushed, she says, "No!"

"Explain it then."

She tries to move toward bringing him into confidence. "Don't— Can you not tell anyone?"

"Why would I do that? You're here to entertain me. And now I'm reasonably entertained. Perhaps someone—probably Oran—thinks I need to be 'handled.' I'll take it as a compliment, I guess."

"Listen, Mr. Plotnik, I have no idea—"

"No, you don't. But when I get back, I would like to hear more. And please, don't give me another retrofit of an old musical."

"What? I . . ." She stumbles again to find the right footing.

"A country girl reeducated by a stern taskmaster named Henry? Do you really think a man my age wouldn't recognize the plot to *My Fair Lady*?" He takes the remaining air out of her unicorn pool float of self-confidence. Ally doesn't know how to respond. So she doesn't. "I'll leave you with your subterfuge, and we can have a conversation without the artifice when I return." He folds his napkin, rests it by his salad plate, and rises. As he does, she remembers her one and only job: Don't let him near the family. She gets up and makes a move to walk with him.

"I'll come too. I once felt—" she starts but stops. "I found I could lose a handsome man in a crowded room."

"I've mastered my way around a banquet hall restroom in my time, thank you."

"I could powder my nose."

"Get me a whiskey sour instead. Three parts spirit." He makes to leave but turns back to her. "Please," he adds.

Hurt, she watches him make it to the restrooms before queueing up at the bar.

Not long after she gets in line at Web's bar, a man swoops in behind her to fill the conversational void. "There's no one at the bar on the other side of the dance floor."

She expects it to be Oran, but it's just some dude. "Sure, sure," Ally responds and flits her eyes to Web. "I'm good."

Not taking the hint, the man stays in line and continues to talk to her. He introduces himself as Cousin Aaron. Rather than making eye contact, Ally takes in the room. She considers how she would exhaust the scene in her notes to Professor Grant. She looks over to see if Plotnik has returned to the table. Instead, she sees a server bring over a pitcher of water. It's not Chanel. This server is white, and her long hair conceals her face. Ally watches her refill Plotnik's glass. As the server turns to head back to the kitchen, Ally catches the side of her face. She looks like the woman from outside the Set Up office. Oven Mitts.

She spins quickly to Cousin Aaron. "Let's get a selfie," she says.

"Wha?" he says, angling his face toward her. She struggles to get him in the frame but catches a view of the server.

"I'm not quite—" he mumbles.

"Thanks," she says absentmindedly. She posts it online with the hashtag #attheparty. She has to prove she was here, right?

Now Cousin Aaron is asking her something, but she's distracted, watching Web chatting up the middle-aged woman ahead of Ally in line. She's wearing a gold lamé off-the-shoulder dress that is a little too on the nose for Las Vegas. Web laughs in harmony with her, and watching him have fun stirs some sulky emotions.

Ally turns to watch the waltz of waiters bobbing through the guests. She doesn't see Oven Mitts again. Is it really her? What is she doing here?

Gold Lamé wraps up her conversation and departs with her drinks, and Ally finally reaches the front of the queue.

"What can I get for you this evening?" Web asks and then, through his smile, says, "Get back to him."

Loudly, Ally says to Web, "A whiskey sour, three parts spirit if you know what that means." Quietly, she adds, "Soda with lime for me. And relax. He's in the bathroom." She isn't sure what she should be telling Web.

"Don't tell me to relax," he says.

"Don't tell me to do my job. What do you want me to do—" she hisses, "—hold his junk?"

Web shakes his head. "Something. Wait outside the bathroom. Don't blow this," he says, looking as if it's his true pleasure to scoop ice into a glass.

"I'm not a stalker, for chrissakes. He's on to me, anyway. Thinks I'm a fucking call girl." She sees Web's smile perk up, so she adds, "He already guessed I'm being paid by Oran." That gets to him, and his smile disappears. "I'm over there faking my way through political conversations while you're flirting for tips. Help. Me."

"My break's in ten. I have an idea. But try to smooth it out first."

"What's the idea?"

"If you can't fix it, tap your shoulder twice when I'm looking at you. Now get back to the table." He presents her with two drinks.

"Great. Another thing you won't tell me. Add it to the list." Annoyed, she says, with some gusto, "Water down Cousin Betty's drinks. She's wasted."

Turning, Ally sees Plotnik arriving back at the table and heads to him. She's pleased to see him. Relieved, even.

As she sits down and places the drink in front of him, Plotnik asks, "Did you get your parts right?"

"Three parts whiskey. One sweet. One sour."

21

WEB

Web watches Ally walk through the crowd. He doesn't have a single idea how to help her, but at least he bought himself ten minutes to figure it out.

The dude who was chatting up Ally orders a whiskey sour as well—Bulleit Bourbon, lemon juice, a shot of simple syrup. Without egg whites, Web adds some bitters for a flourish, shakes it with ice, and strains it into a coupe glass. It's been a while since he had a bartending gig, and it's taking too much of his attention.

He sees the dude stiffen. "You weren't going to tell me you're skipping the egg whites?"

Web knows about modulating tone from a lifetime of experience. He can swap "How can I take your money?" for "How may I help you?" without sounding too angry, too Black. Heaven forbid, no.

After watching Ally rebuff the man's advances, Web gets why he's cranked up. He's looking for an outlet for some aggression, and they both know Web cannot rise to it. "My apologies, sir," Web says, though the man has already left.

Web looks to Ally, who appears to be back in conversation with Plotnik. Good.

He understands why she's freaking out, too. And he still doesn't know how to help her.

The music fades, and then a set of chords causes a shift in the room. The "Hava Nagila." People pour down to the dance floor, pinwheeling in two concentric circles.

"Rum and Coke, por favor," the next person in line orders. White people and their breezy comfort with their poor language skills, he thinks. He's lost count of how many rum and Cokes he's made this evening. Twenty-five? Thirty? Easier drinks, he concedes, allow him to chat with the guests for tips. Make do. This time, though, he focuses on watching Ally and Plotnik talk. It's been a few minutes. Five. She hasn't tried to make eye contact or tapped her shoulder.

But then he sees a troubled look wash over Plotnik's face. He wonders what Ally is telling him. And then it passes. Web sees him rest his hand on the table, relaxed. They drink and talk. Ally seems okay.

The hora is picking up. The DJ is layering the "Hava Nagila" with a dubstep beat. There's a kind of "wah wah thump" accentuating the beat and keeping the circles turning. Wah wah, thump, thump, thump. He can feel the air in the room move. Green lights from the hi-tech mirror ball cycle, slowly but then picking up speed. People are clapping with the beat. Cheerful faces, cycloning, never tripping. He sees Ally and Plotnik stand up and move toward the dancing.

He finishes the rum and Coke.

Web sees the young man, Yoni, seated on a chair, lifted in the center. Clap, clap, clap. Wah wah, thump, thump, thump. A flare of professional envy lights somewhere in the back of his head.

A customer is talking to him, a young woman. "I'm sorry?"

"I asked if you had any tequila and grapefruit," she says.

"Yes, I do. Paloma?"

"Nice," she says, leaning in while maintaining eye contact. "Yes, two."

"Salt?"

"Yes, again." She curls a lock of dark hair behind her ear.

He accepts her stare while his hands work. "Having a good night?" He salts the rim. Tequila. Lime juice, grapefruit soda.

"A wonderful one," she says.

He delivers the drinks with a smile. "I hope it only improves from here," he says, looking into her eyes. Flirty, without leering.

"We'll see about that," she says with a wink and departs with her drinks.

Oh shit. He can't find Ally.

And then he spots them, not dancing but off to the side. Plotnik is leaning on a chair with Ally bent over to him. At first, Web wonders if the old man wanted to watch rather than participate, then he sees Ally's face is full of fear.

Everything slows down and speeds up at the same time.

The crowd continues to spin and Web sees Oran and his wife, Esther, being lifted into the air on chairs. Esther's white knuckles curl over the edges of her seat. Then, Plotnik tilts toward Ally, and she catches his arm as they both slide to the floor. An older woman with purple hair bolts up and blocks his view.

Ally's fifty feet away. He looks at the exit in the opposite direction. He considers leaving her to fend for herself. Instead, he runs to her, knocking over three wine glasses from his bar.

He arrives as someone yells for help, but Web doesn't notice a key change in the tenor of the room. Plotnik's head is resting on Ally's lap, and Web can see his lips moving. Ally's hair partially blocks their faces. Web crouches behind her, unsure of what to do. She is leaning over Plotnik, and Web can see his eyes rolling back. Her hand rests on his cheek.

Two men arrive and pull Ally back while protecting Plotnik's head from hitting the ground. One of the security guards starts chest compressions.

When she's on her feet, Ally turns to Web. "I think— I think he's having a heart attack."

The clapping slows along with the circle dance, then stops. The DJ is the last to read the scene. The music continues for a few moments more before cutting out. Wah wah, thump, thump, th—.

Oran and Esther push their way through the growing crowd and kneel next to the fallen man. Web hears someone scream.

Somewhere along the edges of his vision, Web notices the lights still pulsing. The clapping of the hora has been replaced by the rhythm of chest compressions. He hears only muted voices, as if through a pillow. Web watches the guard count to himself, "One, two, three . . . ," and the man's dark interwoven hands press down on the crisp white button-down shirt. He sees Plotnik's ribcage bend unnaturally inward and bounce back, over and over. He hears a rib crack, and that snaps him out of his daze.

Web turns to Ally and mouths, "GO!" but she's frozen. He decides to abandon his bartender act and hooks his arm under hers. He feels another presence grabbing at Ally's other arm. Web makes a move to push the man away before realizing it's Erv.

They pull Ally backward through the crowd. After a few feet, she breaks from their grasp to retrieve her bag from under the table and joins them in their departure.

On their way out the door, they pass a woman in heels running into the crowd with a white plastic defibrillator unit.

"He stopped breathing," Ally says to no one as they take the stairs down. "He stopped breathing." Thunderous beeps and whoops radiate from the nearby casino floor.

Erv directs them to the van before hopping in front, with Ally in the passenger seat and Web in the back.

"Drive. Now," Web yells. He squeezes his eyes shut, and light patterns dance on the backs of his eyelids like mini-hallucinations.

"I am. I am," Erv barks.

Web's relieved to see Erv put the van in reverse with an urgency matching the tone of his voice.

No one would ever accuse Erv of being too chatty. Web's grateful he knows to just drive with the windows down to clear everyone's heads. It takes a while for Web to notice the music playing on the radio, some eighties station, the cheap power ballads doing nothing to push the image of a man dying in Ally's lap out of his mind. The soaring synths are only making things worse. He leans forward and clicks it off.

He's vaguely aware that Erv is tracing a wide western arc through the Spring Valley neighborhood. It's darker out here, of course. Through the windshield, the Strip is a Stonehenge, rising out of a field of lights. The warm air calms, like an ibuprofen pushing pain to the fringes of his mind.

Ally is silent, lost in what just happened. They likely have the same questions. Is Plotnik really dead? Would someone want to speak with Ally? And how did Erv get there so quickly?

After thirty minutes, as they reach the Westside beltway, Erv breaks the tension. "I guess we're not invited to the after-party," he says.

At that, Ally finds her voice. "'A bread-and-butter gig,' you said. A 'highly irregular week,' you said."

"That was a fucking disaster," Web says, trailing off. He's never had a job go that sideways. He's never seen a person die before, and from her response, he doesn't think Ally has either. "What did he say to you?"

Ally stares out the front window. "He said he was going to Sheol," she says.

"Going to school?" Erv asks.

"Sheol. It means 'See you at the talent show.'"

"Talent show?" Web asks.

Almost to herself, she says, "It's the in-between."

He drops it, chalking up her incoherence to understandable shock. Web looks out at the mountains on the left and tries to trace their outlines in the dark. On the other side, the city, cocooned in its bubble of light, so rarely punctured by reality. *Pop*, he thinks.

"Web. I need you to tell me that this is an insane job. Tell me you went through what I am going through," Ally says.

Web decides it would be better not to dodge the question a second time. He thinks through a response. "I don't—"

Erv interrupts. "Web, she—"

Cutting Erv off, he continues, "I was a college student, waiting tables, looking to make some extra money." Web knows Ally needs a story, even if it isn't true. Lower the temperature.

"I answered a Craigslist ad for a secret shopper gig. I figured I'd get an occasional meal out of it. One bet, two payouts. I enrolled online at a link for a company called Pang Bob. I gave them my address, and in a few days, I received a money order for six hundred dollars in the mail."

With no complaints, he continues.

"That was my entire rent then, so I was all in. I deposited the money order. My first assignment was to go to Walmart and buy three $100 iTunes gift cards and I'd get reimbursed."

He pauses for a few seconds to think about where the story should go. He wants to make the Set Up seem harmless, to her and to himself. For a moment, he falters. Who *is* behind it? It's not legit, that's for sure. He's ignored that for too long. Could be cartel. Maybe whatever's left of the mob. Either way, he's unsure why he feels compelled to defend it.

"I bought a nice polo shirt while I was shopping too. Pang Bob sent me a questionnaire. Was the staff friendly? Was the store clean? That kind of stuff."

Web tries to read Ally's body language, but it's hard to tell from the back seat. "When they asked for the numbers on the gift card to prove I bought them, I didn't think twice. Three days later, my bank called. They said the money order was fake. I checked the gift cards, and the balances had been zeroed out. *And* the bank penalized me $75 for a false transaction."

Ally turns around. "A scam?"

"Totally. But before I called the police, a customer on my next shift left me a massive tip. People tip all sorts of things in Vegas, you know? Chips, gift cards, coins . . . one time I got a room key card. But this time, when I opened the check holder, there was $975—the exact amount I'd lost, save for the cost of the polo shirt—and a phone number."

"So," Erv adds, hoping to conclude. Web can tell that Erv is bringing them back into town. Reacclimatizing them.

"I still wear the polo shirt on gigs," he concludes. All in all, he is satisfied with the story and hopes Ally buys it. He's grateful Erv played along, or at least stayed silent. Maybe they can still work as a team when this blows over.

"So, you trust a business that hooked you with an internet scam." Ally says flatly. Then, "Did you spike his drink, Web?"

There's the *pop* sound of another bubble in his head. Erv asks, "What? Why would you think—"

"Plotnik died right after I brought him the whiskey sour that Web here made him," Ally says. "Plotnik said that he thought Oran had hired me, and I told Web. After he drank your drink, he died."

Web feels Erv let up on the gas and the van slows. Web grimaces at this retelling of the evening's events. He served other whiskey drinks—the guy in line right after Ally got the same drink. And even if he wanted to poison someone, he wouldn't know the first thing about it.

But if Plotnik dies, Ally's read of the evening would certainly lead to the police looking for Web. He thinks of the eyes that watched him make drinks. So many attendees and so many staff whirling around. He feels another presence grow in the van. Something far darker than the night sky outside. Maybe they shouldn't have run out so fast.

"He said he was planning a ruse," she pressed on.

"A ruse?" Web asked.

"Yeah. What does that mean to you, Web?"

He doesn't know the answer. "I don't know what you're suggesting, but it's not a technical term, Ally."

Still, the word is troubling. Did Plotnik have something to do with the Set Up, or was he hinting that he knew why Ally was there? And if Plotnik suspected his son-in-law hired them and told anyone about it, they could have a real problem. Should he text? Will Erv text? Who is in charge here? And come to think of it, how did Erv know to show up at the party just when he did?

Erv breaks the silence. "You're out of your depth, Ally."

Pop, pop. Web starts to think that he might be out of his depth as well.

Ally continues. "What if there really is more than one Set Up team?" she asks. Web feels the van slow down further.

"What do you mean?" Erv asks.

"I'm pretty sure I saw someone at Drai's I've seen before."

"Who?" Web asks.

"I don't know who she was," Ally says, shaking her head. Erv and Web stay silent.

"Has the Set Up ever killed before?" she asks. *Pop, pop, pop.* He has absolutely no way to confirm what happens outside of his partial view. He's getting the sense that he's less of a lead in this story and more of a minor speaking part.

Web hears the engine whine as Erv prods the accelerator in an automotive subtext to the conversation. "Of course not, Ally," Erv says. "We babysit. We lightly intervene. We're only given—"

"Only given the bare minimum information. I know," she says, cutting him off.

Erv starts, "Etcet—"

"Etcetera Principle my ass," Ally says. "I'm not crazy. You were at that hotel yesterday, Web. I saw you drop a bag off at the front desk. Don't play dumb with me. Tell me *something*."

But before anyone has the chance to say more, both Web's and Erv's phones emit a "cha-ching." With a few clicks, he sees a deposit notice for $1,000 in his account. He stares at the amount for a moment. Is that a lot for bartending half of a bar mitzvah party, or way too little for being a party to murder?

Ally's phone, he notices, remains silent. He watches as she reaches into her bag. He sees her enter her passcode: 525600. And then he hears a third notification. It is not, however, the same sound as his and Erv's phones. The difference is slight. More of a "cha-ching" rather than a "ka-ching." Odd, he thinks. And then he thinks about the different passcode. Why, he wonders, are the settings on her Set Up phone different from his?

Web realizes the only possible answer is that Ally isn't using her Set Up phone at all.

SUNDAY

22

MARSHALL

For the first time in a while, he wakes to his home phone ringing.

Marshall looks at the caller ID. Tutti.

He's sleepy, but not enough to mess with his editor. "Yello?"

"You sober?" his editor asks.

"Enough to go a round or two if you're game."

"Let's skip the pugilism, Marshall. You asked me a favor and I'm calling in my chip."

"That was fast."

"You asked me about this Kollis guy, and I'm answering your question in the form of an assignment. Don't be a dick. Take it."

"Okay . . ." he says.

"You know a developer named Chess Plotnik?"

"Only by rep," Marshall says.

"Well, he died last night. Dramatically. I want you to write a piece on him. Not an obit. An explainer. A thousand words on the man and what he's done for the city. By tomorrow night, okay?"

"And you're helping *me* here?"

"I am," Tutti says flatly.

Marshall swings his legs out of bed with a grunt but realizes Tutti might interpret it as commentary on the offer. "Great," Marshall says. "I'm on it." He hears the line go dead.

He fires up his laptop, places it on the kitchen table, and makes coffee while still in his robe. The smell alone triggers wakefulness. He looks at the clock on the oven. 7:26 a.m. isn't the best time to make calls. Might be hard to rustle up quotes on a Sunday. It used to be that he would have to wear out some shoe leather for this kind of job, but these days, he can do more in a few minutes of web surfing than an entire day of research in the nineties.

He starts with a simple search. Plotnik was the principal at OmariCity, a development company. The website is glossy. "Vision + Expertise" appears on the screen before fading to a collage of buildings that look as if they are designed to impale. The images wash over each other. A few blurbs fade in and out. One about being a LEED-certified and award-winning company.

Marshall clicks on the "Projects" tab, which includes several developments he recognizes. He's been in a few of these buildings. The largest seems to be the Vegas Place mall, but there are a few dinky projects too, all organized by zoning: medical, industrial, retail, office, and residential. This guy had his fingers in many pies.

He clicks on the "Our Team" page and sees a picture of Plotnik posing in front of the mall. OmariCity appears to have a staff of ten. A series of managers: finance, projects, properties. A CFO and director of operations. He's not sure who he'd reach out to but figures whoever shows up at the offices on the day after their CEO died is the right person to speak with. He copies the address. Marshall considers asking Losado's chief of staff to see if he can get a comment. Ava Reyes is expecting an email for Losado's class visit tomorrow anyway. Why not? He adds the ask to a message about coordinating their meetup before class and hopes Reyes will come through.

Marshall moves on to *The Record* archives. Seventy-two hits for Plotnik. He searches for OmariCity and gets a few dozen more. A redevelopment proposal for a 208-unit apartment project in Summerlin. An office building breaking ground in Henderson. A celebrity gala to open the new MGM Park hotel. Marshall clicks on an article from 2011 about the Container Park, another OmariCity project.

It is mostly a semi-glowing profile of the entrepreneur millionaire Tony Hsieh. Marshall looks at the byline. Written by an intern, and he feels a flash of anger at his beat being an editorial afterthought.

There's a reference to the downtown's struggles to maintain relevance in the nineties, Hsieh's relocation of Zappos HQ, and how the Container Park was designed as a hip landing pad for downtown. Marshall remembers the shadowy zone surrounding Fremont and knows the history of the onetime network of tightly packed, affordable bungalows. Zappos moved into the old city hall. Symbolic enough. The article says the Container Park area was in disrepair for decades and seized by the city in 2002. Hsieh bought it cheap and partnered with OmariCity. It was the splashiest thing to happen downtown since the Fremont Street Experience.

Marshall's eyes settle on a picture of Hsieh, brash and young. He's surrounded by five of the business owners opening businesses on the site, including three restaurant owners. On the left, somewhat out of place, is Plotnik.

He hears a ping from his inbox; Reyes has already responded. "Elena and I are surprised and saddened at the news of the passing of a great man and a great Las Vegan, Chesed 'Chess' Plotnik. We are grateful that he spent his last moments at a celebration surrounded by his wonderful family and friends. Joining them for such a special occasion was an honor. Las Vegas would not be what it is today without him. Our thoughts and prayers go to his family and friends." She adds, "See you tomorrow," with a sideways smiley face. Reyes wrote all of it.

Marshall's slightly annoyed with the almost mechanical nature of the statement, but he'll find a use for it. Before moving on, however, he notes that the statement suggests that Plotnik and Losado were at the same event last night.

Another notification pops up. It's from Reyes's personal Gmail account. It has one line: "Check out the son-in-law." Not uncommon to get an off-the-record nudge, and they're always welcome, although not without some suspicion. He writes that down too.

9:36 a.m. is a respectable time for a phone call. Ernesto hasn't taken a day off since his daughter's wedding. There are no weekends for realtors.

"Espejo Realty. We're sellin' your dwellin'."

"My god. That's awful."

"No? I'm just trying it out. I'll put you down as a 'maybe.'"

"Can we meet up?"

"Yup. What is it this time?"

"To be honest, I'm not sure," Marshall admits. "Again."

"I'm showing a property out in Summerlin. Meet me at the Café Lola on Hualapai at ten," Ernesto says and hangs up.

He needs to hurry to get across town. He puts his notebook in his bag and, right before leaving, he grabs his '95 notebook too.

"Plotnik's high altitude," Ernesto says, perched on a stool by the café window. Marshall has his notebook out, having successfully interrupted a sweeping tale about nineties battles between Summerlin and the city. "We did solid business with him before I went independent. They probably still work together. Made money every time."

"He *was* big time," Marshall says.

Ernesto sucks air in through his teeth. Tsk. "Died?"

"Yup. What did you know about him?"

"Chess was kind of an apex predator in his early days. He was one of those guys who'd buy distressed properties, places landlords neglected, and he'd flip 'em. He had some friendly relationships, but it seemed like he would use them to relieve people of many burdens of property ownership."

"Urban redevelopment?" Marshall asks.

"Yeah. That's the more hygienic phrase. Eviction, forced segregation, dislocation. He'd offer sweetheart deals, and soon enough, folks were wondering where their neighbors went. Plotnik flipped the homes, whitening the neighborhood."

"Any idea what he was working on lately?"

Ernie shakes his head. "No idea, M."

"But, broadly, OmariCity buys and finances real estate properties. You make a lot of friends doing that?"

"You must. Contractors, investors, city government. Equal to the number of enemies, I imagine."

"Any names?" Marshall asks.

"Friends or enemies? I know people. But those folks are on another level. Medical? Warehouse sector? Big money."

Marshall thinks about how Losado and Plotnik were at the same event.

"Who would Plotnik work with in city government?"

"Who *wouldn't* he work with? Building and Safety, Planning, Public Works, Economic and Urban Development."

"Who do those offices answer to?"

"Development and Community Services."

He waits a second before asking, "And who would they answer to?" Marshall reads Ernie's brow like a headline and senses the resistance before Ernie responds.

Ernesto sucks his teeth again, responding, "Are you coming back to Losado?" He doesn't wait for an answer. "Look, yeah, everything that sizeable gets a nod from the city manager's desk, for sure. Why are you trying to dig up dirt?"

"I'm not! I'm looking at Plotnik," he says, leaning back before adding, "It turns out they were at the same event last night."

"Man, you went after half of the city council and lost, and then you lost more," Ernie says. It stings knowing that, even if Ernie has never brought it up before, Marshall's history influences how Ernie sees him.

"What are you going to lose this time?" Ernie adds.

"Ernie," Marshall says, although he is trying not to take offense. Digging up dirt is, of course, his entire MO. "It's not about Losado. Plotnik. His importance for the city. His story. Losado's only a part of that."

Ernie shakes his head. "Don't write old news."

"It's all old news when you're dead," Marshall says. He thinks about what Reyes wrote in her email and asks, "Are Plotnik's kids involved in real estate?"

Ernesto pulls back to mirror Marshall's pose. Both pantomiming disengagement. "No one wants to hear about that either, man," Ernesto says. "Work is work. Family is family."

"You're saying I shouldn't write about his business deals. I shouldn't write about his family. What should I write about, Ernie? My articles aren't in the style section. Give me an angle."

"Write about the buildings, M. Who used them? People don't want their lives exposed. Nobody wants their business in print."

It reminds Marshall of that old quote: "News is something somebody doesn't want printed; everything else is advertising." He thinks about how to redirect the conversation, salvage the contact without getting into advertising. Ernie isn't usually this guarded.

"What else do you know about the company that owns those two small lots on Ogden? The In-Hwa Group?"

The change in temperature is swift. Ernie finishes his iced latte and gets up. "I'm sorry, I gotta go."

"What . . . Ernie?" Marshall tries.

"Be careful, friend," Ernesto says as he walks out. "Like karaoke, curiosity can really bring out the worst in people. Forget about Losado. Forget about In-Hwa."

After watching Ernesto drive off, Marshall flips his notebook to his page of questions and adds fresh notes.

- What am I missing about the Rothman story? *Randall Carter/driver: dead end. Lived at compound.*
- Unification Church? "Third Family?" *Moved to Laughlin. Joshua Kollis (Minister)*
- Ogden/15th St compound? *In-Hwa development.*
- Who is reviewing my old articles? *Unknown.*

His Plotnik assignment pushes the church and the In-Hwa Group research to the back burner. It's not lost on him that there is an overrepresentation of developers on his to-do list. His series of minor questions are adding up to a modestly sized mystery.

He leaves a space and adds an additional line:

- *Plotnik: Latest OmariCity Development? Connection to City Gov/Losado? Is there a connection to In-Hwa Group?*

Marshall flips through his notes from Lévesque: bad press in the seventies and eighties. The Third Family is a splinter sect . . . Brainwashing isn't a thing . . . Going legit is . . . Are they selling the old compound on Ogden to expand their legit operations in real estate?

Then he pulls his '95 notebook from his bag and flips to his notes on the traffic accident. He closes his eyes to imagine himself there, back at the scene.

He sees the police, including a younger Tracy McCall, interviewing passersby. He remembers speaking to Interviewee

#2, who told him she saw the police pull a gold necklace from Rothman's hand. It reflected the sun, she said. He remembers Brenda, who was sitting on the curb twenty feet from Rothman's body, trembling and crying. Marshall sees himself asking if he could sit next to her, asking questions. She was so distressed. Too distraught to remember exactly, only offering a partial description of the events. It was in those first few moments of trauma. The first moments of empathy became fertile soil for other emotions to bloom, although he couldn't have known it at the time. Shaking his head to the present, he puts the two notebooks in his bag. He needs to speak to Brenda one last time.

But first, OmariCity.

23

ALLY

The reception desk at OmariCity is overflowing with stacks of paper, confetti-colored sticky notes frilling the edges, like battlements. Ally wasn't sure the office would be open on a Sunday morning but found a red-eyed office manager, Tina, who seemed too emotionally distraught to have remembered to lock the door behind her and who also didn't seem to mind when Ally walked right in.

Ally is just starting to warm Tina up when the office doors open again. Turning, she sees her journalism professor approaching, dressed as if for class. She freezes and then sighs. It's about time she comes clean to him anyway.

“Hi there,” Marshall says to Tina, without waiting to approach the reception desk. “I’m writing a piece for *The Record.* Maybe a book. But was hoping to talk about Chesed Plotnik.”

Tina nods to Ally. “You’ll have to take a number.”

“Oh,” he says, turning to Ally for the first time. “Sorry. And you are?”

“Complicated. Can we step outside?” Ally says.

Marshall’s eyes alternate between the two of them. “Um, sure.”

“We’ll be right back,” Ally says to Tina, who appears to take the news as if it makes absolutely no difference to her day.

“I’ve got nowhere else to be,” Tina says without looking up.

———

After Web and Erv dropped Ally off last night, Phoebe let her know she was fired from Chroma. It was hardly her biggest problem.

“Expected.”

“Dana said you walked out,” Phoebe stated without tone.

“No, I . . . I got sick,” Ally offered.

Phoebe wasn’t having it. “Sick in the head, maybe. She saw you get into a car with some guy, which was information neither your manager nor your girlfriend wanted to know.” Ally didn’t know how to explain.

In a bid for sympathy, Ally told Phoebe about the job and Plotnik dying in her arms. Rather than mollifying her, it only solidified Phoebe’s resolve.

“So, you lost your job. You’re getting paid through an app for causing mayhem with your merry band of Hamlet Hooligans. You’ve changed your clothes. You’ve traded your textbooks for comic books. Now someone’s dead?” Phoebe shook her head. “I only *wish* you were caught up with Herbalife. Whatever you're mixed up in, I . . . I . . . want out."

Ally thought of *My Fair Lady* again. The casual insidiousness of being trained. She thought about pretending things were normal for Beep's benefit. She thought about Web. About kissing Howie. If she knew everything, Phoebe would be more than speechless. Her short mental loop only riled Phoebe further.

With Ally unable to muster a defense, Phoebe took Ally's car keys and left. Adding physical space to their widening rift seemed a little unfair. But then again, Ally knew she'd been taking more than she'd been giving as of late.

In the silence after Phoebe's departure, Ally spun in her thoughts before opening her laptop. The Set Up hadn't given her the chance to study up on Chesed Plotnik before they met, she figured, but there was nothing stopping her from researching him after the fact.

She looked through a series of development projects made by his company, OmariCity, tying plots of land across the city. In her notebook, she listed the addresses of the larger projects. She fumbled through, uncertain of what information would help her understand who this guy was. She plotted a map on her computer, then cataloged two dozen of the development sites using public records data and a real estate website called Zoner.

Then she tried to list all that she had gleaned from her interactions with Plotnik at the bar mitzvah. Daughter. Family. She found the obituary of his wife, Judy Plotnik, detailing her philanthropy through Temple Beth Shalom.

At the bar mitzvah, Chess hinted he would be unpopular for what would be his last big project. He called it a ruse. Or *the Ruse*. He was smart, or at least smart enough to size her up as a phony. What was his final trick, though?

She also wrote in her notebook that the Set Up job didn't go according to plan. She put a question mark at the end of that. What if it did? She might never know.

Then Ally remembered the woman she saw at the Set Up's offices, the woman with the oven mitts in her car. That first day on the job felt like months ago, not six days. She tried to recollect the server's face, partially obscured by hair. She pulled up the selfie she posted on PicSnapR and zoomed in. She was about 52 percent confident it was the same woman.

When she looked up the address for OmariCity's offices, she paused at the realization that they were at the Container Park. Same complex as the Fallout Bar. The bachelor party could've been anywhere, but it just so happened that two nights before Plotnik lay dying in her lap, she spent time in the same complex as his business office? Two blocks from the strip club Web works at. In a big city of chance, it made for an uncomfortably outsized coincidence.

The details danced in Ally's head like glittering stars without constellations. She was searching for shapes in the dark.

Ally leads Marshall to the open-air walkway connecting the third-floor offices and finds a shaded table. It's still early, and the heat is a manageable swelter.

"I'm—" he starts.

"Professor Marshall Grant. I know. I'm Ally Parks."

He looks, understandably, puzzled. "Do I—"

"Yes and no. You should. But you don't. I'm one of your students," she says.

She watches his eyebrows raise and lower. "Presently?"

"Yes. What are you doing here?"

"As I said, I'm writing a piece on Plotnik. Why are you here?"

"To be honest? I'm not sure," she says, sitting back into the warm metal of the chair. "I can tell you how I got here, though." Ally inhales, holds it, and lets her breath out slowly through her nose. She unloads nearly everything in a disjointed recitation. The audition. The secret shopper and bachelor party jobs. The bar mitzvah. Chess dying in her lap. She decides not to mention the considerable and probably sketchy payments, nor that she suspects she is, somehow, complicit in Plotnik's death.

Marshall tries to sum it up. "You think this marketing-acting agency—"

"The Set Up," Ally adds.

"—played a part in killing Plotnik?"

"No," she fumbles. She thinks about the Ruse. "Or maybe? I . . . I don't know."

"So," Marshall starts, as he looks over the railing, onto the groups milling around the shops below. "You're an aspiring actor who is taking my journalism class but gets a side job in a shadowy agency to pay for college and then gets wrapped up in a murder plot? Do I have that right?"

"Yes? Oh, I'm also a barista at Chroma," Ally adds with a smile before reminding herself that she *was* a barista until yesterday. "You take your coffee black, like Norwegian Death Metal."

An embarrassed look crosses his face. "Sorry for not recognizing you."

"It's a big class."

"And you were doing this as a class assignment?"

"I was doing it because I thought I wanted to be an actor, and I needed the money. But once I got the job, I saw it as a great topic for your class paper. 'The performance of city life.' Something like that."

"You were planning to write your final paper on a murder plot?"

"That," she says, looking back to the OmariCity offices, "wasn't the plan. But it seems to have legs?" Ally says. "Shuyin loved it. I mean, I didn't tell her about the murder. That's new."

"The Set Up," he says again, nodding to himself. After a moment, he asks, "Given the subterfuge and that we're both here now, I take it you're the one who's putting articles on my lectern?"

"Yes," she says. Not sure how to say more.

"Why? Was that part of the job? You were setting me up?"

She lets out a long breath. "No, no. The class is about the city, right? History. Revisiting. And I wanted to know more about you as a teacher. So it occurred to me that I could revisit your work to get to know both you and the city." This was barely true. Ally was, in fact, annoyed that she found Marshall to be an endearing but clearly distracted teacher. Listless and unengaged. Rather than wait for a course evaluation, she decided to perk him up. What teacher wouldn't want students who were interested in their work, right? *Less of that truth*, she tells herself. *More kibun*. "You said this was a city that hates its past," she says, before adding, "I figured you'd be happy to know one of your students was interested enough to dig up old material."

"Why those specific articles, though?" he asks.

"The first one was your first. Then I found articles that resonated with whatever I was doing with the Set Up throughout the week." She thinks of Web telling her the story of the homeless character in *The Sandman* comics and seeing the Oakwood Housing offices when she parked her Vespa. Pieces coming together.

Marshall considers it. "Why are you investigating Plotnik?"

"Because," Ally starts. "Because at the very least, I need to figure out what he was talking about before he died. I feel I owe it to him." Also, she keeps to herself, she needs to find out if she played a role in his death. "And you're here to do a piece?"

"I was asking my editor about . . ." He stops himself midthought. She watches her professor process it. In class, she feels he is often too quick to speak, but he's puzzling through something now. He looks away before resolving himself. "Eh. It's a long story. My editor asked for a story about Plotnik."

"Let's go talk to Tina," Ally says.

"Let's go to the police," he says. "I have a friend, Tracy. She's an Assistant DA."

"No."

"No? Look." Marshall shakes his head. "If half of what you say is true . . ."

"No, I need to know more. We need to know more."

After making her hold an uncomfortably long moment of eye contact, Marshall relents. "Well, okay. Let's see what Tina can offer?"

"Deal." She gets up, and he stays seated.

"So," he asks, "are you a journalist or an actress?"

"I'm a double major."

Tina hasn't moved from her position at the reception desk. She holds up a single finger to them as she finishes a phone conversation. Once she rests the phone in the cradle, Tina asks, "Who are you two again?"

Marshall says, "I'm a reporter for *The Record*, and she's—"

"His student," Ally says quickly. "What is your role here?"

"Office manager," Tina says.

Marshall asks, "Who knew Mr. Plotnik the longest? Is there someone we could speak with? Someone who's been with OmariCity a long time?" As she thinks, Marshall directs her further. "Didn't he work with a son-in-law or something?"

Ally bites her tongue at the mention of Oran Kollis.

"There was significant turnover three years ago. I got here a year and a half ago. No family in the business. I'm not the person to speak on the record."

"I'm just looking to learn about his life. A friend, then?" Tina considers it.

"You could speak to Walker."

"Walker?" Ally asks.

"Walker Preddy," Tina says. "He owns Second Choice, downstairs. He and Chess have a standing Monday night dinner together." She flinches. "Had, I guess."

She gestures to the piles on the desk. "Look, I have to get back to—"

Ally doesn't let her finish. "Plotnik told me about the break-in. He said everything seemed to be accounted for. Is that right?"

"Yeah," Tina says, turning to face Ally again. "You spoke with Mr. Plotnik?" Marshall steps to the water cooler and helps himself to a drink, which Ally takes to mean that he's letting her direct the conversation.

Ally makes Tina a compatriot. "I sat next to him at his grandson's bar mitzvah. Last night. I was with him as he was dying." Ally feels squirmy at this crass manipulation of this woman's emotions. She looks to her feet, imagining for a moment what Chess might be doing in the talent show. When her eyes meet Tina's, an honest tear runs down her face.

It elicits the desired effect. "Oh god, I'm so sorry," Tina says, covering her mouth. "What were you—"

But Ally doesn't want to answer her questions and presses on. "I imagine you can't share anything, Tina. But the break-in was one of the last things he talked about, and I feel like it was important."

Ally looks at her shoes again, feeling Tina's sympathy build. When she looks up, wiping her eyes with both palms, the suspicious arch she saw in Tina's eyebrows has disappeared. She hands Ally a tissue. Tina's back in.

"That's the thing," Tina says, sitting back in the chair. "No one can tell if it was important. They didn't seem to take anything."

"Was there something out of place?" Marshall asks.

"Everything was out of place," she says. "They trashed our office with real joie de vivre."

Ally thinks about Chess talking about a ruse. About people playing a role that they didn't know they were playing. Ally asks, "Were there any open projects he was working on?"

That triggers something in Tina's face. Some recognition, alongside a beat of hesitation. "Yeah. Let me . . ." She flips through the stacks. "Here's one of them. But that doesn't make sense."

Ally remembers what Plotnik told her: He was "broken into, not robbed."

"Why *wouldn't* someone rob this place?" Ally asks.

"There's not really anything to take. We don't keep cash in a safe or anything. We just have . . . plans." She places a thin book in front of her. Ally cranes her neck a bit to see the cover.

Marshall asks, "Why doesn't it make sense?"

"Well, first," Tina says, "it's a proposal for a collaborative partnership on a project. It's an architectural proposal."

"What does that mean?" Ally asks.

Tina says, "It's like an elaborate thought experiment." She flips through the contents, and Ally and Marshall wait her out. "It's for a museum and international conference center for peace," she says. "Mr. Plotnik said the project wasn't going anywhere, so I don't know why anyone would look for that either." Tina closes the folder, placing her hand on the cover, as if suddenly uncertain why she's sharing it. Ally sees a blue and black logo on the cover of the folder. She recognizes it but can't place it.

"You said 'one of them.' Is there another proposal?" Ally asks.

At that, the smile fades from Tina's face. "No idea if I'll have a job in two weeks," she says. "I probably shouldn't say more."

Outside, Marshall and Ally find a table in the shade near the fake grass lawn. The stage is empty. She looks at the place where she took a picture of Web under a fire-breathing mantis three days ago on their way to the Fallout Bar.

"What do you think?" Ally asks.

"A lot of loose ends."

She pulls out her phone and sees him shuffle his feet. "Ally?" he prods.

"Sorry. First: Yes. You're right. A boatload of information. But second, I'm not texting friends. I'm looking for a picture." She clicks to her PicSnapR account and scrolls through to her posts from Wednesday afternoon, placing scooters around town. She clicks on the one where she's in front of the office building and passes it to Marshall.

"You and a scooter? So?"

"Not me. The sign behind me."

"Oakwood Properties. So this is why you brought the discrimination article to class?"

"Yes, but no." She grabs the phone again and uses her fingers to zoom to the part of the sign with the black/blue logo on it. "Not Oakwood. Look at the sign: In-Hwa Group."

"Okay. I'm not getting it," he says.

"That was the logo on the development proposal Tina didn't want to show us. The peace center? The In-Hwa Group," Ally tells him while searching for the company's website on her phone.

"The architectural proposal?"

"Right, and . . ." Ally says, touching the "About Us" link and giving it to Marshall, saying, "In-Hwa Group has two cofounders. The first one: Oran Kollis."

"I recognize that name," Marshall says. Marshall pulls a notebook out of his bag and flips through the pages. "Right. I came across In-Hwa a few days ago. What's the connection?"

"Oran is Plotnik's son-in-law. I met him. It was his son's bar mitzvah."

"Hm. A friend told me to check out the son-in-law. Wait . . ."

Marshall flips through his notebook and finds what he's looking for. "Here it is. The In-Hwa Group owns a couple of properties a few blocks away. Where a Moonie compound used to be."

"Moonies?" Ally asks.

"Yeah, the Unification Church. Their leader's also named Kollis. Joshua. Can you look him up?"

As the search results load, the fine hair on Ally's arms raises to attention. "The machatunim," she whispers, thinking of the long-haired man spurned by Plotnik.

"I'm sorry?"

"I recognize him from the bar mitzvah. Joshua Kollis is Oran's father."

Marshall nods at the image. "Okay. Can you pull up a map?"

"What am I looking for?"

"Ogden and North Tenth," he says, moving a little closer. Ally tilts the screen to share the view. "Okay. That's it. Do you see those two buildings? In-Hwa Group owns them. Is that the block you saw in Tina's proposal?"

"Yes," Ally confirms.

Marshall, still flipping through his notebook, rests on a page and looks up. "Can we figure out who owns the rest of that block?"

"Fifty bucks says it's Plotnik," Ally says. *Wait,* she thinks, *when did I turn into the kind of person who goes around betting fifty bucks? Thanks, Web and Erv.* She finds the Zoner real estate site again, zooms into the Ogden/North Tenth block with her fingers. There's only a little information on the site, but she remembers it as one she cataloged in her notebook earlier this morning. She clicks on the "Ownership History" tab and sees OmariCity bought the property from the city. "Yep. He purchased the lot for $389,000 in 1999."

Marshall says, "I suppose it makes sense that when writing a piece about a developer's life, I should start with the properties . . ."

Ally tries to keep Marshall focused. "So," she says, "I think someone broke in to get information, not to take something." Ally keeps going, "Together, Plotnik and his son-in-law own an entire city block, right? Tina talked about a proposed peace center that Plotnik said wasn't going anywhere. And Plotnik told me about pulling a kind of trick."

"What do you mean 'trick'?" Marshall asks.

"He called it a ruse or 'the Ruse.' He said it was his last project."

"I'm not sure. What's the 'peace center' project?"

Marshall looks at her and then her phone, and Ally realizes it's her job to keep looking things up, but of all the teamwork she's done over the last week, she's enjoying this collaboration. She searches for "Moonie peace center" and comes up with several hundred hits.

"Try 'Unification Church peace center Las Vegas,'" Marshall says. She finds a 2015 article in *The Record.*

"I missed all this," Marshall says, shaking his head.

Ally pulls the phone closer to read the text. "It's a press event at the Cosmopolitan to announce the plans for an 'International Peace Education Center' in Las Vegas. To be the Unification Church's West Coast headquarters . . ." She summarizes, "Local politicians attended it, but several of them spoke off record to say that the affiliation with the Unification Church only became known to them when a reporter asked about it."

"Who was there?" Marshall asks.

"The mayor, city manager, and three councilors," Ally says.

"Losado?"

"Yup. He sure has a knack for working his way into pictures." Ally continues. "There's also a quote from Joshua Kollis saying the church wanted 'a foothold in the city' to 'transform Sin City into a city of educational enlightenment.'" She scans, then reads more. "The goal was to build a nongambling—I mean *gaming*—facility for conventioneers."

"2015? Huh," Marshall says. "I guess it didn't happen."

"Not yet, anyway," she adds.

"So the block we're looking at was the proposed site for a museum, education, and meeting center. The Las Vegas Unificationist sect wasn't the main branch of Moonies from what I understand. They broke themselves off, calling themselves the Third Family."

"Unificationists, or no?" Ally asks.

"They were. Just separate."

"I wonder if someone was trying to stop Plotnik from developing the International Peace Education Center," Ally says.

Marshall is on a different track, however. "I think they had something to do with the death of the Cal Rothman kid."

"Wait. What?"

"Well, I don't know. It was a long, long time ago." She watches him shake his head. He asks, "Who benefits from Plotnik's death? Who would want this project not to happen?"

Ally considers cycling back to the Rothman kid but answers Marshall instead. "I have no clue," she says, resting the phone in her lap. She can't decide if she should put it in her bag or not. "But I'm gonna bet his ruse involved that plot of land."

"Ally, I am sorry I didn't recognize you," Marshall says.

"It's a big class," she says again. She can tell that there's a lava lamp of information swirling in his head and tries to be kind. "What next?" She sees Marshall sneak a second look at his watch, and asks, "You gotta go somewhere?"

"No. Just thinking about getting back to my editor."

The thought of Marshall writing about Plotnik is an uncomfortable reminder about her own role in the story. She's unwittingly placed herself into a big story, and now she's dragged her journalism professor into it too. Or, she realizes, perhaps he's been involved in it for a long time.

It's all seemingly wrong, all too close. She starts to think Phoebe was right. This was all a mistake. Maybe Phoebe's at home, or maybe she can catch her at the café. Ally hopes. She checks her phone. A bus leaves in seven minutes.

"I— I should go too," Ally says as she stands. Her chest flutters with the overwhelming desire to flee. "Look. Don't mention me in the article, okay? Don't mention the Set Up, either? Please."

"Okay, okay. Hold on. We've got more to do," Marshall says lamely. "We can do it. Together."

"I gotta catch a bus," she says and starts walking away.

Her instructor catches up to her. "Wait. Maybe I should have your number?" he asks.

Ally grabs the notebook from his hand and gives him Phoebe's number. She adds, "You know, I've been emailing you field notes from my girlfriend's email address all week."

"What?" he says.

"I have been taking notes on my phone and sending them to you. They're probably in your spam folder."

"Phoeboopboop?" Marshall asks.

"Beepbeep, not boopboop," Ally says, smiling. "It's the work I did for the Set Up. You'll see." Thinking about Phoebe makes her cheeks burn.

"Okay. Thanks. I'll investigate Plotnik."

"I'll check out Walker Preddy," she says, and he nods in return. Ally turns but doesn't make it far. Marshall catches up to her again.

"Here," he says, handing her a notebook. "Here."

"What's this?"

"It's my notebook from '95. Can you look through it?"

"Why?"

"I think I missed something about the death of Cal Rothman. Can you look?" He adds, "Maybe on the bus?"

Ally cannot imagine finding something her professor has missed in his own notebook, but she puts it in her bag. She just wants to get back to Beep. Maybe she can help.

"See you in class tomorrow," she says.

As she's walking by the pool, one of the Neon Witches pipes up.

"Hey. You said 'Toil and trouble' the other day. Shakespeare, right?"

"Right," she says, not breaking her stride.

"Speaking of trouble," the second one says, "Two men in suits went to your apartment a few hours ago. Came and left."

That slows her to a stop. "Oh? Huh. What did you tell them?"

The third chimes in. "They said you were a person of interest, but we said they must be mistaken. 'Least interesting girl in the complex,' I told 'em."

As she walks away, she hears one of them repeat to the others, "Toil and trouble."

When she opens the apartment door, the apartment screams emptiness. Phoebe's still gone.

24

WEB

"No, thank you," Ally says through the door, which is just barely cracked open. She waited a full thirty seconds after he saw her shadow pass over the peephole. He understands why she'd need time to process.

"I wanted to see if you're okay." For all the time he had, Web winces over the opening line. "Can we talk?"

He's been waiting for her in his car down the block. Her car wasn't in the lot this morning, and the barista at Chroma said she'd been fired. He's not quite sure why he wants to see her, but he can't think of anything else to do with his day, either.

A little after one, he watched two saggy middle-aged men in baggy suits get out of a black sedan and enter the complex.

Cops, he guessed. Web casually walked by the car, and the rig of police lights on the dash confirmed it. He walked around the block and back to his car. After fifteen minutes, they were gone.

At 2:37 p.m., he watched Ally arrive on foot. Web considered meeting her on the sidewalk but chose patience. Give her time to settle in and avoid the appearance of stalking.

"No," she says again. "I've had enough of the Set Up for a few days."

"You decline a gig, they won't call you for another one."

"It won't be the only job I lost this week," she says.

"Then let's talk," he says. "If not here, somewhere else. You pick."

"Pass," she says, quieter.

"How about this? I'm going to the Hedgehog & Fox to have a pint. If you meet me, great. If not . . ."

She doesn't respond but doesn't tell him to fuck off, either, which he interprets as progress. The door shuts.

Walking to his car, passing the pool, he hears, "You a cop?"

Web turns to see three men sitting in deck chairs, catching the afternoon sun on their leathery chests.

"What makes you think that?" he responds. He's lamenting that he didn't take the long way—the one that avoids walking the length of the pool—back to his car.

"Well, you're not delivering pizza," he says.

"And we know you're not her type," the second one chimes in. Web's antennae go up.

"He's not a cop. Cops are ugly and old," the third tells them both. Web considers it a compliment.

"Maybe a drug dealer," the third says. *There it is*, he thinks.

"They don't do that anymore, Jack. People just go to a dispensary now. They're like Apple Stores."

"What do you know about dispensaries? You get light-headed from ibuprofen."

As they turn their bickering on each other, Web puts his head down and picks up his pace.

He's pleased to find the Copa América Final on the TV when he gets to the Hedgehog & Fox. He doesn't really follow soccer, but at least the Brazil vs. Peru match has drawn a diverse crowd.

He finds the only available table, open due to its poor sightlines to a TV. Most people are standing, milling about. When the server arrives, he orders a Boddingtons and a basket of chips.

Peru scores on a penalty kick. The game looks tied going into the half. It's stoppage time, and with the amount of extra time the refs added, he figures there was a fair amount of requisite and expected antics and fakery common in the men's version of the game. Web admires the theatrics most of all.

Web checks his phone. No texts from the Set Up. He senses a crescendo of enthusiasm in the room and looks up. The crowd's chant at the bar matches the crowd on TV as Gabriel Jesus buries a cross past Pedro Gallese.

As half the room erupts in cheers and laughter, beer raining on the wood floor in all directions, the door opens, and he sees an Ally-shaped shadow outlined by daylight. As she walks in on the rollicking scene, he recognizes a nice skirt from the storage unit and a muddled look from their earliest conversations.

He waves for a few seconds before she locates him, and as she makes her way over, he drags a stool from behind a celebrating fan to the two-by-two table. They're pressed into a corner, and Ally puts her phone and purse against the wall.

Something about meeting at the bar gives him a rush of first date feelings. He shakes his head to clear it.

"So, what the fuck do you want?" Ally says. Maybe not so much a date.

"The game-time crowd was a surprise," Web says.

"The absolute least of my concerns," she says taking a sip of his beer. "It's better to be around people."

"Look, I—" Web stops. He's grateful when the server emerges from the crowd and takes a beer order from Ally—a pint of Old Speckled Hen.

"I didn't do Plotnik, okay?" he says. "I get why you'd think that, but my job was to serve drinks and to back you up. Trust me."

"He was in the middle of some land deal, Web. Trust me when I say that there are reasons someone would want him dead."

He hates the sound of that, even if implausible. "He wasn't murdered, Ally. I think he had an old-fashioned heart attack."

She shakes her head. "Now you're a doctor?" She looks at a screen and he's not sure if she can understand Spanish enough to follow the running commentary or if she's just letting him ponder her wariness.

The server interrupts a second time with Ally's drink and a plastic basket of fat, greasy fries. Ally unscrews the cap of the HP sauce, creates a dark pool of brick-red sauce, and stabs it with a fry.

"Ally, c'mon. We're backstage now," Web offers.

She looks at him. "You don't have a backstage, Web. It's all front. Comic books and make believe." She wiggles her fingers for effect.

She's right, of course. He's holding back—not least that Erv referred to her as a "temp," and he's never known one of those before. There's also his growing certainty that Erv knows more than he's saying about the week's gigs, which is a needle of truth slipping under his skin.

"That's cynical," he tries. "You can't go through life thinking everyone is a version of your parents in costume."

Something he says lands, but he can't tell what it is. She shakes her head. "The offices are a stage. A restaurant is a stage. Sidewalks are a stage. 'All the world . . .' Right? People just slip to and from the wings. Even this bar: the distraction of the match, the safety of a crowd, the casual normalizing of a shady operation."

He watches her avoid eye contact. "C'mon Ally, you don't feel that way. I think we've had—"

"Don't try to put on the truth. It doesn't fit."

"What are you implying, Ally?"

"How about that you work at a strip club, not a twenty-four-hour gym?" she says. "The same one Howie was supposed to go to?" Before he can respond she adds, "And I can tell that you won't be honest with me because you're touching your lips the same way you do when you struggle with your lines."

New information to him. He lets his hand drop from his face. "Wait. You followed me?"

"Erv didn't tell you?" At his confusion, Ally continues. "He caught me tailing you. He caught me considering breaking into the Set Up offices. He scared the shit out of me and Howie."

Web rocks back. While he's been trying to tail her, she's successfully tailed him, and neither of them knew Erv was tailing her. He's kept her in the dark, sure, but it seems she's kept him out of the loop as well. Meanwhile, Erv is keeping them both on the outside.

And Howie: the bachelor? What were the two of them up to, anyway? She's pushing him, but he isn't sure where she's going. Perhaps, Web thinks—an uncomfortable realization—he knows less than she thinks he does. He also registers a flicker of jealousy, unmoored, and isn't sure of its psychic destination. Over Howie spending time with Ally? Ally getting a step on him? Or Erv seemingly having more action while he's in the dark?

"You know, there's an English company that packages everything you need to build an authentic British pub," she says. "It's amazing. The stools, the signage, and stained glass windows—all of it in a shipping container. They send them around the world, so an average schmo in Buffalo can own an authentic British pub."

He looks over the bar, taking in the banners and jerseys. The crest of a lion and mare, the Union Jack pennants streaming a chalkboard listing the beers on tap. The round Guinness sign.

She looks at him and sighs. "I bet they even have Ye Olde Gift Cards to scam people like you," she says.

"People like me? What's that mean?"

Her eyes stop scanning the bar and return to his. "The scam that got you into the Set Up in the first place? I'm not trying to sound racist, asshole."

"Oh. Right," Web considers. "That . . . wasn't obvious." Add that to the list of things he's lied about and then lost track of. Web has too many spiraling thoughts, and her steady and directed pace is getting the better of him here.

Ally picks up on the pause and says, "That wasn't how you got into the Set Up, was it?"

Web's unnerved by how much he's missed. It doesn't entirely have to do with Ally, but it isn't a coincidence, either. "No," he says. "It wasn't."

Ally exhales. She gets up and walks toward the door, but Web sees that she's left her things on the table. She turns toward the restroom.

A group of men chant, "*Eu sou Brasileiro, com muito . . .*"

He looks at her phone for a long second. Another chance to try the password. He'll have to do it fast if he's going to. He reaches over and slides her phone out from under her bag. Several other people in the bar join the chant. "*Eu sou Brasileiro, com muito orgulho, com muito amor . . .*"

Web taps in the passcode he saw her enter in the van—525600, a reference to a song from *Rent,* he realizes only by singing out the number—and gets in. The model and the case are the same, but this is not the Up Phone he dropped off at her apartment. He quickly assesses the inventory of apps, podcasts, pictures, and browser pages. This isn't a hacked phone. She brought her personal phone. Okay. Fine.

He looks to the restrooms to make sure Ally isn't coming. He has a minute more. Two, tops.

The soccer chant dies down, replaced by a cheer over a corner kick opportunity.

He clicks on the photos app. There are columns of pictures of Ally, not selfies but posed images. There's a picture of her having breakfast. A picture of her working at Chroma. There are more pictures of her and the woman on the home screen, the one with a pixie haircut. It's her arm that's holding the phone, not Ally's. He exits the photos app and looks at the menu of icons. He sees an app called PushR and clicks on it. He knows it. It's a notification aggregator app—users can link notifications from one phone to another, assigning distinct sounds for each kind of pushed notification.

He realizes this is why her phone's notifications sound different and come later than his: She's pushing her CashStache notifications to this phone. "Ka-ching" vs. "cha-ching." He returns the phone to its place.

When she returns, she takes a long gulp of her beer and sits back on the stool.

"Ally, I've tried to be as real with you as I can be."

"Can't be all that much. But who sends the orders, Web? Who's behind it?"

"I don't know," he says. He tries to redirect her, "Who are you, even? Just a stack of stories, dressed up in off-the-rack casual wear."

"That's what you wanted from me," she responds with some extra vinegar. "That's what you got."

He weighs his options, but it quickly spills out in a word salad. "You're not really from New York, are you? Your parents aren't therapists. Why didn't you say you're a student?" He decides against giving her a chance to think up additional stories. "You're not using the phone. What are you up to exactly? What's your other angle?"

She looks at her pile of bag, phone, and keys on the table. "Fucking lack of pockets," she says. "Again: Who is behind the texts?" she asks.

"I honestly don't know," Web answers.

"Are there other Set Up teams?"

"I don't know." He realizes she's throwing him off his questions. She's sparring. He's not the only one with cards to play. "Why?"

"Your friend at Fallout when I was trying to work over Howie?"

"What friend?"

"The blonde who hovered a little too close? And what about the extra server at the bar mitzvah?"

"You saw the same woman twice?" he asks.

"No, different women. One in her twenties. Tattoo on her shoulder. Blonde. The second woman was older. They've been playing me."

"Ally, you're sounding conspiratorial."

"Am I?" she asks, a little wild-eyed. She's spinning out. Maybe a lot.

"So . . . what, exactly? There's a murderous theater troupe running around Las Vegas? Ally, that's crazy." But is it? he wonders. He can't really blame her for chasing ghosts and grasping at anything.

The idea of other marketing actors, however, doesn't lie outside the borders of his imagination. He's always thought there could be other offices around the country, joking with Erv that he was going to get transferred to the Omaha office if he fucked up. The jokes were riffs on *CSI* or *Law and Order*. "Set Up: Miami." LA or New York could have half a dozen teams. And what if a series of teams were coordinated? Could they change an event? Start a riot? Alter the outcome of a local election?

A new chant emerges from the same table of men, "*O Campeão voltou, O Campeão voltou, O Campeão voltou . . .*" He realizes that he'll have to shout to be heard.

Web speaks in as hushed a tone as possible, hoping Ally will reciprocate. "Who wanted him dead, then?"

"His son-in-law. Oran Kollis."

"And you saw someone familiar at the bar mitzvah?"

"Yeah, well. Yes," Ally says.

"She served the food?"

"No," Ally says. "Just refreshed our waters. While you've been watching strippers work the pole, I've been trying to figure out who killed him." She starts to scroll through her phone again. "Look, I have a pict—"

But just then, Ally's phone ka-chings.

Her thumb moves to mute it, but then she remembers he already knows the gig is up on her phone. Still, they both look at each other, processing the meaning of the notification.

"Did you do a job this morning?" he asks.

"No, I—" Before she can say more, her phone cha-chings again. And then again. Ka-ching, ka-ching, ka-ching, ka-ching, ka-ching, ka-ching.

"That sounds more like a slot machine than a phone," he says as he watches her scan her new notifications.

"They're all deposits of $2,999.00."

"Is it just a glitch? Multiple notifications for the same deposit?"

"No," she says, scrolling her thumb up and down. "They're from eight different numbers. Consecutive but different. Check your phone. Did you get paid?"

He looks at his phone. "No."

"Did you do this?"

"No."

"Did you do this?"

"No, Ally. I've been sitting here," he says. He thinks about it. "That's more than I've been paid for a gig by a wide margin."

"It's almost 24K."

"It must be a mistake," Web says.

They look at their phones. All around them, a volatile wave of excitement crests in the room and then dies as quickly as it rose, with a collective groan.

Ally looks up, and he sees a dark curtain pull across her face. "I think . . . Am I being framed?"

He doesn't know what to make of it.

Ally gets up, this time taking her belongings.

He stands too, but she makes for the door. "Wait!" he tries, but she doesn't turn. He considers following her but figures chasing would only make things worse.

Now what? What, exactly, is going on?

Beer half empty, he absentmindedly stares at the game. He asks for the check. At the seventieth minute, Jesus gets a second yellow card and a dismissal from the match. He kicks water bottles, punches a wall, and heads to the clubhouse in tears in as dramatic an exit as Web's seen in sports. On a different day, he would laugh at the tantrum.

Web considers the different forces working in opposition. He considers telling Erv what he's learned about Ally. That she's not using her company phone. That she's secretly a college student, although he's not sure why it's relevant. That she's questioning the Plotnik job and is drifting out in the world, loose. But then, for all Web knows, Erv is fully aware of all of this. Maybe he's sitting outside the bar in the van. He could text the Set Up something like: "Ally is asking questions. Visited offices w/o permission. Possible problem." He cannot tell what would jeopardize his job more—notifying them or not notifying them.

And then, a new thought. Does he even want to keep this job?

Something's very wrong, that much is obvious. He just doesn't know the shape of it, and he has too little to go on. He also realizes he's a little charmed by Ally, even if it might be some residual transference going on. She's kicking up more dust in a week than he has in two years. What has he really been a part of for the last few years? What is the Set Up, exactly?

Web looks at the clock. With a few hours before his gig at Mademoiselle's, he decides that Brazil being ahead by one and down a man for the rest of the match is a compelling enough reason to not decide just yet.

25

ALLY

Back out on the street, Ally is struggling to breathe. This is all too much: Plotnik's death, Phoebe's leaving, and now the deposits. If the cops come back to the apartment, she won't know what to say. If anyone from the Set Up comes, she doesn't know what they're capable of. She has to get somewhere safe, just long enough to calm down. To figure out her next step.

Ally books a hotel room under Phoebe's name. She stuffs Marshall's notebook and some marketing clothes in a duffel bag and summons an Uber.

As she waits by the parking lot, a voice says, "Going to the airport?" Ally nearly jumps out of her new Everlane ballet flats.

It's just the youngest of the witches, bringing a white garbage bag to the dumpster. "Didn't mean to startle you." He points with his chin at her duffel bag. "Your bag. Airport?"

"It's okay. Sorry. Yeah, no, I'm checking myself into a hotel for a night or two," she told him. "My car is . . . at the mechanic's."

"Let me take you."

"Oh, thanks. I can wait," Ally said.

"Of course. But why wait when you can arrive in style?" Sensing hesitation, he adds, "Plus, you'll be doing me a favor by letting me take Super Blanche out for a spin. Cancel your car on your app thing. I'll go tell the missus." Ally relents with a quick nod, deciding to go with the stranger she knows rather than the stranger on the app—just one more thing tracking her movements. Her heart hasn't stopped racing since the payments showed up on her phone. He comes back after a few minutes, jingling a set of keys.

Super Blanche, as it turns out, is the 1970 Triple White Cadillac Deville convertible in the back of the parking lot that Beep and Ally occasionally admired from afar. As they back out from under the carport, Ally feels exposed, but when the wind starts to blow through her hair, she feels a sense of escaping. From what, though?

Her new friend introduces himself as Claudio but says the other guys call him "Clotho" for his fashion sense. Clearly, he sees her escape as an opportunity to give a little tour of the city. Ally finds she doesn't mind. It's better than being alone with her thoughts.

They drive down to the older casinos. Somewhere in her mind, it registers that they have passed the Container Park, with its praying mantis and movie set vibe. "Driving Fremont real slow with the top down, watching so many lights . . . Now, that was one of my favorite things to do back in the day. Have you ever seen the video for 'I Still Haven't Found What I'm Looking For'? You're too young? It was pretty pretty," he said. "Cowboy Vic's elbow could be mine. Arthritically locked in place." He goes on and on, his schtick unaffected by her silence. She notices his hair doesn't move, even in the wind.

As they pull under the sparkly umbrella of lights at the Plaza, Claudio says, "You don't have to tell me who you're running from, but you can tell me if I can help."

"I— What gives you that idea?"

"Eee-o Eleven," he says.

"What's 'Eee-o Eleven'?"

"Cops stopped by today to ask us questions, we haven't seen your girlfriend for a few days, you've got a packed bag," Claudio says. "It means experience, kid."

"I—"

"Being a 'person of interest' doesn't make you as unique as you might think," he says with a smile. "Here's my number." He hands her his card, and he folds a hundred-dollar bill under it. Ally balks, but he waves it off. "If you don't need it, give it back when you can. You know where you can find me."

The Plaza isn't as bustling as she had hoped it would be. She checks in and then walks through the hotel's modest casino toward the hotel elevators. She catches the mirrored wall reflecting her at a corner. Antique mirrors used mercury for their reflective quality. She's reminded that the element is named after the messenger god, the god of transportation but also the trickster.

For a moment, she catches her face from three different angles, three different versions of herself: Ally from two weeks ago, the Ally that walked into the Set Up's offices, and the Ally she is now, who has lost her job and her girlfriend, and who watched a man die in her lap.

MONDAY

26

ALLY

The day starts with a 7:00 a.m. text. "Meet at the corner of 7th and Ogden at 8pm Confirm." No contact from Phoebe.

Ally gets up and opens the curtains. Looking down at the city is like seeing a movie set. The thought makes Ally never want to act again.

Seventh and Ogden is only a few blocks away from here. Do they know where she is? She doesn't have an answer. She knows what Beep would say: "Al. Don't go. This little class project of yours is way off the rails."

Ally gets dressed in non-Set Up jeans and a vintage Van Halen 1984 tour T-shirt. She tries to convince the Phoebe in her head that this is a good idea. Maybe the Phoebe who is not in her head—the real Phoebe—will come back to her. For what feels like the fortieth time, she thinks about calling Phoebe before remembering that she's been using Beep's phone.

She looks down at Claudio's business card and tells herself that if the colossally gray area she's been operating in gets one gradation shadier, she'll go to the police and tell them all about the weirdo performance marketing troupe that may or may not have a side hustle murdering old men. Probably, they'll send her to the psych ward.

For all the flashing warning signs, she can't shake the image of Plotnik dying in her lap. She needs to know how he got there. She wants to know what Losado knows. Losado said that he had unattended business with Plotnik, and she wants to confront him. All night, a scrolling LED display has been running through her head: In-Hwa. Preddy. Losado. Moonies. Parking lots . . . Over and over. She wants to push on it all. Was Plotnik part of the Set Up, or did the Set Up want him dead, or both? Is Phoebe in trouble . . . or just done with Ally? After all of this, she better earn an A for this class.

She types "Confirm" back to the Set Up.

Professor Grant will be concerned about her too, she figures. She can return his notebook after class. Maybe they can debrief. Maybe he's found something new. Or maybe this is all Lincoln-Johnson 9/11 numerology DaVinci Code conspiracy nonsense.

As she walks through the casino floor on her way to class, she realizes she doesn't want to carry the notebook and her phone in her hands. She heads to the souvenir shop to grab a bag before catching the bus.

27

MARSHALL

Marshall watches as Ava Reyes and her boss, Elías "Landslide" Losado, make their way up the long V-shaped staircase to the plaza of Greenspun Hall. Both of them are in suits. With a misting of sweat, they gleam like newborn skyscrapers. Even under the shade thrown by solar panels six stories up, Losado emits a glow.

With a practiced move, Reyes skirts in front of Losado to greet Marshall. She conveys a certain social proximity to her boss by giving Marshall a quick kiss on each cheek. He feels like he's the recipient of a kind of political pheromone tagging system. Social animals do that sort of thing. Ants. Bees. Wasps.

"Marshall, it's *so* lovely to see you," she says. "Please let me introduce Elías Losado."

Marshall's self-consciousness spikes. The two of them look like they've come to raze his plywood shed. And with his history of accusing Losado of a grave ethics violation, Marshall feels it would be a justified demolition. Losado would not have forgotten about it. Reyes, he thinks, must have worked hard to broker this appearance. Or perhaps Losado's here to gloat over just how far Marshall's fallen.

"The pleasure is mine. Thank you so much for taking time out of your busy schedule," Marshall says. He can't help but bow his head a bit when he expresses his gratitude. Why, he wonders, did he do that? He introduces his four TAs, who he almost forgot were standing behind him. Losado smiles and shakes hands. After witnessing a display of deference from his TAs, Marshall looks at the clock in the entry. "Speaking of time. Follow me."

Entering the lecture hall, he sees his TAs have positioned two chairs in the front and pushed the lectern aside, as instructed. He walks to the stage and glances at the lectern to see if Ally has left him another article, but it's empty.

Looking up, he sees that Ally has taken a seat in the front row. She clearly hasn't slept much; he can see her wide eyes burning holes through Losado. They exchange a nod before Marshall gestures for Losado to join him on stage. Losado undoes the button on his suit jacket and sits. Marshall follows, reaching into his satchel to retrieve a notebook and a pen.

"Good morning, class," he says. He receives about a 90 percent response rate. "Today, as you know, we will simulate aspects of an interview with a politician. You all prepared questions and, with some minor tweaking, I'll ask a select few. Depending on how things go, we will then give students a chance to ask questions."

"Sounds good," Losado says. "Thank you for having me. I'm always happy to accept an invitation back to my alma mater. Go Rebs." The class claps, a sea of warmth. Students always love a guest, especially a successful alum. Marshall feels the contrast between the politician's smooth delivery and his own frumpy discomfort.

He forges ahead. "Since you all did your homework, I'll offer just a brief introduction. Elías Losado began his service to the city as the CEO of the Valley Hispanic Health Council, a community-based organization directed at improving Hispanic and Latino health care access through education and direct action. He served two terms as Ward Three council member, winning so handily he earned the nickname 'Landslide Losado.' The mayor appointed him as city manager three years ago. His office oversees several municipal departments, including Urban and Economic Development, Cultural Affairs, Parks and Recreation, and Community Services. There isn't much you don't have a hand in, is that right?"

"It's an expansive job, yes," Losado says, smiling.

"Mr. Losado hasn't done many interviews since leaving city council," Marshall continues, "so we'll forgive him if he's rusty."

Losado laughs. "City managers are workhorses, not show horses," he says. "I hope I haven't lost my ability to trot." The class laughs.

"Well, our first question is right in your stable," Marshall segues into the interview. "City government often houses culture and economic development offices in the same administrative unit, yet arts and cultural development and economic development can, and maybe should, have contrasting plans. The Blu Condo project, for example, ended up including a performance space instead of the mixed-income housing that was part of the initial plans. How do you weigh the different values in the arts and in, say, affordable housing?"

"Right for the intra-agency intrigue, eh?" The class laughs again. "It's true. Agendas don't always mix comfortably. Our Office of Cultural Affairs and the Urban and Economic Development worked together on our scrappy little Arts District development. It's the job of our office to balance the needs of all our downtown communities, and that means . . ."

As Losado speaks, Marshall tries to coordinate the times when Losado turns toward the class with his glances down to the notebook in his lap to search for the next question. He also steals a glance at Ally, hoping to read how she's doing, but she doesn't break her focused attention on Losado.

He looks to Ava Reyes, who seems to be just as enchanted as the students. Perhaps more so. Through thirty-five minutes of conversation, Losado's a pro, handling himself well. There's a question about economic development and social justice, and one about how the private security forces of casinos police public spaces. Losado plays some answers straight and leavens the conversation with a bit of humor for the audience's sake—a practiced combination. For all his experience, he's still young and eager, has the right balance of constituencies. He's widely expected to make a successful run for city hall next year. After a term or two there, Congress. Who knows? Maybe higher. Reyes could be in for a long ride.

"Term limits confine our current mayor, Mr. Losado. Have you had any discussions about next steps?"

"I won't comment on the discussions I've had with the mayor."

"You won't do us the favor of making news today?" he prods.

"If I were to make news, this would be the class to do it in, but I'll decline at the moment." The class laughs and claps a little, and Marshall feels his jealousy perk up again. "Next question."

Marshall thinks the Q&A has been enough of a success to give the class a chance to ask questions.

"With our remaining time, perhaps we can have a few students ask questions?"

"Excellent," Losado says.

Ally's hand shoots up, and before Marshall can call on someone—anyone—else, Losado points to her. "Yes?"

"What do you know about Chesed Plotnik's death?" she asks.

Marshall watches Losado's brow furrow at Ally, and then his eyes click to Reyes. The class falls silent. He tries to think of something to redirect the exchange, but Losado gets there first.

"I remember you from the bar mitzvah. Mara, isn't it?" Marshall's thrown by the sudden modulation in Losado's tone, and he can see that the class is breaking into little hushed discussions behind her. He's also not at all on the same page as Ally. Did she learn something yesterday afternoon? Something incriminating? Why is Losado calling her "Mara"?

"Yes," she presses on. "What do you know about Chess?"

"Well, nice to see you again. I can't tell you anything more about Chess Plotnik's unfortunate death than what you already know. I was at the same event you were."

"I think you know more than you're saying," she says, her voice shaking a little. Marshall imagines a steering wheel drifting underneath his fingers; he can almost feel the fast *thump thump thump* of the rumble strips as his class veers off course.

Losado, however, radiates nothing but calm. "I am sure people are looking into that," he says. "I believe you were next to him, weren't you? I recall him being in your arms?"

A rosy burst of color blooms just below the skin of Ally's face. Words erupt from her mouth just as quickly. "Do you know who'd profit from his death?"

At that, the classroom fractures into a hundred barely hushed conversations, and Reyes stands up. Marshall does the same, putting his hand up to Ally, but she keeps going. "Do you have any business ties with the In-Hwa Group, Mr. Losado? Or Walker Preddy? Did the city manager's office approve or block any of Plotnik's recent real estate deals? Did you block his development of the International Peace Education Center?"

Without modulating his voice, Losado says, "I am sorry for that evening's tragic ending. Things certainly got . . . complicated. And my deepest sympathies go to the family." He offers a kind of grimace-smile and adds, "I imagine people are looking for you. You might be the one who can answer some questions, no?"

At that, a bit of color drains from Ally's face, and her cheeks slacken. She freezes for a moment.

"Okay, okay," Marshall says, putting both hands up. "This is a classroom exercise, not a— not an interrogation."

The students are talking excitedly, craning their necks to identify the student in the front row and pulling out their phones to record the interaction. All four TAs attempt to quiet the class.

Marshall tries to intervene. "We should speak after class, Al—" He watches her get up, grab a plastic bag, and push through the doors at the back of the hall. Students pan their phones to record her exit.

"Okay," Marshall puts his hands up again. "Okay. Let's move on."

While he's addressing the class, Marshall sees Reyes raise her phone to waist height and make a quick nod to Losado. He rises and buttons the top button of his suit jacket. The signal is clear.

"Well, my chief of staff says I have an unexpected meeting. It seems like things are going unexpectedly here too. Thank you, Professor Grant. Thanks, everyone!"

Attention returns to the stage, and the students slowly catch up to the scene, clapping and waving goodbye as the duo walks up the aisle.

Marshall improvises with the remaining time, saying it was an opportunity to unpack some discussion while it's fresh in their minds. As per some implicit agreement, and to his relief, no one mentions Ally's outburst.

The TAs hover after class, but he pushes through them apologetically. He bolts to the bathroom, finds an empty stall, and can barely lock the door before heaving brown stomach acid into the toilet.

Marshall's disappointed but unsurprised Ally's not waiting for his office hours. He finds the number she gave him and calls it from his flip phone.

"C'mon Ally," he says to the dial tone as it goes to voicemail. "Your call has been forwarded to an automated . . ." He hangs up.

He sits at his computer and reads the webpage for the dean of students' office as if some campus resource would be available to a student in Ally's situation. As he finds the number for University Legal Services, he hears footsteps echo down the hall. They come closer and pass without stopping.

He sits at his office computer, feeling helpless.

"Of course, the day I'm in my office hours, Dorris *doesn't* come," he says to himself.

With a deadline looming, Marshall absentmindedly tinkers with the phrasing in his article about Plotnik, but it doesn't prevent his mind from cycling back to Ally. He conducts fruitless web searches for things Ally mentioned. Combinations of "acting company," "the Set Up," "guerrilla marketing," "Las Vegas Ruse." It's all connected; he's just not sure how.

He returns to his notebook, flipping to the page with his set of questions and notes.

- What am I missing about the Rothman story? *Randall Carter/driver: dead end. Lived at compound.*
- Unification Church? "Third Family"? *Moved to Laughlin? Joshua Kollis (Minister) Going to sell Ogden to go legit?*
- Ogden/15th St compound? In-Hwa development. *Oran Kollis (Developer) (Son-in-law of Chess Plotnik—dead) In-Hwa vs OmariCity?*
- Who is reviewing my old articles? *Ally*
- *Plotnik: Latest OmariCity Development? Connection to City Gov/Losado? What's the connection to In-Hwa Group?*

Thinking about Ally, he attaches her name to the fourth question and adds two new bullet points:

- *What is the Set Up? OR the Ruse? Related?*
- *How is Losado involved? OmariCity? Development?*

He goes back through his inbox to find Ally's emails. Before he clicks on the last one, though, he sees a new email from Len Dorris and decides to see what the department chair has to say:

> I visited your Friday office hours, and you were absent again. More concerning are the emails I just received about today's class. I'm afraid your reappointment for the fall semester will be under review immediately.

He rereads it, which doesn't take long. Marshall thinks back to Friday. Instead of holding office hours, he went to see Lévesque.

Marshall considers finding Dorris and mounting a defense in order to keep his job. Instead, he closes the message without responding. It can wait.

He returns to Phoebeepbeep. He replies to the last email with his list of questions and notes. He hopes it will reach Ally. Maybe, he thinks, they can work on getting answers together.

Why did she go after Losado? His heart twists a little over his student's emotional state, and he feels his stomach churning again. He closes his eyes to focus and thinks about exhausting the scene. He's on the stage with Losado. She's in the audience, clearly upset. She met Losado. They were at the same event on Saturday night. She asks a series of questions. Then she gets up and leaves the lecture hall. She has a bag. A plastic bag, like from a hotel gift shop.

That stops him. He opens his eyes, then opens last week's lecture presentation and flips to the slide with his notes from '95. He finds it and focuses on Interviewee1:

> Interview1=white woman. late 20yo. jogging by. Saw the vic in traffic. "couldn't be his fault" driver was crying. black running shorts. FQ bag. Contact #: ████████.

"FQ bag." Four Queens bag.

He closes his eyes and now returns to his memories of that day. The ambulance. The crowd. He recalls the exhaustion in his voice on the recording. What Brenda looked like when he walked to her: she was sitting on the curb, in tears, vulnerable. Twenty feet from Rothman's body. He remembers approaching her. He remembers the plastic bag by her feet.

"Why would a jogger have a hotel gift bag?" he asks himself. There's only one answer, and he doesn't care to say it aloud: It wasn't her bag. She took something from the scene. And it belonged to Cal Rothman.

28

ALLY

Looking down at her Plaza Hotel gift shop bag, the bartender asks, "You lost?" with a little tone.

Ally walks up to the bar. "No. No. I'm—" she pauses. "Can I speak with Mr. Walker Preddy?"

"He's busy. What can I do for you?"

It didn't take long for Ally to figure out where to find Preddy. The Choice—his original restaurant, on the Westside, not the one in the Container Park—is dark and cool. There are two pool tables in the back and, to Ally's right, a bustling restaurant with a short and chatty queue. A menu board filled with specials teeters on an easel. Ally is the only white person around—has been since she got off the bus a few blocks from here.

"Thank you, but I need to speak with Mr. Preddy," she says.

"Um-hm," he says. He finishes making a drink, sets it at the server station, and heads to the back without a word.

She isn't at all sure if the bartender is getting Preddy or just ignoring her altogether, but she waits and surveys the room, the pictures on the wall. She sees Preddy age in slow motion, from left to right. There are old pictures of Black men and women wearing suits and ties, and the whitewash of the pictures gives the impression of an oppressive heat. Everything looks hot in old pictures. She guesses they were from the neighborhood, although the neighborhood she walked through from the bus—vacant lots, chain-link fences—isn't what she sees in these street scenes.

The man in the pictures emerges from the back in a polo shirt and black jeans, followed by the bartender, who returns to his business.

"Can I help you, Miss—"

"Mr. Preddy, you can call me Ally."

"I don't think I'll need to. We're not looking for servers."

"No. Sorry. I'm here to speak to you about Chess. Did you hear?"

At that, she watches his shoulders droop a half inch. He has a trim beard that only amplifies a shadow of a scar on his left cheek all the way down to his jawline. Something medical, she guesses.

"Yes, yes I did," he says, with a suspicious look. "What's it to you?"

"I hear you had a standing date with him on Mondays for dinner. Is that right?"

"That's right," he says, sighing. "And again: What's it to you?"

She considers not using the one card she has, the same one she played on Tina. Using it again seems gross and slippery. And yet, she *was* there. A man looked into her eyes as he felt his life slipping away. She can't walk away from that so easily. Ally's the player, not the dealer, and decides to use what she's got. "Well, I was with him when he died." After a shaky breath, she adds, "I'm hoping you can clear some things up for me."

And at that, she sees Walker's eyes relax a little, as she expected. There's a thrill masking her revulsion at the manipulation. He gestures to a barstool away from the bustle of the restaurant. He grabs a bar rag, wipes the counter twice, and places it over his shoulder as effortlessly as she tucks her hair behind her ear. Automatic.

"Okay, so you met Chess," Preddy said.

"Only briefly. I didn't know him well, but he was nice to me."

"Chess was a hard person to know," Preddy says with a chuckle.

"He was politely conversational. How about that?" Ally concedes.

Preddy fills a glass with ice and pours himself a Coke. He lifts the soda gun nozzle in Ally's direction as if to ask if she wants something.

"Water, please," she says. He scoops some ice into a glass, pours water into it, pulls a slice of lime from the garnish caddy, and places it artfully on the rim of the glass.

"I'm not eager to talk about him, Miss Ally," he says, passing her the glass. "What is it you wanted to ask me?"

"He told me he planned to set things right, and it seems you might be the only person who can tell me what he meant by that."

Preddy looks at her for a long time and nods before letting out a long whistle of an exhale. "I suppose it all doesn't matter anymore," he says as he looks over her shoulders to the wall of old photographs. "I've known people like Chess all my life," he continues. "I can't say that I liked him for most of that time. You know how he made his money?"

"No," she says.

"He did it the frontier way: stealing land. There's a reason this bar is on this side of town and not the other. People like Chess bought properties everywhere, and the banks helped them plenty. Somehow, people like me could only get loans on this side of town."

"Redlining," she says, deploying information from Marshall's lecture on the Oakwood apartments.

"I know what white people call it," he says. "I knew Chess by rep. He was a landlord. One Sunday, my buddy's toilet clogged, and Chess came to see if he could fix it rather than pay time-and-a-half to a Black handyman. I was there and helped. We got to talking. Had a few laughs. He gave me his card.

"Over the years, we crossed paths. I started this business, made some money, I bought houses here and there. Well, not 'here and there' so much as 'here and also here.' I built up to some larger properties. Occasionally, Chess would stop in for lunch and we would get to talking business. When he got in on the Container Park project, investors wanted to mix cosmopolitan hipster amenities with some 'local color.'" At that, he laughs. "I guess Chess figured I'd add some color."

"I'm sorry," Ally says.

"Why would you be sorry? I'm a grown man who knew exactly what I was being used for, and I made my money. Plus, Zappos bros pay twice as much as folks do here," he says with a nod to the dining room.

Ally builds up to her biggest question. "Before he died, Chess told me he had some last trick up his sleeve."

"Oh he did, did he?"

"Yeah. I'm wondering if he talked about it with you. He said he planned a ruse.'"

Preddy chuckles, and Ally feels suddenly exposed. She wonders if she's on a wild goose chase. Or if it all is, indeed, some big joke.

"I'm sorry, Miss Ally," he says, reading her body language. "I don't mean to laugh." He sighs and continues, "Sometimes there's a right and wrong side of doing things, just as there's a right and wrong side of town. Chess often operated on both sides, in both ways. But he never forgot where he got his money from. Four years ago, we got to talking about how he wanted to set things right."

"And that's why he planned to do the Peace and Love Center? Did someone want to stop the center from being built?"

"Someone? You could say that. It was Chess. Chess wanted no part of some Moonie Peace Center."

"Then what did he want?" Ally asks.

"He was going to sell the land to me."

"You?"

"He didn't say 'ruse,' Miss Ally. I'm going to guess he said 'Rouge.'"

"Rouge? Like a cosmetic?"

"No. Like a casino."

This clicks in her brain. She remembers Web talking about it.

"Wait. The Moulin Rouge? The one on Bonanza, right?" she asks. He looks at her, a little impressed.

"That's right. He was going to sell the lot to a group of us. Ron Barden, too. Heard of him?" Ally shakes her head, and Preddy waves his hand. "We were going to build a second Moulin Rouge casino, this time on Fremont Street. All African American ownership group. On-site worker culinary and service training for promising youth . . ." He trails off, as if his possibilities are now just pipe dreams.

Preddy wipes the counter again. "I said it didn't matter anymore, because his son-in-law—"

"Oran?"

"That's right. He called to tell me Chess died. But that was only the first blow. He also told me his wife, Esther, would inherit the land and that Chess's plan would be buried along with him."

"So Plotnik's last trick was going to be the Moulin Rouge?"

"Right," Preddy says.

Ally inhales quickly and asks, "Do you think Oran could have learned about the Moulin Rouge plan by breaking into Plotnik's office?"

"It's possible." Then, "I suppose."

They stare at each other for a while.

She recalls Plotnik's head resting on her knee, his white hair fanned behind him like a crown on her dark blue dress. Her hair blocking out the tumult surrounding them in those seconds, his eyes locked to hers.

"The Moulin Rouge wasn't to make things right with me but with himself," Preddy says with a shrug.

Ally takes her first sip of water.

"Although," he smiles. "He did have a good sense of irony. He was quite tickled by the idea of a place for Black folks to legally extract money from the pockets of white folks."

Ally doesn't quite know what to say to that, and they sip their drinks in silence. Then, she thanks Preddy for answering her questions and says she'll walk back to the Plaza hotel. He offers to walk her back under the overpass. "It seems my regular Monday night dinner date won't be making it, and it gives me an excuse to exercise both my walking tour and my sciatic nerve."

Preddy punctuates the thirty-minute walk with several stops along the way for Ally's second old-timer tour of the last twenty-four hours. A compact building housing an African American history museum on Van Buren. A gravel lot on Jackson where a few of his businesses once stood, which now hosts a blue/gray tent, a red lounge chair, and a shopping cart. The original site of the Moulin Rouge on Bonanza. Along the way, there are introductions to passersby curious about the white woman Mr. Preddy is on a stroll with. The gift shop bag, she imagines, almost makes her make sense—as if Walker's escorting a lost tourist back to the white side of the tracks.

Before parting, he tells her, "Come back to the Choice any time. We put out a nice spread for dinner."

29

MARSHALL

The GPS leads him to a stone gateway and guardhouse flanked by rows of palm trees. Spanish Hills. Summerlin is pockmarked with this kind of gated complex. They're grayed out on his GPS. Marshall supposes it would be silly to expect anything less from a community founded by the Howard Hughes Corporation.

He's surprised when the guard waves him in after taking his name and making a phone call. "5087 Rustic Ridge," he says. Marshall notices the Glock-style gun on his hip.

You'd have to wait tables at a pretty splashy spot to live here, Marshall muses as he heads along a gently winding road into the complex.

After his realization that Brenda had taken Cal's plastic bag minutes before they met, he located the sticky note with the phone numbers and addresses of the witnesses that Tracy offered on Thursday. He spent the rest of the afternoon distractedly cobbling together his article about Chess Plotnik, emailing grading instructions to his TAs, and holding out hope that Ally would stop by. At 3:30, after sending the article to Tutti, he decided to surprise his ex-girlfriend.

5087 Rustic Ridge is a standard looking, million-plus-dollar house. High-end sunbelt suburban. Green Subaru in the driveway.

Brenda is waiting by the door. "I don't want to know how you know where I live." She lets the discomfort sit.

"I'm sure you don't," he says.

"Come on in."

Looking around, Marshall notices the house is sparsely but nicely appointed. It's ready for a catalog photo shoot. A set of magazines fanned on an end table; a vase of fresh flowers centered on a table that wouldn't be out of place in an executive boardroom. Rugs, vacuumed. Windows in the back that open to a mini-desert landscape.

"Lovely," he says, as she leads him to the living room. "You live here on waitress money, do you?"

"You've got me," she says playfully. "I keep this house for my boss. He lives in Maui and only occasionally comes back to check on the restaurant. This isn't my kind of place anyway. The tall ceilings make me feel . . . lonely. Can I get you something to drink?"

"No, thank you," he responds.

"I'm hoping something comes through for me soon. I'm ready to move on." She gestures toward the couch and they both sit. As she does, she leans forward. He sees a simple gold necklace dangle below the neckline of her shirt. He's not immune to it.

She tucks her foot beneath her before turning to face him. "So, what brings you to my door?"

He sees a glass of white wine on the coffee table, next to her phone. He's been thinking about this all afternoon; he wants to pressure her, find out if she played a role in Cal's death. But now, facing her, he falters.

She doesn't wait for an answer. "I'm surprised to see you. Pleased, actually," she says. For a second, he registers a look that might be flirtation. She sits close, and her arm stretches along the back of the couch toward him.

He realizes he should try to be professional and looks at the chair opposite the couch. He should have sat in the chair. Head in the game, Marshall. "Well," he sighs, "the reason I wanted to talk—"

He sees her face switch, knows she will cut him off. "I said I didn't want to talk about that day, Shally," Brenda says. She takes a sip from her glass. "I've been hoping you were using this as an excuse to be back in touch with me. So, please. Let's talk about something else," she pleads. "Anything else. Make me feel less alone."

He questions what he is doing chasing a decades-old story.

What *is* he doing here?

"There's something specific. Something I need to know." He waits for her to protest, and, when she seems resigned to his agenda, he asks, "What was in the plastic bag, Brenda?"

"What plastic bag?"

"That day. You had a plastic bag, from a hotel."

"I couldn't possibly remember, Marshall. And what's it got to do with anything?" He notices that she's dropped his nickname. She sits up straighter and pulls her arm away from him.

"You said you were out for a run. What would a jogger be doing with a plastic bag?"

He feels a momentary change in the room's atmosphere as she sucks air through her teeth. Her expression softens as her eyelashes flick and her hand rests on his shoulder. "Can't we talk about this . . . after?"

At that, her hand moves to his forearm, and he feels her thumb caress him once again.

Before he knows it, she's closed the distance between them. His thoughts scramble as familiar scents and embraces collapse time and space in the familiar-but-different bodies and shadows and echoes of old gestures, and he tosses his plans to the floor, along with everything else he brought with him.

She wraps a throw blanket around herself, covering little, as she leans over to the coffee table. "I have some more white in the fridge," she says, taking a sip from the glass, which narrowly missed being overturned twice.

"No. Thank you," Marshall says, preferring to mull familiar mixed emotions sober.

They make small talk about the house, the weather—anything other than the last half hour or the last few decades. He hopes to return to his questions, although he feels marooned, with his vast continent of notebooks and questions and puzzles an ocean away.

He tries to keep his journalist hat on, which is challenging when undressed. He grabs a pillow from the couch, attempting modesty. Well, that's something he's never talked about in class, he thinks.

Thirty seconds seem like twenty minutes for an interviewer. If you can stand the discomfort, he knows, most people talk. The trick, sometimes, is to not talk at all.

Finally, he stammers. "I'm sorry. L-Look. I just want you to help me understand what I am missing."

"I think I just showed you what you're missing," Brenda grins.

"About that day, Brenda. Not . . . not this."

She pulls the blanket tighter around herself, giving a disappointed schoolteacher head shake. "What makes you think I know what you are missing?"

"I— I think you know."

"What do you think I know, Marshall?"

"You had a plastic bag with you. From a souvenir shop."

"So you said. What are you getting at?"

"Why would a jogger have a plastic gift bag with her?"

Her look of disappointment transforms into a scowl. She sighs again with twice the sorrow.

"How could I possibly remember, Marshall? Maybe I was dropping off something for a friend. I told you it was very, very traumatic for me. Forcing me to talk about it is unkind." Brenda gets up, wrapped in the blanket. She turns. "Now, I have to say, that was fun, but you're well on your way to ruining it." She walks to the other side of the coffee table to get her phone. He sees her thumb scroll around as she walks to the kitchen.

She brings him a water bottle, not wine, sets it down on the coffee table, and starts putting on her clothes. "Here you go," she says. "It's good to hydrate after exercise . . . especially if you're out of practice."

"Thanks," he says, focusing on gathering his clothing, having to reach behind the couch awkwardly. She turns to him in the silence, the kind of silence that happens in movies before something meaningful happens, but Marshall struggles to meet the moment. Her eyes look at him, hopeful and then, again, disappointed.

"I'm sorry," she says, upbeat. "I have a meeting across town. Maybe we can talk another time. Perhaps over drinks? Like a date date."

He doesn't have an answer, and she breaks eye contact to indicate she's not looking for one. She sends another quick text and collects a large bag, the water bottle from the coffee table, and her keys. He follows her to the front door and slips on his shoes.

He doesn't protest as she leads him into the hot air. "Can you hold this?" she asks as she hands him the water bottle. She sets her house alarm, locks the door, puts on her sunglasses, and clicks her key fob.

"Bye, Shally. I really wish we went on that date," she says.

His head's a jumble. Can he ask her one more time? Meet her for a drink and forget all about guerilla marketing, off-brand Moonies, murder, and real estate? For a moment, he realizes he's chosen a bizarre ghost chase over connecting with a living person. Marshall watches her get into the car, flash a smile through the glass, pull on a pair of white oven mitts from her bag before touching her steering wheel, and drive off.

He stands there for a few ticks. He snaps from a melancholic lull and returns to his baseline state of curiosity. He should see where she's going.

Marshall rushes to his car, puts the water bottle he forgot to hand back to her in his cupholder, and does a U-turn to the front gate. He catches up to her, heading out to Tropicana. He watches her pull into a strip mall and park. He does the same, several rows over. He looks at her through the windshield of a car parked in front of him. She doesn't seem to notice that he's followed her, but she doesn't get out either. She sits at idle, with her head down. He guesses she's on her phone. He considers walking over to her car but decides to see what she does next. He looks at the clock on his dash. 7:03.

"What are you doing?" he asks, both of Brenda and himself. He snaps the green cap off the water bottle and takes a few gulps.

He looks at the strip mall. Her important meeting is here? People filing in and out of a gym, a Walgreens. Twenty minutes go by. He sees her put down her phone and pull out of her spot. Marshall puts his car in reverse, but there's a vehicle parked directly behind him. A van, waiting for a spot, directional blinking. Marshall watches as Brenda's green Subaru leaves the lot and heads east on Tropicana. The van is still blocking him. He honks the horn twice, but the driver doesn't seem to notice.

Marshall gets out and approaches the passenger-side window. He knocks on the glass once and then a second time. Finally, the driver rolls down the window.

"Help you?" he asks.

"You're blocking me in."

"I'm waiting for a spot," the driver says, nodding vaguely forward. He's a tall, young, white dude. Maybe half Marshall's age, wearing a plain red polo shirt. He looks entirely serene, but not someone Marshall would want to get into a physical altercation with either.

He looks around and doesn't see a driver getting into a car, nor any taillights.

The young man has a few decades on him and is more athletically built, so Marshall tries to strike a polite tone. "Can you move your van, please? You can have my spot."

The man says, "Hey, ace, why don't you get back into your car? I'll move when I'm ready."

"I'm not—" Marshall stops himself as the window rolls up, almost brushing his nose. Right before it closes, the man says, "I'll leave in a minute. Don't worry. You're not going to make it."

"Make it? What?" he asks, but the window closes, and the man turns back to looking forward. "I—" Marshall starts, without knowing what to say.

Does he know this person? A jealous boyfriend of Brenda's? He's too young to be an ex-husband, he guesses. Is this a warning? Should he copy the license plate number and call the police? He returns to his car, defeated. He's lost Brenda, he knows—in every sense.

As his hope fades, he considers following the man in the white van once he gets moving but cannot find a compelling argument for it. He gets in his car and looks at the clock. 7:28.

His breathing calms a bit after the interaction. While he waits for the van to move, he takes a few more gulps of water.

After another few minutes, he feels a little lightheaded, and he turns up the AC. He finishes the water, hoping it might relieve what seems to be a swelling heartburn. He sees movement in the rearview mirror and watches the van finally pull away. Then he senses a kind of constriction in his chest. He knows enough to recognize it as a potential sign of a heart attack. He reaches to open the car door, to get help, but his fingertips miss the lever. He feels a sway and a surge. Like the feeling of falling in love, Marshall thinks.

And then he feels nothing at all.

30

ALLY

Ally wakes from a nap at 7:30 p.m., groggy. She tries Marshall's number, but it goes to voicemail. She takes a quick shower, puts her jeans back on, and shoves the phone in her pocket. Better not be late. She packs everything else in the duffel bag and brings it with her. She doesn't know where she'll stay tonight. Maybe she'll come back here. Maybe she'll go home. She wonders again about the choice of pickup spot.

Outside, she walks on Ogden toward Eighth Street. Walking through Zappostown, she looks up at a five-story mural. It's the bust of a man, his face obscured by cacti emerging from smoke and a blue-purple owl resting in the flat pads of a prickly pear cactus. The man's thin green hands reach up, as if not daring to touch what has become of his face. Another owl, orange, nestles in his arms. Waves swirl around the edges. The desert-faced man unnerves her.

"Excuse me?" A voice startles Ally. "Can you take my picture?"

"Sorry?" Ally says, focusing.

"Can you take my picture with the mural behind me?" The woman is a youngish blonde, early twenties. She's standing in front of another of the dozen or so murals in this part of town—a block-long image of a horned lizard with blood squirting out from its eye.

Ally has time; she's only a block from the pickup spot.

"Sorry. Yeah, sure," she says. The woman hands Ally her phone with the camera app open. She sees the little rainbow vortex icon. *Ha. Maybe stealth advertising works, after all.*

Ally takes a step back, but the woman matches her steps, so Ally backs up further to get more of the mural in the photo, at an angle. She takes another step back, and now she's at the curb. The light on the mural is nice, but the sunset is backlighting the woman. As Ally's finger hovers over the little white button, her attention shifts to the woman's face.

For a second, Ally thinks the app is in selfie-mode. The face on the screen isn't quite hers, but the woman's bone structure, coloring, and height are similar. Seeing this other Ally on the camera screen gives her an uncanny circus-mirror feeling.

And then it clicks. Ally recognizes her. It's the woman who was wearing the Bikini Kill T-shirt at the bar where she picked up Howie.

"Oh shit," Ally manages to say. "Were you at Fall—"

And then she hears the *beep beep sjjjjooop* sound of a van door sliding open behind her, and the blonde woman steps forward a third time, too close, and shoves her. Ally feels her knees give out as she trips backward. Someone catches her, and the blonde pulls Ally's legs up and in. Before the black hood falls over her eyes, Ally sees she is in a van a lot like the one she's been riding in all week.

She hears her duffel bag drop on the floor beside her. Before she can say anything, she hears another woman's voice say, "Relax, Ally. Relax," and then the familiar sound of a GMC cargo van door sliding closed as they pull away from the curb.

About thirty minutes later, the van stops and they drag Ally out, half stumbling. "On your knees, please," a woman's voice says. Ally obliges, seeing no alternative. Gravel digs through her jeans.

Someone pulls the hood off, and Ally's eyes adjust to the low light. The headlights bounce off some vegetation to her left, and there's a faint glow of red taillights to her right. The van idles behind her. Her eyes adapt more, and she sees a dune ahead with a necklace of saltbush and creosote around its base. It's pretty.

"You know, we're in the only major city that isn't directly connected to a thriving waterway? Even LA has its shitty little river." The woman walks from behind to face Ally.

Even with the stark shadow and light exaggerating the woman's features, Ally knows this is the white woman who was at the bar mitzvah. Oven Mitts. She's fiftysomething, with long dark hair, a white V-neck with a gold necklace, and one of her hands behind her back. She's about eight feet away. The right half of her face catches a little red from the van's taillights.

"Isn't there a background you should be lurking in?" Ally asks. "What am I doing here? Where's Phoebe?"

"Adorable, Ally, but none of your questions matter," the woman says. "What matters is that the Set Up needs you to do one more job." The woman pulls her hand from behind her. "The good news is that it will be a short assignment."

Ally half expects her to be holding a gun, but it's a water bottle. "I suspect microplastics aren't what I need to worry about with that bottle," she says. The other blonde steps out of the van.

A wind roars up, muting the sound of the van. "The other option is . . . messier," Oven Mitts says.

"You're going to set me up to take the fall for Plotnik?"

"Ally, we already have," the younger woman says, moving from the van to join Oven Mitts.

"No one's gonna believe some college student wanted to kill an executive of a development company," Ally says.

"Sure they will," Oven Mitts says with the corner of her lip upturned. "For a price, the Set Up provides the hit *and* the perp. You were the last person with him. You were seen at the Container Park, near his offices, the night we broke into them. We took a glass you drank from at the office and placed it in Plotnik's house so the police can pull a fingerprint. Thousands of dollars were just deposited in your bank account. You even signed your name to a confession at the focus group."

Ally thinks about the waiver Erv had the group sign. She didn't read the fine print. One of so many mistakes she's made.

"And," the younger woman says, "there's your phone."

Ally scowls, her face in the shape of a question, and the blonde offers an answer.

"Your phone places you in Plotnik's proximity five different times this week—the Container Park, his office, the In-Hwa offices, a restaurant you left a scooter at . . . Plotnik even had a meeting at the Park MGM at the same time you were snapping pics of tourists on the Strip."

It brings her no comfort to realize that her guess was right. There was a second team all along. A kind of void crew. What they're out to void, tonight, appears to be her.

"And of course," Mitts continues, "you were with him at the bar mitzvah. The police will put it all together."

"I filled in some blanks too," The other blonde says. "Dressing as your double and making sure it looks like you were on all the right security cameras. Your texts will add to the data. The phone pinged all the right cell towers."

Mitts steps forward a little. "So, you are going to kill yourself out of guilt, Ally." She takes the green cap off the water bottle and takes a step toward her. "And if you don't, we'll just go after your cute girlfriend. You said her name was . . . Phoebe, right?"

She feels her face go numb, like a mega-shot of Novocain blowing through her body. "So I just walked out here myself?"

"Of course not. You rented a van, Ally. It will be here shortly."

Ally tries to keep them talking and, suddenly, a new fear opens a door. "Do you know a Cal Rothman?"

Oven Mitts pauses and lowers the bottle a few inches. "Now, that's a name I know. But why have I heard it twice in one day?" Marshall, she figures. Ally remembers that he didn't pick up her call and suddenly worries about what's happened to him. "I should tell you I'm not really an actor," Ally tries. "I'm a journalist." The women exchange looks.

"Is that why my ex showed up at my home today?"

Professor Grant dated this woman?

"Who is— Who was Cal?" The younger woman asks. "What ex?"

Ally tries to keep the conversation moving, putting what she knows about the Set Up together with what she read in Marshall's notebook. "I only wanted to do a paper on aspiring Las Vegas actors. I came across the article on Cal's death just because my professor wrote it. But . . ." She takes a deep breath and thinks. A little door opens in her mind. "Always teams of three, right? So I'm going to guess how it worked: One person drove the car, one person pushed Cal into the street. And a third to serve as a corroborating eyewitness to the supposed accident."

"What is she talking about, Ruth?"

Okay, Oven Mitts's name is Ruth. Ally presses on. "If Marshall came to Ruth here . . . And judging from her response, Ruth played a role back in '95."

Ruth says, "Pedestrian deaths are so much easier now with distracted drivers. We barely have to do anything but let it happen these days. Back then, death by misadventure needed a little more coordination, yes."

"I only see two of you, and I'm going to guess you have a third. A man. Someone who . . ." She stops. Of course. "Ah, Howie."

Ruth exhales and looks back to the van. "Well, fine, yes. You can come out. It doesn't matter anyway."

Ally's duffel bag drops by her knees, and Howie joins Ruth and the blonde a few feet in front of her.

He says, "You finally got me in the desert, Ally. How'd you describe it? 'The city fades to dust' out here?"

"Aw, really?" Ally says. "You even played hard to get. Is your name even Howie?"

"Of course not. Did you really go to a boarding school?"

"Of course not," Ally says. "It's from *My Fair Lady*."

"Ah," he says with a nod and a contented frown. "Cute."

"You set me up to fail the Girlfriend Job, didn't you? That's, what, 'the Crisis' stage of the con?"

"We did," he says. "Good effort, though. I liked the move to book the hotel. I'm going to borrow that one."

"I don't feel ownership over it," Ally says.

"Well, soon you'll feel nothing," the older woman says, with a bit of music to it. Ally recognizes it as a reference to Maria's number from *A Chorus Line*. Well, actors know their theater. Ruth shakes the water bottle in the air between them.

Everything gets wobbly for Ally. She takes a deep breath. The numb feeling subsides. Her eyesight sharpens. Things come into crisp focus.

"But I— I know some things," she responds. "I know you're getting paid to clean up Oran Kollis's business. I know Plotnik didn't want to sell land to his son-in-law." Ally continues, pointing at Ruth. "I posted a picture of you at the bar mitzvah. I know about the Set Up. And my professor knows about it too. I've been writing notes to him all week. He knows about Plotnik. He knows—"

"Your professor can't help you now, I'm afraid," Ruth says. "You know some things, granted. But you do not know enough. The Set Up offers limited information for a reason, Ally. The police, however? We'll hand them plenty of data."

"Can't believe I'm going to die because of a final paper," she mumbles. "Summer session was supposed to be easier."

"Okay, enough," Ruth says, nodding at Howie. "Get her phone."

"Aren't we going to wait for the others?" Howie asks.

"It doesn't matter," Ruth answers. "They'll be here."

Ally reaches into her pocket for her phone. A puzzle piece pops out of place in her head. They don't want this phone, though. They want the one Erv gave her.

"Oh. But this isn't the Set Up's phone."

"What?" Ruth asks.

"Your phone is in my apartment, in its manila envelope. I . . . I never trusted it." She holds up Phoebe's phone as if they could tell what she's saying is the truth from its sleek black screen.

Howie looks at the phone and demands, "Tell us the passcode, Ally."

"Whoops. Maybe you have less data than you thought?"

And that's when she hears the engine of another van roaring through the desert air.

31

WEB

Erv picks Web up at 7:30 p.m., as per their instructions. They head south, riding in silence until finally Web says, "You owe me $100 for the Set Up calling Ally back."

"You'll owe me $900 for her not making it a month."

"We're not picking her up?"

"She got a ride."

"Where to?"

Erv doesn't respond. Etcetera. He's curt but rarely mute.

This isn't lost on Web.

Web thinks about his conversation with Ally at the Hedgehog & Fox and asks the same question Ally asked him: "Are there other teams, Erv?"

Erv responds with a look of acute indigestion, an expression that, even after seeing him eat hundreds of meals, is new to Web. The look fades quickly.

"I'll pass along the question, Web." He doesn't like the sound of that, either.

"I'm not saying to pass it along. I'm asking you. Are there other Set Up teams?"

"Can't say."

Web hears Erv receive a text, watches him read it and then put his phone back in the cupholder, making the van's key fob jingle.

Without a conversational partner, Web takes out his phone. He opens PicSnapR, clicks on @SetUpAlly, and scans through the photos she's been posting to the site. There are a few pictures of her with the same woman he saw on the phone she's using. He scrolls further back to see Ally's series of Vespa pictures. He looks at her smile, her face, and he feels a brief stir in his stomach. He pauses at the one at the office building. The afternoon light looks good on her. He zooms in a little on her face.

And then he scrolls to her selfie at the bar mitzvah, where Ally's pointing at the server she thought was suspicious. The woman looks like . . . No, it can't be. Web zooms in, but the photo is blurry. He can't say for sure. But if it is, Ally might be right that there's far more going on than he's realized. It might be time to press Erv.

"Why were you at the bar mitzvah?" Web asks.

"What do you mean?"

"You were supposed to be in the van."

"I was," Erv says. "I didn't trust her and was checking up on you. Glad I did. When it went sideways, I stepped in. Same as you."

Plausible, Web thinks. Still.

"Erv," he asks, "did we kill Plotnik?"

At that, Erv eases off the gas. "What?"

"The old man. Chess Plotnik," Web says.

Erv doesn't answer.

Why, Web wonders, hasn't he been more curious about the work that they've done this week? Why so many gigs in close succession? Why rush Ally? He thinks about Ally telling him about Plotnik and his son-in-law and saying it's all about development.

"Do you see a connection between our jobs this week?"

"The only connection I'm concerned about is the growing gap between your budding sense of curiosity and your very best interests."

Web looks around and realizes Erv is driving them out of town, south on Las Vegas Boulevard. The traffic is thinning. There's another white van in front of them, identical to their own. "Wait. Where are we going?"

"Out a bit," Erv said.

Web looks at Ally's picture from the bar mitzvah one last time. He thinks about Ally, sitting with Plotnik while he served drinks. How frustrated she was when he outsmarted her acting. How he learned she wasn't who she said she was.

"Am I being set up?" he asks, more to himself than to Erv.

"No," Erv says, keeping his eyes trained on the road. After a few minutes, he adds, "You're not being set up. I'm not being set up. Sit back and shut up. Just a little longer, Dub."

Web quietly unbuckles his seat belt as Erv brakes for a light.

As the van stops, Web reaches for the key fob and his door handle. The move requires too many steps, and Erv is able to grab his forearm with his right hand to prevent him from taking the fob and leaving the car.

"What do . . . ?" Erv starts to ask. Then, suddenly, he strikes Web in the face with his left fist. When someone is as tightly coiled as Erv, there's a great deal of force when that spring inevitably flies loose. Web's head snaps back and then falls forward, hard, onto the gearbox between them. *Ow.* The force pushes the stick into park and a measure of clarity into Web's brain.

With his knee on the floor of the van and his head so low it's almost in Erv's lap, Web twists to reach up and grab Erv's collar. Face to face, Web sees darkness in Erv's eyes but then a flicker of concern. Web takes it as his cue. With a quick pull, he cracks Erv's head against the steering wheel. Because of the geometry of the angle, it's a hard hit, and he feels Erv go limp. Surprised, Web struggles to get his arm out. He hears a car horn sound and realizes the light has changed.

Web quickly unclicks Erv's seat belt and pulls him into the space between the seats. A sustained horn blast is sounding around him as he awkwardly climbs over Erv and into the driver's seat.

He notices that his own nose is bleeding, unleashing a stream of red blood onto his shirt.

Web gets full control as the light turns from yellow to red. He can see the taillights of the other van far ahead. If he sits through the light, he'll lose it.

"Let's find out where this rabbit takes us, Erv," Web says to his prone partner, blowing through the intersection and hoping a cop isn't watching them. That would be really, really bad.

After the light, Web slows down. Erv's steady breathing by his side calms him. He reaches over Erv to find a stack of napkins from Rita's Comidas in the glove compartment and pinches his nose.

Web keeps a car or two between him and the other van, but after ten more minutes, the two vans are the only vehicles on the road. Both glide along just below the speed limit. Neither runs a red light nor makes sudden turns. It isn't a chase; they are together.

As his adrenaline from the struggle lowers, Web gets to thinking. What was Erv planning to do to him when they arrived at their destination? He doesn't think Erv is a killer. But if he's to believe Ally, they've all played some part in the death of Chess Plotnik. Even knocked out, Erv is starting to feel dangerous.

But what if Ally is wrong? What if he's just following some cowboy going out to his ranch? He considers turning around. But where would he go? Home? To Ally's apartment, to wait for her again?

The emptiness of the highway makes him feel conspicuous. He slows down and lets some distance open up between the vans. Then, he flicks his directional and swerves as if he's pulling over. After a minute, he cuts the headlights and steers the van back on the road.

Ahead, he sees the other van's taillights disappear. Web slows down to find the turnoff. He catches sight of other van's red lights and follows along a gravel road. There's a sign: "Wood Rough Ranch."

He watches as the van pulls through a break in the fencing. Web stops at the metal cattle tracks. He sees the van park two hundred feet ahead. If he's going to trespass on some rancher's property—which, to be clear, he'd rather not do—he figures he'll be less noticeable on foot.

Web lets the bloodied napkins fall, checks Erv one more time, and then leaves the van running with the driver's side door ajar. He walks toward the first van and hides behind a short bush a little distance away.

The better view isn't a good one.

Is that *Alice*? And Howie the Bachelor?

And there's Ally, on her knees.

There's another woman, whose face he cannot see. He watches her shake a water bottle as she talks. Searching for a way to get closer to hear what they are saying, Web can't find easy cover. He's at the edge of a clearing.

Perhaps this should all be less of a surprise. How the bar mitzvah went sideways. How they rushed Ally into the job. How Erv has been acting all week, so certain that Ally won't last.

His nose has stopped bleeding, though. That's something.

He hears a skitter at his knee. A talon or claw retreating. He sees a dark hole in the roots of the bush. Too big for a snake, he hopes. A burrowing owl, perhaps. Either way, it's time to move.

Web creeps closer, thinking of joining the trio. He's part of the Set Up too, right? Erv was bringing him here, so maybe they're expecting him.

Sure. Maybe. But are they expecting him to be standing, or on his knees with Ally?

He commits the license plate to memory and walks back to the other van. Erv still seems out. Web figures the group is expecting the second van. Erv wasn't trying to be sneaky as he followed them.

Web drives forward slowly until he's about twenty feet away from the group. Then, he turns on the high beams and steps on the gas. Here goes nothing.

Web quickly swerves between Ally and the three others—and presses the button to open the sliding door behind the driver's side.

Beep beep sjjjjooop-click. He leans out the window and says, "Let's go. Confirm?"

Ally grabs her duffel bag and jumps in. "Confirm," she says.

He hits the gas again, closing the sliding door and locking the locks. He glances to his right, long enough to see the other three, slack-jawed, trying to get a read on the situation. He almost hits the brakes in surprise as he sees the second woman's face. It *is* Ruth, and she's holding a water bottle out, as if offering it to the van.

But Web doesn't linger. He circles their van and heads back over the cow grates to the road. He hears two pops behind them. Maybe Ruth threw her water bottle, but maybe it's gunshots. Shit shit shit. He hits the gas once he reaches pavement and makes a quick left on Las Vegas Boulevard heading south—away from the city. It's dark out here, and he cuts the van's lights again. What now?

After a quarter mile, he coasts to a stop along the shoulder. In the rearview mirror, he sees the other van leave the Wood Rough Ranch and head north.

He turns around to face Ally. "Okay, we're okay," he says. "For now." He figures the other team will hit a few lights before they start to wonder why they're not catching up to him and Ally.

He pulls back onto the road, headed south. He's driving fast but not fast enough to attract attention. There's not much traffic in any case. They can catch the turn onto the I-15 to head back to the city.

Ally finally speaks. "Your nose?"

Web nods toward Erv resting awkwardly in the space between the driver and passenger seats.

"So," Ally starts, "one of those people was Howie. The older woman was named Ruth . . ."

"Ruth trained me. I worked with her for two years."

Quietly, as if telling herself, Ally says, "They were going to kill me."

Web lets that float in the air. He's sure she's right.

Web takes them to the airport warehouse. They park the van inside their unit and climb out. They leave Erv in the van.

"He'll be okay?" Ally asks.

"He's breathing." Web can feel the pressure building in his nasal cavity when he speaks. His voice sounds like he has a head cold.

"What will happen to him?" she asks.

"Etcetera, Ally. Come on."

He pulls his phone out of his pocket.

"Don't!" Ally closes the gap between them, reaching to take the phone from his hands. She doesn't reach him in time, but it doesn't matter.

"Bricked," he says. Can they track them? Who are "they" anyway? He drops the phone on the floor of the storage unit and feels a spark of relief.

He pulls out one of the olive-green Vespas, and Ally gets on behind him, placing her duffel bag on her lap. He waits for her to put her phone in the bag. She taps him on the shoulder, and he pulls out.

"Take me back to the Plaza," she yells over the wind. No wonder he couldn't find her at her apartment. She got spooked and ran. Smart.

Once they get close to the hotels on Fremont, she points to a parking lot and shouts into his ear, "Actually, pull in here."

He parks the scooter and they both hop off, removing their helmets.

"I should've listened to you."

"Ruth was your boss, Howie was my mark, and the other woman was at the Fallout Bar too," Ally says.

"That was Alice."

"Did you know her, too?"

"I was on a team with Alice for a few years." He pauses. "I trained her."

"She kidnapped me using the photo app trick."

"Was it Ruth who you saw at the bar mitzvah?"

"Yup," she says. And then, "A second team."

They both stop to watch as a car passes. It slides into a spot and the driver walks across the street to Atomic.

"How many times have you done this?" she asks.

"What? Set someone up for murder? Ally. Christ. Never. I was in this for the free food and the money. I never—"

He doesn't know how to complete the sentence. He's not offended.

"This lot is what it was all about," she says. He watches her look around, and he does the same. The lot's half full. Decent for a Monday, he thinks. "This is what Plotnik died over," she says. "Plotnik. Oran. The In-Hwa Group. OmariCity. The Rouge." He watches her as she looks up to him. "Why me, though?"

"I don't know, Ally."

"What do you know, Web? Was I the fall gal? Were you sent to convince me to stay with the Set Up last night? Or was it for you, Web-I-Don't-Even-Know-Your-Last-Name?"

"Erv was saying you were only supposed to be with us for the week, but I didn't get it. I— I should have told you."

"That didn't sound suspicious?" she says, folding her arms. Ally clearly wasn't who they'd hoped she'd be.

Ally's eyes look around, and he feels it too. They're exposed, standing in a downtown parking lot. After a minute, her face centers on his. He realizes they are close, well within each other's personal spaces.

Web and Ally stare at each other for a minute and, blood pumping in his ears, he leans into her.

"Oh. Oh, no. Web, that's not. That's not— That's not gonna happen." She steps to the other side of the Vespa.

"Right. Right. I was just—"

"You were just. *I. I* was *just* about to be murdered."

A low-rider convertible drives down Fremont, and the sound system interrupts her. After it passes, she lets it drop.

"When Erv comes to, he'll figure out I took a Vespa. You have a few options," he says. "Your hotel's five blocks in that direction," and he turns ninety degrees and points to the north and says, "And five blocks in that direction is a police station. You could go tell them everything. Tell them they kidnapped you in a white cargo van. Nevada plates. EJ1-Y26."

"EJ1-Y26. Okay. What are you going to do?"

"I'm . . ." He considers it. He isn't sure. "Fuck if I know." Putting on his helmet, he turns to say goodbye. "See you at the talent show, Ally," he says.

She smiles a little, and he flicks the button on the Vespa and pulls into the street.

In the side-view mirror, he sees Ally toss her helmet on the asphalt and head toward the police station.

TWO WEEKS LATER

32

ALLY

Lounging by the pool at the Cosmopolitan, Ally lazily watches the white-aproned servers as they weave between the chairs.

Ally and Phoebe are splurging on a last-minute discount vacation—well, Phoebe is, since Ally's bank account has been frozen as "tainted assets," even though she never transferred any of the money the Set Up deposited in her CashStache.

After she left Web, Ally told the police everything she knew about the Set Up. She told them she thought there were two groups in the city, at least: one with off-the-street actors like Ally and Web, and another team—Ruth, Howie, Alice—operating in the same spaces but with different rules and different ethics. She told them about Plotnik.

At first, they treated Ally as if she were looney tunes, but once she asked for the assistant DA and dropped Marshall's name, she was given a touch more respect. Tracy McCall told her how Marshall had been found in his car, dead, at the same time Ally was on a drive out to the desert.

The medical examiner had determined Plotnik had a heart attack, but Ally's statement to the police triggered a closer inspection into both deaths. They found lethal levels of fentanyl in their systems.

Tracy has been sending Ally regular updates. Police picked up Oran in his home and caught Alice at the airport, trying to catch a flight to Ecuador. They pulled CCTV footage of Alice heading to the OmariCity offices, blurry enough to be Ally if things had unfolded differently. Apparently, Alice was content to plead guilty to kidnapping and breaking and entering, and head to state prison, rather than corroborating Ally's story about the Set Up.

Ruth, Howie, and Erv are still at-large. Web, also a person of interest, remains missing. Police found his phone in the storage unit but couldn't recover anything from it. Same story with the phone Ally left in her apartment.

Tracy told Ally that the In-Hwa Group rented both the space on 2305 Desert Inn—abandoned and emptied of its contents—and the storage space by the airport. All the tech was either gone or wiped. No leads, as far as she could tell. Only closed circuits. Erv had done quick work.

Ally's still in some legal jeopardy, though no one seems to be sure exactly what kind. Her lawyers think the emails she sent Marshall from Phoebe's phone should be helpful evidence for her. There's some question about her participation in guerrilla marketing for PicSnapR, but that's tied up between the app developer and the FTC, all of which is well above her head.

She's the beneficiary of some residual goodwill, or at least guilt, over Marshall's death. *The Record*'s lawyers provided consultation, and she was allowed to access the paper's archives, looking for anything having to do with the Set Up, for all the good that did her.

Mostly, Ally has been stuck turning the events of that week over in her head, trying to find new angles. Was it just Ruth and Erv using Alice and Web? Is there someone else at the top? Etcetera, etcetera. She concludes that Phoebe was right all along. The Set Up, whatever it is, is similar to a multi-level marketing scheme, preying on a loose and competitive community of unsuccessful actors, exploiting the surveillance and communication powers of smartphone technology, and diffusing responsibility into a gray mist of anonymity.

Elías Losado made a statement to the paper, expressing his hope that Plotnik's Fremont Street block will be gifted—or at least sold at a very fair price—to Walker Preddy and his investors, to do "what's right for those caught in this shadowy web and as my good friend Chess Plotnik intended: The Moulin Rouge will be a jobs and human development mecca for our great Westside community, and for our entire city." She marvels at the politics spinning around it all. Plotnik was right. This guy will be mayor.

The chair of the journalism program, Professor Dorris, took over Marshall's class for the last four lectures, giving students wide latitude to complete their final papers. Ally finished hers a touch late, and Dorris sent the draft to Marshall's editor, Vaughn Tutti, at *The Record*. The story has the requisite mixture of journalistic titillation and meat-and-potatoes social issues—connections between murders spread decades apart, urban redevelopment, a multi-level marketing scheme dressed as a theater troupe, a religious sect trying to shine up their image with an International Peace Center. Tutti told her it might make the front page, depending on the news of the day, of course.

Ally knows Marshall's death will haunt her for some time. As satisfying as it might be to crack a blockbuster story, it hasn't erased the responsibility she holds for midwifing her instructor's death. She only wanted to encourage him to be a better instructor. The least she can do is write an article that would make Marshall proud.

She's also been offered a paid internship at the paper, which will more than make up for her lost income from Chroma, and be a lot more interesting, she hopes. Maybe even a career foothold.

Their server brings two club sandwiches and their check.

Ally pulls their refillable travel bottles from a tote. She won't be drinking water from a plastic bottle any time soon. The server retreats in reverse so deftly, she imagines hearing an echo navigation as he backs up from their deck chairs. Beep, beep, beep, beep. She watches him merge back into the ballet.

There's a DJ tent and a set of speakers by the kitchen. Bikini-clad women are dancing provocatively to the tame morning beats. Ally watches the DJ's bobbing head, and her thoughts migrate to Web. She hopes he's alive.

She reaches down to rub her bare knees. When she's awake, Ally can still feel the gravel and sand there. In her dreams, she returns to the dunes with Howie, Ruth, and her doppelgänger, Alice. The dream dunes are unnaturally jagged, and the three figures stand tall and immobile as pillars, their faces lit in white and red halves. Only, instead of Alice's face, it's her own. Sand spreads out from the base of their feet, solidifying into thick ropes and snaking toward her.

She turns to Phoebe, as she does whenever she shakes awake from that dream. "Love you, babe," Ally says. Beep returned to her after a few days, having stayed with her friends in LA. She felt bad for abandoning Ally, but Ally has reassured her every day since: If she hadn't been so suspicious of the phone, Ally might have never returned from the desert.

"Love you too, Al." They hold hands for a moment, and Ally feels Phoebe's thumb caress her palm.

As Ally folds Claudio's hundred-dollar bill in with their lunch check, she jumps at a phone notification coming from her right. Phoebe catches her eye as they both remember they had the good sense to leave their phones back in the hotel room.

33

WEB

Thankfully, Green River, Utah, is just big enough to have a library; he walked over earlier, as he has most days, and used an old Dell computer to scan the Las Vegas news. There hasn't been much to see, save for an article about Plotnik by someone named Marshall Grant, and it didn't answer any of Web's questions. Today, he happily bought a used copy of Octavia Butler's *The Parable of the Talents* from the library's $1 rack, exchanging pleasantries with a librarian wearing a "Rural and Proud" T-shirt.

After leaving Ally in the parking lot, Web retrieved his bug-out bag from his storage locker at Mademoiselle's and changed his clothes before riding north, out of town.

He ditched the Vespa in St. George, took a Greyhound to Provo and then to here, this small town he picked from the bus station map at random.

With no phone, no music, no text directives, Web felt anxious at first, and then, six hours into his exodus, a warm rush of calm came over him. He couldn't remember when he had been so alone with his thoughts, so free in his actions, limited in range though they were.

He likes it here well enough, and he hopes this nine-hundred-population, no-stoplight town is the last place anyone will look for him. If anyone is looking at all. He's staying in a roadside motel—attracted to the novelty of using "free HBO" as advertising in this streaming age. Inside the small room is everything he owns. Some clothes. A baseball cap. Pair of metal chopsticks. What's left of the ten grand he stashed. That will keep him going for a while longer. It's all still in his bag, just in case.

Web spends a lot of time wondering whether he really needed to run. There was the assault, but would Erv really press charges? Surely, Erv is in more trouble than Web is. The police are probably looking for both of them. What did Ally tell them? He's thought about the bloody napkins he left on the driver's side of the van. Knowing what the Set Up is capable of, though, the police might be the least of his worries.

Web knows he can't stay here forever, but he's still deciding on his next move. He could head back to Vegas in another week or so, see if he can just slip back into a quiet pocket of the demiworld of Fremont Street. Maybe he can call in a favor for some work off the books. Maybe it'll all blow over.

Sitting on a white plastic chair outside his motel room, he looks up from his novel for a few minutes. A few lines hang in his thoughts. He's survived, he thinks, and maybe that's enough.

Web watches traffic lazily move along Main Street and looks out onto the arid Book Cliffs. Brushstroke clouds crawl through the darkening sky, and a transparent quarter moon rises above the RVs and four-room shacks strewn across the valley. He thinks of his mother's moon jar and looks for the seam, the uneven halves, the mismatched spheres. All the partial stories that led him to where he sits.

He wonders when people will notice his absence. They've already pulled his name from the schedule at Mademoiselle's, no doubt. It will be a while before someone checks in on his condo. Like his parents before him, he's vanished.

He falls back to his book, flipping through pages, but jumps out of his chair at the sound of a text notification emanating from under him. Standing a few feet away, he waits, holding his breath. The chair pings again and, almost comically, he flips it over with the toe of his sneaker. A manila envelope is taped under the white plastic seat.

He looks around. The parking lot is empty. The highway is silent.

Web opens the envelope. The weight is a giveaway.

He stares at the phone for a long moment. Then he punches in 709416 for the passcode: Route 70, 94 Main Street, room 16. A text appears on the screen: "No need to run We have a job for you."

Web gapes at the phone. He considers responding, but before he can figure out what to type, another text comes in: "It's your mother."

Web wonders where to buy a phone charger in Green River.

ACKNOWLEDGMENTS

For their insights into real estate, Québécois sensibility, journalism, music, and rabbinical expertise, respectively, I would like to thank Becky Brown, Alexandre Frenette, Greg Saulmon, Alex Falk, and Aaron Fine. For their unshakable cheerleading, my gratitude goes to Rachel Ayotte, Scott Brown, Margot Douaihy, Ron Goodmark, Janice Irvine, Sarah Smith, Allen Shelton, and the too-good-to-be-true Taro Tsujimoto. For giving me all the life skills I didn't know I needed, I tip my prop fedora—which I still have—to my high school drama teacher, Richard Hess and the rest of the WEHS Drama Club. For dealing to me my sense of place and sense of self, through the mid-highs and lowest of lows, I flip a chip to all the Las Vegas denizens who know who they are. For excellent editorial work, I give a knowing nod to Kate Senecal, Hattie Fletcher, and Michael Jauchen. For giving this book a chance, I offer a penitent bow to Anne Trubek and her badass punk publishing outfit at Belt. For betting on me, I thank my dear family, Robyn, Ellis, and Sol. And for providing lively feedback on early drafts and for always being the best part of my working day, I express my deepest gratitude to the University of Massachusetts Amherst Emerging Scholars (especially Sam Cadwell and Anna Calamis). This book is dedicated to you all.

ABOUT THE AUTHOR

Jon Wynn is a professor and the department chair of sociology at the University of Massachusetts Amherst. He has written *The Tour Guide: Walking and Talking New York* and *Music/City: American Festivals and Placemaking in Austin, Nashville, and Newport*, and co-authored *The City and the Hospital: The Paradox of Medically Overserved Communities.* His work has also appeared in *The Guardian*, *The Atlantic*, *Salon*, the *Washington Post*, and other venues. *The Set Up* is his first novel.

Belt Publishing

beltpublishing.com